THE GIRLS WHO GOT AWAY

KILLER SIGNATURES 2

CHRISTINE WINSTON

THRILL.INK BOOKS

Copyright © 2024 by Christine Winston

All rights reserved.

No part of this publication may be reproduced, distributed, or transmitted in any form or by any means, including photocopying, recording, or other electronic or mechanical methods, without the prior written permission of the publisher, except as permitted by U.S. copyright law. For permission requests, contact www.christinewinstonauthor.com .

The story, all names, characters, and incidents portrayed in this production are fictitious. No identification with actual persons (living or deceased), places, buildings, and products is intended or should be inferred.

Book Cover by Alison Celis

Developmental Editing by Emerald Edits

Copy Edit by Bright Owl Edits

Proofreading by Orla Doyle

Read through editing Deirdre Winston

First edition 2024

For Izzy

Contents

Prologue	1
1. Chapter 1	5
2. CHAPTER 2	11
3. HUNTER, AGED 10	19
4. CHAPTER 3	23
5. CHAPTER 4	32
6. CHAPTER 5	37
7. HUNTER, AGED 11	43
8. CHAPTER 6	48
9. HUNTER, AGED 12	53
10. CHAPTER 7	57
11. HUNTER, AGED 13	65
12. HUNTER	68
13. CHAPTER 8	70
14. HUNTER, AGED 14	76
15. CHAPTER 9	78

16.	HUNTER, AGED 15	88
17.	CHAPTER 10	90
18.	HUNTER, AGED 17	103
19.	HUNTER, AGED 20	105
20.	HUNTER, AGED 27	107
21.	CHAPTER 11	109
22.	HUNTER	112
23.	CHAPTER 12	114
24.	CHAPTER 13	119
25.	HUNTER	121
26.	CHAPTER 14	122
27.	CHAPTER 15	129
28.	CHAPTER 16	137
29.	HUNTER	145
30.	Chapter 17	146
31.	CHAPTER 18	153
32.	CHAPTER 19	163
33.	CHAPTER 20	169
34.	CHAPTER 21	181
35.	HUNTER	184
36.	CHAPTER 22	185
37.	CHAPTER 23	191
38.	CHAPTER 24	201

39.	HUNTER	215
40.	CHAPTER 25	216
41.	CHAPTER 26	226
42.	CHAPTER 27	237
43.	CHAPTER 28	249
44.	HUNTER	254
45.	CHAPTER 29	256
46.	CHAPTER 30	265
47.	HUNTER	280
48.	CHAPTER 31	283
49.	HUNTER	289
50.	CHAPTER 32	291
51.	CHAPTER 33	296
52.	CHAPTER 34	304
53.	HUNTER	309
54.	CHAPTER 35	312
55.	CHAPTER 36	320
56.	CHAPTER 37	323
	The Thrill Begins Here...	328
57.	Acknowledgements	329

Prologue

HUNTER

Last night we ended up in the emergency room. Doctors, with furrowed brows, ran test after test to find the mysterious origin of Beth's illness. Their conclusion came in cold and clinical - elevated liver enzymes. The cause could range from medication nuances to alcohol abuse or even cancer. Beth clung to me, the color draining from her face, her frail body trembling in the midst of such uncertainty.

The doctors wanted to run more tests, I refused. She's so delicate. She didn't need the overpowering stench of bleach, the constant beeping of machines, or the whining of irate patients. All she needed was me. When I let them know this, I saw the narrowing of the doctor's eyes, the pinch to his already sour expression. The same suspicious look had darkened my father's features when Lorraine fell ill. Foolishly, I relented and allowed the hospital to schedule a home visit. This morning, a phone call revealed their true intentions: a nurse from Adult Protective Services was on the way.

When the doorbell chimes, my eyes slide to the ceiling above me.

Beth is usually a light sleeper, but she doesn't stir. Her easy breathing filters through my earpiece and slows my racing heart. I glance in the mirror, adjusting a wayward strand of my dark hair with swift precision. My neatly pressed blue shirt compliments the sharp lines of my pants falling effortlessly to my polished black shoes. I give a final, cursory inspection, ensuring every detail of my carefully constructed facade is in place.

When I pull open the door, the nurse's face comes into view and a jolt of recognition courses through me. The rehearsed smile climbing my face stalls, the greeting I'd prepared to put the nurse at ease forgotten as I'm suddenly transported back to my youth. At first glance, her face resembles the countless others I'd seen along the sterile halls during my mom's hospital appointments. However, it's not the faces hidden behind medical masks that flood my thoughts. Instead, I find myself in father's old office, staring at a photo. My breath catches, the clean lines of my polished appearance blurring with the dirty secrets of my childhood curiosity.

Joanna Deveraux.

The door hangs open, seconds stretching as I take her in. Despite the fine lines of time, she looks like she did twenty-five years ago. Long auburn hair with freckles of the same shade, she's as captivating in the flesh as any photo I've ever held.

She is one of Father's 'survivors.'

That label, one I'm sure she wears with pride, is a dagger to my heart. Her presence pains me as though she's grabbed hold of the handle, twisting the blade, opening old wounds. My insides roil with the memories, all the pain, that *he* caused.

I was the survivor!

"Mr. Fisher. I'm Joanna Deveraux, the care facilitator with Inova

Fairfax hospital..." She extends her hand for me to take. As our fingers meet, I graze the steady throb of her warm pulse, suspending me further between the past and the present. My blood sizzles, a myriad of forgotten desires and a perverse temptation to take, to possess, to finish what *he* started all those years ago grabs hold of my imagination. Her head tilts, her bright smile faltering at my lagging response.

"I'm here to check in with your wife? She visited the emergency department last night."

"I'm sorry, Mrs. Devereaux. Of course. Come in, come in..." I step aside and open the door wider. "Beth is sleeping, will you need to speak with her?" I ask, as she steps over the threshold.

"Yes, I'm afraid so. But we could run through some general questions first, check the ingredients on some of the over-the-counter medications she's taking, rule some of those out?"

"Of course..." I turn from her, closing the door. My trembling fingers turn the lock. The dead bolt drops into place with a heavy thud that echoes around us.

It's too risky, I can't ... The words rattle around my mind in shaky disbelief.

Turning back, I force a warm smile. Her eyes dart to the door behind me, her fingers gripping the strap of the briefcase hanging from her shoulder.

"This way..." I step towards the dining room. The air thickens with her hesitation "Is everything OK?"

"Yes, but..." She looks over her shoulder and back to me, a shadow of doubt clouding her eyes before she straightens her spine, "I'd like you to unlock the door." She asserts.

"Beth has moments of confusion. Last week she left the house and a car almost hit her."

"It's policy Mr. Fisher, I'm uncomfortable proceeding with the door locked." She holds her ground, unmoved by my response. My stomach tightens with the need to control but I resist the urge to deepen her unease and meet her gaze with cool acknowledgment before unlocking the door.

"Of course. I apologize."

Her shoulders relax, but the tension remains etched on her face as she follows me into the dining room. I hold out a seat for her at Beth's prized elmwood dining table.

"I'll run through some general questions first, to make sure all the information I have is correct..." She takes out some documents, flicks open a folder and begins to read the information. "I'm here to establish a care package for Elizabeth Fisher, date of birth..."

I nod along as she reads, watching her tick the boxes.

"And you are her husband? Full name Hunter Fisher..."

Her pen pauses. A slight tremor travels through her hand, her milky complexion paling again.

Does she recognize my name? Did Father speak of me?

Haunted eyes lift to meet mine across the reclaimed wood. She swallows audibly.

"Is your father—?"

I nod. "Yes."

Chapter 1

Four months later

MAC

A sheen of sweat coats my skin, soaking my pink tank top. Filling my lungs, I breathe out slowly. Jogging through the Wolf River woods in July is stifling, and despite the shade of the birch trees around me, the struggle on the final uphill trek toward my uncle Sailor's camp burns in my chest.

Only a hundred yards to go ...

Rounding a bend I move off the trail. My sneakers kick up dirt as his tent comes into view.

Fifty yards ...

The smell of this morning's campfire draws me closer to where he sits. As usual, his long gray hair is curling around his ears and shoulders.

Made it.

I stop next to his fisherman's chair, bending forward, my hands drop to my knees, to catch my breath. I check my watch. *Damn it, it took me an extra five minutes.*

He turns to greet me, his full beard, still holding a tinge of his once jet-black hair, brushes against his chest.

"You're late!"

"This heat is slowing me down," I complain.

"Did you hydrate?"

"Yes."

"Have you shortened your warm-up time?"

"Yes."

"Electrolytes?" his brows pinch.

"Yes! My turn: have you taken your medication?"

"I did, not that I need them. I'm as strong as an ox ... "

His eyes, the color of the forest he loves so much, widen in conviction.

"Even an ox will get a sore hump from overworking!"

"Do I look overworked?"

Sighing heavily, I drop onto the log across from him.

"Not today, but I do worry about you."

"Me? No need girly, did I ever tell you about the time I fought off a black bear with just my pocketknife?"

"You did." *Many times.* "But tell me again." I indulge him.

"It was in these woods; your mother was alive then ... " He looks down at the walking stick in his hand, carved of wood from this very forest. He twists it in his hands. Regret and sadness color his tone as he continues. "You were just a little tot. I was traveling downhill toward the Wolf River at dawn. A thick fog was rising from the forest floor as I made my way to a ridge ... " He gestures in the air, reliving the memory before my eyes.

"The black eyes of the bear bored into mine ... " he continues.

Sailor has always been a fighter, just like my mother, his little sister. She was a financial wizard in Wallstreet and benefited greatly from buying and selling stock. Tips she shared with Sailor too, but to look at him, you'd never guess how wealthy he is. When she fell pregnant with me, she returned home to Wisconsin and gave it all up to raise me here. This story always reminds me of the night she died. She went up against a different beast, but unlike Sailor, she didn't live to tell her tale.

"His claws swiped at my head—!"

Mom's murder hit us both harder than that bear ever could. She's been gone twenty years. But with every anniversary, every bad dream or happy memory, the blows keep coming. I doubt they'll ever stop. As he recounts his tale about the bear, his voice carries the weight of battles fought and my gaze is drawn to the scars that litter his calves and thighs. Each mark represents not just his physical struggle with the bear but is a reminder of the untamed world he chooses to live in. My eyes travel up his wiry body, that never seems to hold any fat, to more scars on his hands and up again to his eyes so much like my mom's. I can see her courage in his eyes, it's mirrored by his resilience out here in the wilderness.

"How did you get out of the woods and to the hospital?" I ask, even though I already know the answer.

"I had some first aid supplies in my bag and managed to wrap some gauze around my head before crawling back uphill. Some hunters found me."

"Did you ever see that bear again?"

"No, but I quit hunting that day. Took it as a sign to respect the animals that live here." His eyes drift toward the river then upward to the rustling leaves of the trees that keep him cool in this heat.

"Be careful out here, won't you?" My voice takes on a pleading edge.

"I belong out here." His words scratch at a bone-deep guilt I feel for ever having taken him from this place. Sailor is as wild as this forest, but he gave it up to care for me.

"I know," I sigh, "but I worry about you, alone out here, sometimes."

"Come by as often as you like. But make sure you're switching up your trails," he warns.

Being a father was never in the cards for him, but he so easily switches into that protector mode. I roll my eyes playfully, before checking my watch.

"Gotta go: I've got a client at nine-thirty."

"Will you be by tomorrow?" he asks.

"Yeah."

"Ok. Lock the doors and leave the hall light on, ya hear?"

"I always do."

"Yes, Mac, and you know better than anyone, that if somebody wants something bad enough, they'll find a way to get it … " his eyes tighten their hold on mine. *Promise,* they plead.

"I promise. Do you need me to bring you anything tomorrow?"

"I'm good. Now you get! And keep an eye out, over your shoulder. If you come across anyone suspicious, remember: they're less likely to attack you if they think you'll put up a fight—"

"I know, Uncle. Eyes trained on them at all times."

"Good. Have you been practicing your self-defense?"

"Yes!" I laugh now, we're each as bad as the other. Mom's anniversary is coming up in a few days. It always brings me fears of losing him. I'm sure he's plagued with similar worries about me.

"I'll be by at the same time tomorrow."

"I'll be waiting." He smiles before bending to grab the fishing rod by his chair. He doesn't turn back until he reaches the edge of the river. There's no doubt about it, he's home. With one last wave, my sneakers pound the faint path back toward my car. I'll be back tomorrow. And if I didn't show, I'm secure in the knowledge that Sailor would immediately come looking for me. That's the rule. You show up when you say you will, or the other assumes something is wrong. Waiting twenty-four hours might be police policy, but twenty minutes' grace is the Arnold policy, and we stick to it.

MAC

A shadow hangs over the pitched roof and vinyl siding of the house we call home. Set on the corner of a pretty street in a highly sought-after neighborhood in Appleton, Wisconsin, even with its fresh white paint and blue shutters, it's forever shrouded in darkness. Physically, it bears no signs of the horrors inflicted upon its occupants. The blood has long since been washed from its walls, but not before seeping into its foundations. The blood, the death, the trauma, the stigma of that night continues to haunt it all these years later.

There was no shedding the past, no leaving it behind to start over.

I tried.

I traveled the world. Practiced the art of yoga in Thailand and Bali, walked white sandy shores and looked out at the most magical sunsets. With one eye on the horizon, and the other over my shoulder, I watched the sun sink into a still ocean. Awed by a sky streaked in orange, blue and violet, I was simultaneously checking for any danger lurking behind me. It was during one such sunset that reality dawned. There was no escaping my past. The memories and the pain travel with me, the trauma sewn into my healing heart, a stitch representing every day of my survival. Coming home to the one place I felt loved felt like the only answer.

Like any toxic relationship, staying is bad for me, but walking away from the potential this home once held feels like failure. This is the last place my mom kissed me goodnight, hugged me, laughed with me. It's where she took her last breath. This house and those memories have taught me to be always vigilant and aware of my surroundings.

Parking in front of the double-garage doors, I step out of my white Jeep Grand Cherokee. As I'm bending to stretch out my muscles, a metallic gleam catches the corner of my eye. Straightening, I walk to the steel trashcan at the end of the driveway. Its lid sits askew.

Why is it off?

The garbage truck doesn't come by until noon.

Instinctively, my eyes scan the yard and sidewalk for anyone lingering about. There's no one.

Beneath the lid, the white trash bags with their yellow ties sit, uncollected.

I put the lid on tight. *Has someone gone through my trash?!* The hairs on my neck stand at the very thought.

Again, my eyes dart up and down the wide street. There is no one, not a single soul in sight. Unzipping the fanny pack on my hip, I pull out my phone to check the security cameras. Opening the app, the words "content offline" flash in white text across a black screen.

My heart pounds in my ears. Every worst-case scenario flash through my mind and without a second thought my thumb punches 911.

CHAPTER 2

DEPUTY JONES

Mandy's voice crackles over the radio.

"Jones, come in."

Climbing behind the wheel of my patrol car to drop my coffee into the cup holder, I reach for the radio on my shoulder to respond.

"Jones here. Go ahead, Mandy."

"We have a possible 10-14 at 1212 Silentwind Lane, are you in the vicinity?"

1212 Silentwind Lane?!?...

"Are you sure of that address? I thought that house was vacant?"

"That's a negative. MacKenna Arnold is on site believes an intruder could be in the house."

"Mac is home?"

"Roger that," Mandy confirms. ",are you in the vicinity?"

"I'm about three minutes out. Do we have a description of a possible suspect?" I'm already backing out of my parking space.

"Negative. Homeowner has been advised to remain outside the dwelling."

"OK, I'm almost there now."

Memories of my childhood friendship with Mac and her mom's death resurface. My stomach clenches hard as I make my way to the "Slaughter House," as it's still called. I've never been inside, but my dad was the lead detective on the Julie Arnold murder case. Since joining the force, I've looked over the case files. Crime scene photos of the blood-soaked bed and walls are engraved in my memory. My heart aches, knowing what Mac suffered as a little girl. We became friends after it had happened. For years we played together, laughed together and relied on each other until ...

Focus, Jones.

I straighten in my seat as I turn onto Silentwind Lane, redirecting my thoughts to the job at hand, my mind drifts to my criminal psychology studies. This situation with Mac brings back the lessons on trauma and how it shapes a person. I'm reminding myself to remain unruffled by the chaos of our past when I see her for the first time since high school. MacKenna Arnold, the only surviving child of Julie Arnold, and the girl responsible for giving me a bloody nose in front of our entire school, sits on the curb. She jumps up on long slender legs as I pull into the driveway.

Still beautiful ...

She rushes to my car door, crowding me as soon as my boots hit the ground.

"Hey, Mac." I give her an easy smile.

She cranes her neck around my body, searching the passenger seat of my car "Are you alone?"

"Sure am." I rock back, thumbing the loops of my duty belt "Wanna tell me what's going on?"

She sighs. Loudly.

Still defensive.

"I told Mandy, I think someone is in the house!" She's obviously distressed. At times like this, I appreciate Walter's ability to keep his emotions at bay. Drawing from his example, I Keep my tone calm, and try to reassure her.

"OK, well let's try get to the bottom of it. What has you thinking that?"

"First, my trash can was disturbed when I got back from my jog, and now my home security system is offline."

"Disturbed?"

"Yeah, like someone went through the trash!" She huffs, hazel eyes narrowing. Nodding slowly, I note the deep rise and fall of her chest.

"OK, tell me about the security system."

Her tone sharpens with impatience "I just told you, it's offline!" she throws her hands up.

Stepping back on one foot to gain some space from her, I observe her further. From her sneakers to her long black hair, and the tank top still soaked in sweat, she sure enough looks to have returned from a jog. Mac and I have a turbulent past, to say the least, but I'm not here to add to her frustration. I'm considering how best to navigate this situation when she starts in on me again.

"Well, don't just stand there!"

Her tone pokes at me, tempting me to re-start old fights. Inhaling deeply, I push forward calmly.

"Have you looked back over the footage?"

"Yeah, it cut off about ten minutes after I left. There wasn't anyone near the house before it went, but look, you can see the lid is secure on the trash can." She opens an app on her phone, her arm brushing mine as she leans in to show me the footage. The scent of damp moss and woodfire fills the space between us. We watch her drive off; the lid is definitely secure.

"Do you have footage of the lid being off when you got back?"

She looks up from her phone "No, the cameras were offline. They came back on just a few minutes ago."

"What type of security you got?" I ask, taking my notepad from the shirt pocket of my uniform.

"It's the best available!" she snaps, stepping back out of my space, taking her woodsy aroma with her.

Her aggression bounces off my vest, which helps me to separate our past hostilities from the vulnerable woman who dialed 911 for help.

"Mac, I'm trying to figure out if it's connected to your Wi-fi or through a digital box with cables?"

"Oh ... " Her cheeks flush pink. "It's connected to the Wi-fi. And before you ask, I get a notification if anyone accesses my system."

Dropping my chin, I lean into the radio on my shoulder.

"Dispatch, this is Jones. Could we check if there was a power outage or network fault over on Silentwind Lane today?"

"I'll check that for you now, Jones."

We wait for Mandy to come back on the radio.

"How's your dad?" she asks suddenly.

"Good. And Sailor?"

"Yep, great!"

Mac and I stand by each other in awkward silence, the air between us thick with years of animosity. Her eyes scan my body, intensely enough to make me uncomfortable under her perusal.

She looks good, always has. My eyes fall to her sunburnt shoulder, I nod to the pink skin.

"You got too much sun."

"That's the least of my worries." She rolls her shoulders back, her arms folding under her perky chest, while she fidgets with her silver necklace.

She still wears her mom's necklace.

"Just saying, is all ... " I shrug, walking away toward the front of her house.

"Hey! Where are you going?"

"I'm checking the perimeter."

I keep walking. The landscaping is well maintained, with tall plants and bushes providing some privacy around the ground floor windows. Satisfied that everything around the front yard seems to be in place, I move along the side of the house.

"I like your yard, but I'd cut those trees down." I point.

"You're not here to give me advice on my trees, Jimmy Jo—"

The crackle of static interrupts her words. I've never been happier to hear Mandy's husky voice come over my radio.

"Jones? No reports of network or electrical failures in the area."

"Thanks, Mandy. Be advised I'm doing a walkthrough of the property, bodycam on."

I release the call button and turn to Mac. "OK, let's check inside the house and I'll be on my way."

She directs me to the back porch, her fingers swiping along her phone again before the sound of locks opening can be heard.

"No keys?" I ask.

"I have keys, but I can control all my home security from this app," she explains.

"Wow. What if someone hacks your system? What then?"

"I've taken all the necessary steps to prevent that happening."

"Obviously not, Mac, if you think someone is in your house!"

"Look, can we get this over with?"

"OK, but I'd change the passwords, in case you've been compromised."

"I'm sure you would ... " She pushes past me to enter the house. My hand comes to her arm, stopping her on the threshold.

"Probably best if you wait out here," I advise, stepping ahead of her into the house.

"Wait! I ... " her slender fingers grip my elbow. "I don't like people snooping in the house."

Her hazel eyes cloud. The fear in them disarms me. Mac never asked me inside when we were kids. It was something that bugged me as a teenager. As a man, I understand it wholeheartedly.

"I promise to mind my business. I'll secure the house for you and get out."

"What if someone got in?"

"I'll call out to you from each room. You'll know where I am at all times, OK?"

She nods, her bloodless fingers releasing their grip on my arm.

Unbuttoning my holster and resting my hand on the butt of my gun, I move inside.

"Kitchen, all clear," I call out, before moving room to room. I check every nook and cranny of her home. The cream marble floors and walls carry me through the main floor before meeting with the plush carpet of the staircase. I pause briefly to look down at my boots. Mac will not thank me if I stain these carpets. I climb the stairs, recognizing the room at the top from file photos as the one where Julie was murdered. Nothing seems out of place. My eyes move constantly as I walk the landing, securing every room. Above me, a large crystal chandelier hangs from the ceiling of the third floor. Moving up the final flight of stairs, I find myself in what must be Mac's yoga studio.

"Attic, all clear!" I call down, surprised to find her looking up at me from the ground floor. We check the garage together. Satisfied that no one is in the house, we walk back to my patrol car. Opening the driver's door, I lean sideways, my arm resting on the roof to face her.

"I'll write up a report and file it. If anything else happens, you should call it in. Looks like nothing more than a scare, so I'll be on my way."

"You think I'm overreacting, don't you?" her tone skirts along the edge of anger.

"I think it's a reasonable response, considering ... "

"WHAT?"

"Jeez, Mac. Cool your jets here, I'm trying to be helpful!" Exasperation fails me.

"You've been looking at me like I'm paranoid since pulling up here!"

"Now hold on a damn minute. I was trying to figure out what the hell had you looking so afraid! I was not—"

"I wasn't afraid, Jimmy, I was being cautious!"

"It's 'Deputy Jones.' I'm on duty!"

"Whatever. Point is, I wasn't afraid!"

"Oh, bullshit! You were petrified and rightly so. You've had it tough—"

"Don't you *dare* use that against me!" she growls.

"You're a piece of work, you know that? Fine, you're paranoid. Happy now?"

Damn it! She baited me!

"I knew it! Tell me this, Cracker Jack—"

I burst out laughing. "*Cracker Jack?*"

"Yeah! You think you're a mighty fine thing, Jimmy Jones, but I'm tired of small-town folk thinking shit like this can't happen to them!"

"*I* work as a cop. My dad worked your mom's case! I know all too well that danger can come knocking on any door, in any part of the world."

"When it knocks on your door, Jimmy, maybe you'll understand a little more about being paranoid!"

"Ain't nobody doubting that. Especially ... " I shake my head in bewilderment and look away. I can't win. This is madness.

"Don't bother. If I need the cops again, I'll call."

She's already storming back up the path toward her front door.

"Mac!" I shout after her. "Change those passwords!"

Ignoring me, she continues back into the safety of her home. My hands go up in defeat when the door slams behind her. Mackenna Arnold is still as guarded as she was at thirteen years old.

HUNTER, AGED 10

*L*eaning closer, my breath steams up the windowpane and despite the steady tapping of rain against the glass, the house is quiet. Too quiet. Even Molly, Dad's prized vasa parrot sits behind the wire mesh of her aviary in peculiar silence. The whining nuisance is usually squawking for some kind of attention. I'm not allowed to come in here unless it's to feed Molly with Jan our housekeeper. Today is different. Today the persistent rain means they can't send me outside to play in the back yard while they talk. Instead, Dad marched me down to his office, with two warnings.

"Don't listen and don't touch a thing," he said, before leaving me with Molly.

I hate Molly.

I think the feeling is mutual. Turning on the window seat, my sneakers drop to the floor and with narrowed eyes, I stick out my tongue in her direction.

"You need to fight this, Camilla."

Molly cocks her head toward Father's voice. It carries down the hallway, polluting the air with his disappointment as he yells at Mom. Stepping closer to the open door, I strain to hear her response. Nothing. She never raises her voice. Unlike him, she's kind. Mom hates stupid Molly too. *I just know it.*

Silence descends again. Bored, I reach into the pocket of my gray jeans and pull out the new Road Champs car Dad brought home from his most recent business trip. Turning the blue and white Chevy Caprice over in my hand I read the badge on the driver's side door "Wisconsin State Patrol."

Aha. He was in Wisconsin!

Whenever he goes out of town, he brings me home a new toy car for my collection. I never know where he's been until he gives me the car. I'm too old for them now, but he wouldn't know that. All he cares about is his job, and stupid Molly.

She flaps her black wings, drawing my attention as she flies about in her cage. Her aviary takes up so much space in here, but if I dare to darken the door of this office, he scolds me.

No space for me, it's so unfair.

Training my ears toward the hallway again, I listen for any approaching footsteps. They're in the kitchen, their words too hushed to make out, but I hear Mom crying.

I grind my teeth together. Why can't he make her happy? My fists curl against the urge to run to her, the plastic wheels of the small car digging into the flesh of my palm. I want so badly to punish him.

How can I punish him? My eyes snap to Molly in her cage. I could set her free. The thought sends a shiver of danger and excitement through me. It's too risky, but it feels good to daydream. No, there must be another way.

My focus shifts to the long edge of his desk. Don't touch a thing. *His words echo in my mind, but my feet are already moving to the forbidden territory. Without concern for the shiny surface, I plonk my Road Champs car down, scratching the wheels along its varnish, driving it around the desk until I come to the middle, where his files lie open.*

I shouldn't look ...

But he *shouldn't upset Mom.*

Pushing the car forward, I cruise it up and over the files, stopping on top of a stack of photos. My breath hitches. I'm thrilled with my disobedience. I pluck up an image from the pile. Molly begins to whine loudly. I ignore her, my eyes glued to the photo.

There's blood everywhere!

On the walls, on the carpet, on a lady's naked body.

Whoa, are those stab wounds?

I can see her chest, her boobs falling to each side, a large gash on each one.

Why are her eyes open?

Black and lifeless, they stare up at nothing.

She's dead!

My mouth falls open, saliva pooling beneath my tongue as I bring the photo closer for inspection. Twisting it every which way, memorizing and absorbing the bloody scene. It's the coolest thing I've ever seen.

Did he do this?

The thought of him doing this to Mom brings me crashing back to reality. Just then, Molly blasts out a string of short, noisy whistles. Father's heavy footsteps come rushing down the hallway and without thinking, I stuff the photo into my pocket and rush to Molly's cage, just as he enters.

"What's all the racket, Hunter?" *he grunts, out of breath.*

"Molly's whistling," *I say innocently.*

His eyes narrow suspiciously before glancing around his office. I silently pray that he won't notice the missing photo. He turns back to me.

"OK, keep it down. Mom is with the doctor. I won't be long."

"Is she sick again?"

The adrenaline still pumping around my body drops heavy into the pit of my stomach.

"Yeah, Champ. The doctor is taking her to the hospital for some tests ... " His eyes search the floor, avoiding the pools of tears that flood mine. "Just play with Molly. Everything will be OK."

He turns away, leaving me to cry on my own.

CHAPTER 3

DETECTIVE JOHN WALTERS

The nutty aroma of coffee reaches me before his sneaky footwork lands him at my desk. I've already drained two cups today. Maybe a third will be what I need to ease the strain from my tired eyes. I look up from the report I'm struggling to focus on, just as Jones slides into the seat across from me.

"Why are you bringing me coffee?"

"I always bring you coffee."

"Mm-hmm, and why is that?" I take a sip, leaning back into my own chair.

He gives an easy shrug, keeping good eye contact with me as he ponders his reply.

"Maybe I like you."

I laugh. Jones has a habit of interrupting my work and for some reason, I don't mind it as much as I let on. I hold his stare, wondering at what point this kid's unexpected appearances became almost welcomed.

"OK, I need a favor," he finally admits.

I look down at the coffee in my hand, my gratitude suddenly dwindling. "Fine. Fire away!"

"Well, I got a call this morning, to a possible home invasion ... "

"Oh?" My ears perk up. I hadn't heard anything about it.

"Yeah, turns out it was nothing. Homeowner's security system was down when she got back from her run. She got spooked."

"How did that develop into a home invasion?"

"It didn't. I secured the house, but ... " he pauses, shifting uncomfortably in the chair "The house belongs to the daughter of Julie Arnold."

"Who's that?" Not being an Appleton native, I don't always know the local history like Jones does.

"She was murdered over twenty years ago; my dad worked the case."

"OK. So, the daughter is paranoid?"

"That's the thing. She's got her head screwed on right. Defensive, for sure, but paranoid? I don't think so."

"So what's bothering you?"

"I know her. I'm wondering if I missed something since, you know, we grew up together—"

"Is this an ex?" I interrupt.

"Oh, God no ... " he blusters, "nothing like that. I mean, we were friends for a few years, but then one day, out of the blue, she just turned on me. Said she didn't want to hang out anymore. Cut me out, like *that*." He snaps his fingers.

I gesture to move him along. "As riveting as all this sounds, cut to the chase."

"Oh, right. Yeah. It's been preying on my mind all morning. She has a way of provoking me. She got me again, and I'm worried it affected my read on the situation."

"And you need me to go out there? Talk with her?"

"I'd tag along. We could go after work?" His grimace is equal parts beseeching and hopeful.

I wasn't offering to help. I was just curious as to his motive for bringing me coffee. My inclination to say yes without giving him a hard time first has me suspecting he laced the damn thing with something.

"Fine." My eyes roll in time with my heavy sigh. "But: you owe me another coffee, and I need help going over these reports."

"You need glasses! And you've reached your coffee quota for the day. I'm not made of money, you know!"

"I do *not* need glasses," I growl. "And this coffee is stale."

"Sure thing, whatever you say, boss. " He bounces out of his chair. "Oh, and I watered your plants this morning. " He grins, the cocky bastard. "You're welcome!"

He practically skips off. My eyes slide to the four plants sitting on my windowsill, a smile tugging on my lips as they land on the one Della left me.

"Leave my plants alone!" I call after him. I've been taking care of them just fine.

My eyes scan Jones's gray cotton pants and white t-shirt as he climbs into the passenger's seat next to me. I shake my head, biting back my smile.

"What?"

"Nothing, you just look about fifteen years old."

"Well excuse me, Mr. black-shirt-and-gray-attitude," he counters.

"Black is smart and presentable. You, on the other hand, look more prepared for a game of baseball than to solve a murder."

"This isn't a murder scene. Well, not today," he corrects himself.

The rush hour traffic has long since eased as we turn right onto East Capitol Drive, heading to the Arnold home.

"Tell me about the case."

"You mean you didn't look it up?" his cocky grin is back but I'll give him points for knowing I would look up the case.

"A little," I concede, shifting in my seat to a more comfortable position. I nod at him to go over it anyway.

"Julie Arnold was murdered in her home, twenty years ago. The anniversary is in three days. Mac, her only child, woke up during it all and witnessed the brutal attack. The killer chased her, but she managed to hide in a makeshift bunker her uncle Sailor had built in her closet. The police only found her when they spoke with Sailor. He was away with the navy at the time of the murder."

I shake my head as I listen, my stomach turning with disgust.

"Your dad did a great job hunting down the scumbag."

"Took him five years. Though, he was never giving up without catching him, even if he died trying." There's a mixture of pride and regret in his tone.

"You did the right thing, asking me to come out here" I tell him.

"Maybe you can get through to her, she hates me!"

"Interesting..." I bite back a smile." How does that make you feel?"

He rolls his eyes. "About as comfortable as someone *liking* you makes you feel!" he scoffs.

I laugh. This kid is the only person I'd let get away with a comment like that.

"OK, run me through everything that happened when you arrived on scene today." I bring the conversation back to the job at hand, listening, as I turn right onto North Meade Street. We're only a few blocks away.

When he's finished his report, I ask, "Is there any way we can check if she's been hacked?"

"I checked with Bob—" Bob is the stations tech guy—"He said she should try to log into her router admin settings, and if she can't gain access then she is most likely hacked."

I turn left onto Apple Creek Road.

"How does she do that?"

"Fucked if I know, but I'm guessing she does."

"OK, let's start there. We can double check everything and put both your minds at ease."

"Thanks, boss!" He grins happily. The fact that I like helping him has me rolling my eyes at myself.

This kid's making me soft.

MAC

My white sneakers are stained green as we run through the field, between the rows of tractors. Mr. Jones bought us hotdogs and told us we have five minutes to pick our winners for today's meet, while he finds our seats in the stands. This is my favorite part of the tractor pull. My eyes skim over all the shiny paint jobs before landing on a metallic blue tractor. The words "Keeping Track of Her," written in gold along the hood bring me to a full stop.

"This one's mine!" I squeal to Jimmy, who's still running ahead. He turns back, squinting at my pick.

"That's gonna lose. Ain't no way that thing can pull sixty thousand

pounds!"

Mr. Jones brings us to tractor pulls most Sundays and Jimmy's pick usually wins, but not today.

"You're wrong, Jimmy Jones, this one'll win!" My tongue darts out. He's quick to come up beside me, his hip bumping mine.

"Looks as slow as you! Come on, keep up ..." He's running ahead. I don't follow. Instead my eyes fill.

I'm not slow.

"Come on, Mac!" he hollers, but I want to go home. Turning back, I run through the tractors, trying to find Mr. Jones. My feet move through the wet grass, until I come out the other end of the row. There's nothing but a wide field. I got turned around. My tummy hurts and it feels hard to breathe. Dropping my hotdog to the ground, I crawl under the nearest tractor to hide.

"Mac?" Jimmy's calling my name.

"JIMMY!" I scream back, my chin wobbling as tears stream down my face. When I see him round the corner and dash in my direction, I climb out from my hiding place.

"Yeesh, Mac. What got you running away?" he bites into his hotdog.

"You were mean ... " I sniffle. He screws his face up in confusion.

"Huh?"

"You said I chose bad."

He laughs, and without thinking I grab the stupid hotdog from his hand. He's shocked. There. That'll show him, laughing at me.

"Hey! Jimmy that back," he says.

The fear and anger in my tummy turn into something nicer as I laugh at his silly mistake.

"You said 'Jimmy', instead of gimme!"

"I know. It made you laugh, didn't it?" he grins.

I don't like him.

My body melts into the soft rubber of my yoga mat. With closed eyes, I listen to the sound of crashing waves, as I relax into *savasana* or "corpse pose." I should be releasing internal thoughts, events of the day. This is my time to just *be*. Instead, amber eyes, the color of whisky, intoxicate my mind.

Breathe in for four ...

Jimmy Jones is all grown up. A long time ago, we climbed trees and played cops together.

My eyes roll beneath their lids just thinking about that one summer, when everything changed. His legs grew long and scaling trees wasn't fun anymore. Oh no, he wanted to use those legs to chase girls.

Exhale: 1, 2, 3, 4 ...

That charisma has somehow morphed into a rugged sex appeal and boy, does he know it.

Ugh. He even makes that ugly brown and tan uniform attractive. It kills me to admit it, even to myself.

I really don't like him. Not anymore. A long time ago, he was the *only* person I liked. Until I became the weird kid and he was Mr. Popular.

Let it go, Mac!

Inhaling deeply again, I hold my breath for four, then release thoughts of Jones on a slow, steady exhale. This morning's events take up the empty space in my mind, bringing a heavy sickness to my gut. Its weight pins me to my mat.

Arrrrghhhhh!

My eyes shoot open, staring at the white ceiling of my yoga studio. It's pointless. My mind refuses to relax. Sitting upright, I cross my legs and allow my hands to meet in prayer to show gratitude to the ancient practice that keeps me sane.

"Namaste," I whisper to the empty room.

I was eighteen when I started yoga. Initially it was meant to help me stretch. I wanted to be able to run faster, for longer and prevent injury where I could. That first class changed my life. Eyelids closed, leaden with fatigue, the instructor's words lulled me beneath the veil of the conscious mind. Drifting through my thoughts, my subconscious mind whispered to my heart, my soul, and my eight-year-old self with love. It was bizarre, scary, and completely empowering all at once. Yoga became a safe place for me to explore the past.

Today, there are still corners of my mind, my memories, and even this house that remain unexplored and unhealed. Yoga has taught me to be patient with myself, to process in my own time. So many good times with Mom are locked away, linked too closely to the horrors of her death.

She's in the bunker!

A sick fear knots in my stomach just thinking about the hours spent hiding in darkness. I was terrified, but more than that, I felt like I should be doing something, *anything*, to help her. After the police found me, I knew for certain it was too late, and I was ashamed. Shame became my secret. At eight years of age, I knew my life had changed forever.

I reach for the silver compass necklace resting against my chest and rub the pendant between my fingers. Sailor had gifted it to my mom the Christmas before she died. I've worn it since finding it after her death.

Comforted, I begin rolling up my mat and put it away, before making my way down to the second floor. Walking past Mom's room, I linger to rest my hand on the closed door. I rarely go in, and like now, whenever I recall her final moments, tears gather in the corners of my eyes. They almost break free until the doorbell chimes.

Startled, I open the security app on my phone and examine the men on screen. A flutter of relief and unexpected excitement assail me at the sight of Jones's closely cropped brown hair. With his back to the camera, the line of his broad shoulders come into view. Next to him, and staring right at the lens, is a stranger. He has a set of clear and observant eyes, and enough sex appeal to steam any lens. He tilts his head just a little, one brow lifts as if to say, "I know you're watching."

I smile.

Definitely a cop. So why do I already like him?

I'm impressed enough to put up with Jones for a second time in one day. Closing the app, I make my way to the door. I'm curious to find out what has them calling after eight p.m.

CHAPTER 4

DEPUTY JONES

"Maybe she's out?" I muse, my ribs growing tight at the prospect.

"She'll be here shortly," Walters drops his gaze from the camera above my head. He meets my doubt with impervious confidence. Right on cue, the unmistakable rattle of a chain across the track of a security lock is followed by the heavy clunks of three more deadbolts opening before the thick wooden door swings inward. Mac stands there. Her rosy cheeks complement her full pink lips. Her hazel eyes darken more to brown as they meet mine.

"That's a lot of locks you've got!"

The words are out before I think. *Of course she locks her door!*

Walters throws me an exasperated look before introducing himself to Mac.

"I'm Detective Walters with the Outagamie Sheriff's department, ma'am. Deputy Jones here mentioned you had an incident this morning. We were in the area, wanted to drop by and ask some follow-up questions." He says smoothly.

Mac's shoulders relax, her gaze warming as she turns her attention to Walters.

"In the area?" she asks him, with none of the hostility that greeted *me* this morning. I shift from one foot to the other, my arms crossed over my chest as I watch their interaction.

"Considering the station is just a few minutes from here, I guess you could say we're always in the area." John shrugs. She smiles.

Why is she smiling at him?

"What's this really about, Jimmy?" Beneath her thick black lashes, her gaze and tone slice in my direction. The unexpected turn is a kick to the gut.

"I told you, it's 'Deputy Jones,' Mac—"

"You don't look to be on duty right now," she retorts, her eyes scanning my body.

Shit! Heat creeps into my cheeks.

Walters presses his lips into a thin line, suppressing a smug smile. I'd hoped she would be civil with him here.

"I wanted to make sure I hadn't ... missed anything here today. What with our history ..."

"And what history is that?"

The late evening sun turns up its heat on my back.

"I've known you all my life!" I huff. "I just wanted to be sure."

Her small, pointed nose wrinkles in scorn.

"You did your job well enough. I changed my passwords, so you can rest assured I won't be wasting police time in the future."

"I never said that!"

"You didn't have to. Your arrogant face said it all!"

"Now hold on there a minute—"

"OK, enough of this," Walters interrupts me. With a stern expression but an easy tone he admonishes her. "Whatever your impression of Deputy Jones, he is a fine police officer. We are here because *he* wants to be sure you're safe."

I've never understood her obvious disdain for me. It disarms me, forcing me to look away and down to her bare feet. She has pink nail polish on her toes.

" ... We can run some checks on your router, ensure your system wasn't compromised. If you're unhappy about proceeding, we will be on our way."

There's no arguing with John's logic. Steadying myself, I glare back into her defiant eyes. Her jaw ticks with silent frustration as she steps aside to permit us entry into her home.

"The router is in the downstairs office." She points toward the kitchen. I lead the way, having already located the office this morning. The squeaking of my sneakers on the gleaming, cream marble tiles makes me feel self-conscious.

"It's just before the kitchen, on the right," Mac calls from behind Walters. I want to tell her I know but bite my tongue instead and push open the white door into the office space. I flick on the lights as we enter. As in the rest of the house, the walls are a pale cream. I see my reflection in the large mirror hanging behind the small desk. There's a small filing cabinet below the mirror, with the router on top. I walk to it.

"Have you tried to access your main router?" Walters asks.

"No, why would I do that?"

"Hackers generally gain access through your Wi-fi. Once they're on your system they can go through all of your personal data, emails, web history and security system. Accessing the security system still requires your passwords. If you have a strong password on your Wi-fi, it takes them longer to get in ..."

"I have a two-step authentication," she interrupts him. I hide my smile. He had no clue about any of this until five minutes ago and yet he delivers it with such confidence. It's admirable: he shows no weakness. People believe in him and Mac's reaction to John reminds me that I'm a long way off from being that kind of cop.

They chat back and forth while I watch from across the room. Looking at Mac from a distance is nothing new. We became buddies after her mom's murder: she spent every weekend with us until we turned thirteen. That summer, she went camping with Sailor, came back full of guts and a wariness of boys. For her, those months were spent learning self-defense and how to push people away. For me, I missed her every day and developed a major crush on my absent friend. I was so excited for her to come back, I wore my best clothes, even stole some of Dad's aftershave to go hang out with her. She took one whiff and told me to go home. I'd convinced myself that with time, and talking, I could somehow heal her. Hero complex if ever there was one, it took a bloody nose to snap me out of that notion.

"How does that two-step authentication work?" Interrupting their conversation, I cast those memories aside as I kneel next to the router.

"If someone accesses the system from a different device, I get an email asking me to confirm it's me. If it's not me, I report it and block the device." She shrugs. "I didn't get an email."

"Were you out of service for long this morning?" Walter's asks.

"I jog the Wolf River trails. There's no signal, so my phone and smart devices are offline until I get back on the highway. It took me just under an hour this morning ..."

"Does Sailor still camp in that area?" I wonder.

"Yeah, I was with him this morning."

"Sailor's her uncle," I explain to Walters, who nods, withdrawing his notepad from his pocket. It piques my curiosity that he's taking notes. I've learned that Walters has reason for everything he does. Satisfied that the physical router hasn't been tampered with, I stand up, pulling out the desk chair.

"OK, can you log into the computer and access your network properties?" I nod for her to sit.

She looks to the desktop sitting at the centre of the desk. "That's my mom's computer. I don't use it."

Her suddenly vulnerable tone halts us.

"Do you have a laptop that you prefer to use?" Walters asks.

"In the kitchen." She leaves the office without a backward glance.

Walters and I exchange a knowing look before following. You don't work in law enforcement and miss the subtle signs of trauma. Mac's tough exterior empowers her, but we soften our approach as we enter the kitchen.

CHAPTER 5

DETECTIVE JOHN WALTERS

There was as shift in Jones the second his feet hit the porch of MacKenna's home. She makes him nervous, questioning his own judgment. The battle line drew tight between them as soon as the door swung open. I was mildly amused until she embarrassed him.

Following behind them, my eyes find a piece of art hanging on the wall between the office and kitchen. It's striking: a shallow box made entirely of glass, with swirls of blue moving slowly between its panes. Art in motion, like a calm sky falling into a stormy sea.

A bit like these two!

There's history between them, for sure. A nervous energy that sizzles, revealing itself through biting remarks and awkward glances. I'm sure their disjointed interactions are as muddy and unclear to them as they are to me. I've known Jones for four years now, and this is first time I've seen his doubts get the better of him. Her mother's murder and his father's connection to the case are only the tip of the iceberg. I suspect deeper feelings reside beneath the surface.

"I'm in. What now?" Her round eyes look over her laptop toward me. Sitting at the kitchen table, she forces confidence back into her voice. The mask is back in place, the tragedy and fear etched into the lines of her heart-shaped face fading. I wonder if she knows how obvious her pain is, to people like me and Jones.

"Jones will have to take the lead from here. I'm not much of a tech guy," I say.

He slides into the chair next to her, pulling the laptop in his direction. Leaving him to run the security checks, I wander around the kitchen. Her home is modern, clean, and clutter free. Other than the artwork in the hallway and a few alphabet magnets that spell out "MAC" on the fridge, there is no color in her home. It intrigues me. Jones is the psychology guy but Agent Della Perez taught me a few things about human psychology and just how fragile it is.

Is MacKenna hiding from happy memories in the same way she is hiding from the bad?

"John, come look at this."

I walk over and stand behind them. I lean in over their shoulders to see where Jones points to some kind of activity timeline.

"According to Mac's camera footage, she left the house at 7:02 a.m. But look at this: at 7:14 a.m., there was activity on her router. It's an unknown Windows device." He turns to Mac. "Are you sure no one else has your Wi-fi password?"

"No, I kept the default password. I didn't think to change it."

Both heads turn to me for answers.

"Does your uncle have access?" I ask.

"No. Sailor hates technology. He doesn't own a cell phone, never mind a computer."

"Jones, phone Bob, and ask what this means," I direct him. Nodding, he stands. He's already dialing Bob's number as he walks out into the hallway. I sit in the vacated seat and face MacKenna. Opening the notepad in my hand, I question her further.

"Did you notice anything else strange this morning?"

"The lid on my trash can was off. Just slightly, but I know I put it on tight."

"And before today? Anything unusual?"

"No, nothing."

"What about this afternoon?"

"No, I've been working all day."

My pen pauses, my eyes lifting to meet hers. Her back stiffens and fear begins creeping into her voice.

"Take me through your day from start to finish," I nudge gently.

"Can you stop talking to me like that?"

"Like what?"

"Like you're a cop and I'm a victim."

I already know that her carefully constructed appearance of strength is nothing more than a fragile shell. Her anxiety moves me, encourages me to change direction. Closing my notepad, I lean back into the chair and nod.

"OK. Could I trouble you for some water?"

She nods, jumping up and going straight to the fridge. I point to the glass artwork in the hallway.

"How does the paint move around in that frame?"

"It's not paint ..." her smile turns into a small giggle at my assumption.

"Oh no? what is it?"

"Two panes of glass are framed together. The space between the glass is filled with water and sand, blue sand in this case." She reaches into the fridge, pulling out a jug of filtered water as she talks.

"How does it move around so much?" I'm curious.

"Actually, that piece moves quite slowly compared to others. I can regulate the amount of air trapped between the panes. The air bubbles and gravity help to move the sand around the frame."

She looks more relaxed as she hands me a glass of water.

"You're good." She smiles. MacKenna is astute.

"I wasn't pretending. I like it."

"So do I. I commissioned that piece, actually. I've another one hanging in my yoga studio on the third floor, that one has green sand that forms mountains. my clients love it." She grins.

"You teach yoga?"

Her smile widens. She gives a deep exhale before sitting back into her seat.

"Like I said, you're good." Her eyes roll good naturedly. "Yes, I'm a yoga instructor. I had an early-morning client from 9:30 a.m., and she left a little after 10:30. My second client arrived around 11:15. She was late so we started straight away and again, she left an hour later. I puttered around, cleaned my studio, had lunch and ran some errands in town, before getting back home at 3:00 p.m. I had back-to-back clients, three in total, from 4:00 to 7:00. I was just finishing up my own workout when you guys rang. There was nothing out of the ordinary and trust me, I'd notice. Other than the trash can and now this ..."

Jones walks back into the kitchen. Still on the phone, he pulls it away from his ear.

"Bob says it could be a neighbor piggybacking on your Wi-Fi. Is it OK if he accesses your system remotely to run some checks?" he asks. She nods.

Taking the laptop he walks to the kitchen island to finish his phone conversation. MacKenna watches his every move, suspicion creeping into her expression.

"He's a good cop," I tell her.

"I'm sure he is, but …" She shakes away her thoughts, her attention cutting back to me. "Where were we?"

"Why did you phone the police this morning?"

"I allowed myself to be rattled. My mom's anniversary is coming up, it must be preying on my mind. When I checked and found the feed offline …" She swallows. "I'm sure he told you what happened to my mother?"

"He did. I reviewed her case myself, before coming by. I'm sorry for your loss. Jones wants to make sure you're safe, that's all." I give her the truth. She deserves it.

"OK," Jones addresses her. "Looks like someone gained access to your router. The good news is that they haven't blocked your access or set any bugs. Bob will need to come out tomorrow to reset the router. That will knock off anyone piggybacking on your internet."

His relief is evident.

"Does that mean everything is OK?" she asks.

"Most likely, yes. There doesn't seem to be any data compromised, but the new IP address is scrambled, so it's someone who knows what they're doing. Bob said it happens all the time. Hackers get into different systems and just sit on them."

"For what purpose?" I ask.

"Well, they can look at the user's search history, gain access to emails, online banking, essentially all personal information is at risk." He looks back to MacKenna. "Bob said you should unplug your router and cut off the access until he resets it."

She jumps up. "I can't do that; my security system will go down!" Her defensiveness shoots up higher than ever, as her eyes bore holes into Jones's bewildered expression.

"I get it, Mac. I know it's scary—" he begins.

"I'm not afraid!"

"It's understandable, Mac! You don't have to pretend—"

His words, meant to ease her concerns, just raise her hackles further.

"I am *not* pretending, and if you were any kind of cop, you'd know that!"

Her blow lands.

"Fine. Do as you please. You know I came here to help, right?" he growls.

"I didn't ask you to!"

"*You* called the cops this morning!"

"If you two are done!" My tone is sharp. "MacKenna. All we can do is suggest the necessary steps to protect your system from hacking, but it's up to you whether or not you take them." I'm already tucking my chair at the table back in.

"Jones. Let's leave Ms Arnold in peace." I nod, walking past him into the hallway. Jones looks like he's suffering from whiplash.

I hear the soft clatter of the laptop meeting the table and Jones's uncertain footsteps following behind me.

"Don't doubt yourself. You did the right thing asking me to come here," I tell him, as we pull away from the curb at 1212 Silentwind Lane.

HUNTER, AGED 11

*T*he *clipper lifts from my head. Charlie turns his attention to the door. Glancing from under my lashes into the mirror, I see a Marine enter the barber shop.*

Nodding to the empty seat next to me, Charlie tells him to sit, before pushing my head back down. The clipper resumes its path along the back of my head with vigor. Charlie addresses him as "sir" when they fall into polite conversation. His wrinkled hands move quickly to finish my haircut.

Typical.

Everyone in Quantico loves to credit the Marines for our safe community. As if their heavy presence along the Potomac River here in Prince William County is to protect the town, and not as a direct result of the military base that surrounds it.

From the corner of my eyes, I watch as the muscular body sits, his cap placed on the ledge in front of him. There's no mistaking the insignia sewn onto every cap and Marine flag. The eagle, globe, and anchor, representing each Marine's worldwide commitment to serving their country. The familiar green pattern of his camos holds my attention until Charlie addresses me directly.

"How's your mom holding up, Hunter?"

"She's doing good." *My lie comes out on a heavy sigh. I'm usually good at hiding how worried I am about Mom, but this morning she was confused and vomiting again. I don't know what it means, and with each relapse, her body weakens. Two years ago, she could go months without symptoms, but last year the disease hit her hard. The doctor warned Father there would be rapid decline. He doesn't care. He's away again, even though the attacks are more frequent, and she needs a cane to get around.*

"That's good, son. You go on home now, you're all done." He pats my shoulder. My eyes lift to meet his sympathetic gaze in the mirror. He removes the black cape from around my shoulders before I hop from the red vinyl chair and hold out my five-dollar payment.

"No charge today, son." He shakes his head, waving off the money. With a shrug, I tuck the bill back into my pocket and stroll toward the door.

"You have a good day..." he calls out behind me.

"Thank you, Charlie," I say, lifting my bike from the ground outside.

"Poor kid. Weight of the world on his small shoulders," he tells the Marine. Ignoring their pitying faces, I climb onto my saddle, my feet pushing down onto the pedals as I begin my cycle home. We live on the edge of town, our ranch-style home nestled between Quantico Creek and the borders of the military base. Passing the gate out of town, I stop pedaling, spreading my arms wide as the bike coasts. My head tilts toward the sky, the warm summer air caressing my freshly shaved head. I know there are Marines holding M16's watching me pass, but I don't care. I feel wild, careless and free as I turn up our drive. Jan is away so it's just me and Mom today. Dropping my bike next to the garage door, I run straight to her bedroom.

Empty.

"Mom?" I call, searching the house. She's not here.

"Mom!" I call out again. The panic starts when she doesn't respond. Coming through the kitchen again, my fears subside when I catch sight of her in the back yard. Facing away from the house, she gazes out at Quantico Creek and my heart settles further. She's safe. Stepping through the door, I spy her walking cane leaning against her chair on the patio. She's standing, unaided. A happy bubble expands in my chest.

She must be feeling better since this morning.

"Hey, Mom," I chirp, stopping next to her. Turning, she smiles. Her sapphire eyes puffy from tears. She's been crying. Her long black hair whips around her face in the cool breeze that travels across the creek. She wraps her arms around my shoulders, pulling me to her, leaning into my strength.

"Hey, baby boy. How was your day?"

"I'm not a baby, Mom."

"You'll always be my baby!"

"Well I'm old enough to get a haircut on my own."

"I can see that! You look so handsome."

"Thanks, Mom. How are you feeling?"

"Happy now that you're here."

Her fingers lose some of their grip on my shoulder.

"It's getting cold. Let's go inside, Mom." I wrap my arms around her waist to lead the way. Disorientated when I turn her too quickly, she wobbles.

"Slow down baby, one step at a time. Pass me my cane."

"You don't need it. I'm here!"

"No Hunter, pass my cane." Her voice resigned ",It's not your job to worry about me. You should be outside with your friends having fun."

"I don't want to be outside with them, I want to help make you better."

"No Hunter, I'm not going to get better."

"You will, I'll help you to." I plead with her to listen, showing her how helpful I can be, I pull out her chair at the kitchen table as she sits down.

"Hunter, you said yourself that you're not a baby. You know what's going to happen, don't you?"

"Mom, please don't talk like that, you're going to be fine."

"Oh I wish with all of my heart that was true. I want to stay with you always. There is nothing I want more, but you must be prepared for when I'm gone."

"What the hell does that mean? You're not going anywhere." my fists curl.

"Hunter, I promise to stay with you for as long as I can."

She's giving up: she wants to leave too, just like him!

"I don't want to have this conversation anymore. I'm making pancakes."

Leaving her at the table, I move about the kitchen in anger. Whisking the batter with vigor until she breaks the silence.

"Maybe when you're finished making those pancakes you could go hang out with your friend Trevor?"

My hand stills, my stomach hardening *"He's at that stupid summer camp."*

"Oh Hunter, it's the father-son weekend."

Turning on a sigh, I meet her eyes *"It's a stupid idea anyway. I didn't want to go with him."*

"Hunter ..." full of sympathy, her eyes see right through me. "Your Dad was looking forward to that but he's so busy, it must have slipped his mind. I should have reminded him, I'm sorry sweetheart."

"NO, it's his fault, he doesn't care about us!" I spit.

"He does, he loves you." her eyes swell.

"He loves Molly more! If it was a father-parrot weekend he'd be here."

"Oh Hunter..." she laughs ",that's not true."

"Forget him, Mom, can't we just enjoy our pancakes?"

"I know! let's take our pancakes to the living room and camp out there tonight?"

"That's lame!"

"OK, what would you like to do?"

"We could let Molly out of her cage and try catch her!!"

My eyes light up, my good mood returning when a bubble of her laughter fills the room. I don't ruin the moment by telling her I was serious.

CHAPTER 6

AGENT DELLA PEREZ

Scanning the maple trees beyond the parking lot of the FBI Academy, I exhale deeply. When the dust settled on the Jeffrey Carson case, a serial killer out of Appleton Wisconsin, I was promoted. The profile I developed for the case highlighted a killer aroused by the sound of his victim's bones breaking. It helped to steer Detective Walters's investigation toward a suspect working in a field involving bones, which ultimately led him to Jeffrey Carson.

It led *me* here to Quantico, Virginia, and the position of unit chief of the violent crimes division.

I jumped at the opportunity to travel less. The desire to put down roots, to find a place to call home was more prominent than ever before. But the days are long. Working twelve- to fourteen-hour days leaves me with a non-existent personal life.

Turning back to my desk, I audibly groan over the mountain of case files. I work with hundreds of agents and police officers. For the most part, I've been stationed here at Quantico. That was until an active serial killer came across my desk two months ago.

It's been twenty-one days since his last victim, Gloria Kirkland, was found. The fourth victim in a string of murders, committed by one killer.

March:

His first victim, Joanna Devereaux, was found in Garrisonville, Virginia, not far south from here.

April:

The second victim was Michelle Curtis, from Lima, Ohio.

May:

The third victim was Laura Jarvis, of Cincinnati, Indiana.

June:

His fourth, and most recent victim was Gloria Kirkland, of Illinois, Chicago.

July:

There is no fifth victim. Yet. But he is traveling north, across America, and seems unlikely to stop.

He has two signatures, both highly unusual, and known only to the FBI and local law enforcement teams on the ground. The first lies in how he chooses his victims. They were all survivors of a previous serial-killer attack. In a sick game of déjà vu, he kills them on the date of their original attack, in the same manner as the original killer intended. He is meticulous, skilled. In lieu of physical DNA at the scene, he leaves behind his second signature: a black feather.

It was Gloria's murder that brought me back into the field. I traveled to Chicago when the call came in. I can still hear the wails of her best friend as I arrived on the scene. They followed me through the house as I made my way to her bedroom. The sounds of agonized moans, the weight of misery, and the finality of death echoed around and attached themselves to me like iron anchors. Those burdens tie me to this case and wear me out at once. It's exhausting.

The taskforce set up to oversee this case is spread over four states, with hundreds of officers and agents collaborating. With all the original killers either dead or in prison, our suspect pool has broadened to include family and friends of each killer and the family and friends of each victim. We have scoured through online blogs and articles discussing the original killers, hunting down fans and online trolls who made any threats spanning over the last twenty-five years, since the earliest attack occurred. So far, any potential suspects have been cleared. The *whys* remain unanswered.

Initially, my thought was that his motive was less about the pleasure of the kill and more about asserting himself as some kind of king among killers. However, his behavior during Gloria's murder gave me further insight into his psyche. Unlike the first three victims, she didn't fight back. There were no defensive wounds, nothing to indicate any kind of a struggle. It was as if she accepted her fate, and yet he viciously tortured her before delivering the final blow that killed her.

Bile rises in my throat just thinking of these women's suffering. No person should ever have to face that kind of evil once, let alone twice in their lifetime. It indicates that he was inflicting pain not only to 'finish them off' but for his own pleasure too.

Figuring out how he will select his next victim keeps me awake at night. I've retraced his movements so far and anticipate that he will strike in Iowa or Wisconsin next.

Wisconsin reminds me of my time spent in the Milwaukee office. I miss my old team. Lynam remained there, but thankfully, Agent Ryan was offered a position in the cyber-crimes division here at Quantico. Although we don't work as closely now, it was a relief to have a familiar face around the place in those first few weeks. He's a whizz kid with technology and is already helping to compile a list of other potential victims that this killer could target. I'm having him focus on people who survived an attack in the month of July, spanning back thirty years and starting with Iowa and Wisconsin. Getting ahead of this killer is key right now. We've also requested interviews with the two original serial killers that are still alive and incarcerated. To date, neither have given formal consent to be interviewed.

"Perez, you should go home and get some sleep." My eyes shift to Agent Gary Clark, standing in the doorway of my office. Taller than any man should be allowed, he lounges casually against the frame, the sleeves of his white shirt rolled to his elbows. The tender edge of his husky tone, in perfect harmony with my melancholy, is followed by a warm smile. Gary transferred from counterterrorism to the criminal division a few months before my arrival in Quantico. He's boisterous and at times a joker but has proven himself to be career-focused and determined to get ahead as a profiler. I value his critical thinking, but right now he lacks the ability to intuit certain elements of the crimes. I hope this is something he can develop. With it he will become invaluable to any profiling team.

Meeting his gaze, I smile. "I will, soon."

"That stack of files will be waiting for you in the morning. Come on, I'll buy you dinner."

My eyes burn for sleep my brain is too foggy to think straight. "Oh ..." I manage, scrambling to navigate this delicately. His offer has knocked me off kilter.

The surprise must show on my face, since his fair complexion reddens with each silent second that passes between us.

"As friends," he clarifies, stepping into my office, his blond head cocking as he strolls over to where I sit. I doubt a woman has ever refused a dinner invitation from him. He's not only tall, but broad, with arms that could throw you over his shoulder with ease, and blue eyes that you could drown in if you stared too long. He waits, the offer lingering between us. It should have me weak at the knees. Instead, I find myself remembering wary brown eyes and a guarded heart. I'm pining once again, for my past and a man who wants no place in my future.

"OK, where to?" I hear myself saying. Talking this case over with someone might spark something in me, a new line of investigation and new layer to the profile. And I'm lonely.

"There's an Italian place a few blocks from here. We can walk if you like?" His kind smile is infectious. He towers over me as I grab my purse.

"If it's OK, I'd rather drive behind you. I'm not sure I'd make it there in these heels."

His blue eyes fall to my black pumps, before raking up my exposed legs.

"We can't risk that." He winks playfully, and I laugh. It feels good and with my loneliness forgotten, we walk side by side in easy conversation toward the parking lot.

HUNTER, AGED 12

The incessant whining becomes too much. I bite down on my fist, hard enough that my teeth break the skin. The metallic taste of my own blood sends me into unbridled rage. With a roar, I jump up onto my bed, screaming at the wall that separates Father's office from my bedroom. Spitting and heaving, my fist slam into it, over and over, until I break a hole in it.

"SHUT UP, YOU STUPID BIRD!!" The words are flung from my chest.

"Hunter! What has gotten into you?!" Father's voice pierces through my rage. His hands grip my shoulders as he pulls me back from the wall. I twist and flail in his grasp. My fists, still searching for a target, find his jaw.

"Umph! Jesus, Hunter! Calm down, Champ," he begs. His arms come around mine, pinning them to my sides as we fall onto the mattress. I keep fighting, thrusting my hips up and off his body as he struggles to restrain me.

"I know it's hard, son, but you can't behave this way." He's breathless when he speaks. Exhaustion kicks in, and I go from feeling strong and in control to cold all over, nauseous and afraid. Wrapping my forearms around my stomach, I ask the question plaguing me since Mom's diagnosis.

"Will I get sick too?"

"What your mom has isn't hereditary."

"Why does she have to have the aggressive one?" I cry, hard.

I've researched mom's disease. Multiple sclerosis affects the brain and spinal cord, and the symptoms are wide. Some people can have a mild form, but Mom has one of the worst types. She's dying a slow, painful death and there's nothing I can do. I'd do anything to save her. He doesn't even try. Why won't he even try to save us from this pain?

"I know, it's hard—"

"For me! You're never here. She might live if you stayed home."

He stills beneath me, his silence deafening until he finally answers.

"I can't save her from this, son. I wish I could…"

Liar.

"There is no rhyme or reason. Your mom is fighting to stay with us. She's fighting every day to be here, with you. We have no control over death."

"Don't say that! There are new drugs, new treatments she can try! Don't you say those words to me!" He sounds just like Mom. We have to *do* something.

His cold-hearted acceptance of her impending death feels like a jagged icicle running along my spine. I shiver. He releases his grip, allowing me to move off his body and back onto my bed.

"I'm tired," I tell him. He sits up, staring at me before looking above my head to the hole in the wall.

"We will need to talk about this again," he says, pointing to the damage. I look away. I wait until his weight lifts from the mattress and I hear the gentle click of my door closing. When he's gone, I burrow under my blankets and cover my ears as Molly begins to squawk again.

Six days later...

I press my ear against the door of Father's office and listen.

"How will he take care of the boy now?" Father's colleagues whisper, out in the hall. Their chatter turns my stomach. They can't be dumb enough to believe he ever cared for me. That was all Mom. Even when she was bedridden, she asked about my day. It was Mom who made sure that I'd brushed my teeth or finished my homework. It was Mom who cuddled with me when I was sad.

Now she's gone. I'm on my own and that's exactly how I want it to be. Molly squeals loudly from her cage, as if to remind me that she's going nowhere. Her beady black eyes hold mine as she calls out to her master. Molly knows my secrets; knows how I like to sneak in here when Father is away. She squeals each time, always trying to get me caught.

I wonder if, like me, Molly wants to be free of this house. This giant fucking cage. Lifting my ear from the door, I walk to her aviary. The latch lifts with ease. My hand snakes in to grab hold and catches her by the neck. Adrenaline zings around my body: my hand is shaking as I squeeze, cutting off her air supply. Ending her relentless wailing.

Three hours later...

"Hunter, where's Molly? Molly's gone!" he is screaming in panic from his office. We buried Mom this morning, and he barely shed a tear. This'll teach him, for having mistreated her. He bursts into my room, terror etched in every line of his face.

"Didn't you hear me?" he yells. I remove my headphones, pretending I hadn't.

"What?" I ask, dropping my cd player on the bed and sitting forward.

"Molly. She's gone. Her cage was open, the window was open, Hunter!!"

"I told you it was a bad idea to have people back here." I jump up. *"We'll have to go looking for her."*

"Grab your shoes," he insists, looking at my bare feet. I had changed out of my funeral clothes as soon as I could. "Hurry!" he rushes me. I do. I move with haste, bending to pull on my sneakers and willing myself not to smile.

CHAPTER 7

DEPUTY JONES

M ac's case plagued my mind all night.
Did she take our advice? Was I too quick to lose my temper?
I hate that my professionalism slipped. Embarrassed and unsure how to proceed, I decided to visit with my folks before work. Mom and Dad retired onto three acres of land, about twenty minutes northwest of Appleton. Binghamton is a quiet community in Black Creek and their property is right on the edge of town. Parking my patrol car, I bypass the house and head straight for the old barn Dad converted into a garage out back. As expected, the hood of our orange WD45 Allis-Chalmers tractor is up with Dad on a step ladder next to it, his head in the engine.

Shit! I forgot about Sunday's meet!

Growing up, whenever he had the time off, Dad took me to tractor pulls. He grew up on a farm and always had a love for antique tractors. The power-pulling sport was a natural draw for him. As a kid, I loved watching the restored tractors pull a weighed sled along the 350-foot track, seeing which tractor could pull the sled furthest. Mac loved it too. She often joined us, and before each pull we'd run between the tractors, each choosing the one we thought would win. Dad has a photo of us sitting on the hood of a modified, metallic blue super semi tractor. The memory reminds me of the reason for my visit.

Hollering to be heard over Elvis rocking on the radio, I stop next to the tractor .

"Don't tell me old *On the Run* here is giving you more trouble?" I pat it affectionately.

A small smile creeps up the side of his oil smeared face, though he's still focused on whatever he's fixing. When he retired from the force, he asked if I'd like to help him build the best tractor Wisconsin had ever seen. Despite having a bad back and some arthritis, Dad's in good shape. So, of course I said yes! It took us three years to win a trophy, and while we don't win them all, we're always in the running.

"Nah, she's fine. Just sounded a little funny so I was checking the flywheel..." After one last wrench turn, he stands up straight, holding the housing for support as he stretches out his back. "You ready for Sunday's meet?"

"Yep. She good to go?" My hand glides along the tractor's shiny paint job with pride.

"Last weekend this beauty reached over seventy-two horsepower and pulled near thirty thousand pounds. I was thinking I might move the hood forward a few inches and beef her up with some ceramics and heavier springs, try her in the 4,500-pound class..."

I nod along in agreement. Truth is, Dad's the mechanic, I'm just the driver. I don't have much time to help him. He doesn't nag me about it but a twinge of guilt hits, all the same as he moves around the tractor showing me all the improvements. When he's finished, he hunkers down next to his toolbox, collecting discarded tools from the dirt floor and putting them back inside.

"So, what brings you out here in uniform?" he asks.

"I gotta ask you about something, a case ..."

"Oh yeah?"

"It's connected to the Julie Arnold case." I pause, noting how his back stiffens at the mention of her name. Dad retired with just one unsolved case, but Julie's case was the toughest of his career. He ate himself up every day that her killer remained on the loose, and despite finally putting him behind bars, he still feels guilty about how long it took. He drops a hammer back into the metal box, wiping sweat from his brow as he stands.

"Go on."

"Mac called 911 yesterday. Looks like someone hacked her Wi-fi and had access to her home security and all her personal online data..."

"Is she OK?"

"She's more than OK. She's the same hard-headed woman she was at thirteen, but other than having no home security for a few hours, I think it was a random cyberattack," I explain.

"Then what did you want to ask me?"

I ponder his question, weighing it in my mind. I came here hoping to understand why Mac is hell bent on making an enemy out of me, but I'm not so sure it's my business to be snooping around. He moves to a stool next to his workbench waiting for my response. Leaning on the bench next to him, I finally ask.

"What was it she saw that night?"

"She was only eight years old, a child Jimmy..." a pained expression crosses his face ",Can't you read this in the reports?"

"I've never read *her* statement. Feels like an invasion of privacy, somehow. We were friends," I shrug.

"You never asked her, back then?"

"Once, a few months before she went on that camping trip with Sailor. She told me she didn't want to talk about it, ever. I never asked again."

"And today is different. Why?"

"She was very difficult when I went out to question her last night. I can't figure out what I did to make her hate me."

"She doesn't hate you. You two always butted heads, even when you were the best of friends. What Mac saw that night is her story to tell, son, but I'll say this much. *We* were the first people she was with after that horrific night. She stayed with us until Sailor came to retrieve her. Much of her story is wrapped up in our family too. Let her work through that. She'll come around."

"I didn't remember that." My brows draw together, my mind trawling through my memories and coming up short.

"She was only with us for a few hours then. You two watched cartoons and ate cereal together on the living room floor. She showed you how to build a sturdy pillow fort, you made her laugh. You might not remember, but that was the night you became friends. She was traumatized for years. I think that maybe she feels guilty for laughing with you. You made her happy, son." He shrugs.

"Whoa" My word is a shocked whisper.

I always knew that Mac came into my sphere because Dad worked her mom's case, but there was no time stamp on my memories. It didn't seem important to me until now. Mac's fondness for me was tangled up in tragedy, and her reluctance to have me around makes sense for the first time since my teenaged heart took its first blow.

"Mac is tough, but beneath it all she's scared as hell. You go by and check in on her today. She won't say it, but she'll appreciate it."

"Thanks, Dad."

"OK, let's go inside and see if your mom made lunch. Doing all this manual labor, *alone,* has me hungry." He rubs the oil from his hands onto an old rag and stands.

"Pipe down, old man. I'm the one behind the wheel winning all those trophies."

"Not enough wins to satisfy my thirst!" he laughs as we head into the house together.

"If Mom made iced tea, it might help quench some of your thirst now," I grin, happy I came out to chat with him.

MAC

"Coming back to center, remember to check in with your breath. Bring your head, heart and pelvis in line as we move onto all fours ..." My gaze shifts left to check my client's tabletop pose. Bernadette is sixty-eight and while she's been with me for a year now, I'm always conscious not to push her too hard.

"Great, now curl your toes under and spread your fingers wide onto the mat." She follows my instructions with ease, already hovering her knees off the mat and waiting for me to guide her further.

"When you're ready, and keeping your feet hip width apart, ground down into the mat. Press down with your palms and toes and move back into downward dog."

Her flawless transition into her dog brings a proud smile to my face. When she first started, her muscles were so tight that her heels never met the mat. Now, her spine and legs are straight, her arms and feet solid.

"On the next exhale, come back onto your kne—"

A loud bang startles me mid-sentence. The thunderous clanging of the front door knocker, echoing from the entrance hall up to my studio.

Crap! My security feed is still offline. I was expecting a technician from the police department a few hours ago.

Typical, he decides to show in the middle of my practice!

"Apologies, Bernadette. Bring yourself into *child's* pose, I'll be back shortly."

I gently increase the volume on my meditation playlist and close the door behind me.

Barefoot and muttering with impatience I pull open the door. *Oh!* Jimmy Jones is leaning against the frame. Blinking away my surprise and ignoring the familiar curve of his smile, my irritation returns.

"I'm in the middle of a class," I huff.

His smile disappears. "Sorry, I tried to call ahead, but you didn't answer. I'm just checking in."

My deep breath, meant to center me instead brings the earthy musk of his aftershave right to my core. Its sudden, sensual effect has me wanting to hide behind the door.

His eyes look over my head, searching my home.

"I'm busy with a client right now and your tech guy never showed, so I've nothing to update you on. If you don't mind …"

His foot blocks my attempt to close the door.

"I just want five minutes, OK?"

"No."

"Why are you being so difficult?"

"Why do you care? You did your job!"

"I've always cared about you, Mac—" His lips clamp together.

"Don't be ridiculous. You don't even know me now."

Memories fill my mind, whirling with moments of laughter and a childhood spent with Jimmy. Tractor meets and hotdogs, building pillow forts and running through the woods while hiking with Sailor. Years of regret ache in my chest as the light in his eyes fade.

"I ..." he removes his foot from the door. "You're right. I don't know you anymore."

"I've got a client —"

"MacKenna, dear, I have to go." My miserable excuse is interrupted by Bernadette gliding down the stairs, socks and shoes on, her yoga mat slung over her shoulder as she waltzes toward the door.

"Bernadette! I'm so sorry, this was completely unprofessional."

"Don't be silly, these things happen ... " She eyes Jones and winks. "I'll see you Friday!" Passing us, she turns back. "Oh, and MacKenna? you might have a mouse, dear. I heard some scratching sounds along the baseboards. I can give you the number of an exterminator!" she chirps over her shoulder. Moving fast for a woman of her age, she jumps into her car.

"I can't believe you drove away my client!" I grumble.

"It's hardly my fault!" His derisive tone reignites my anger at his disruption.

"I'd appreciate if you'd phone ahead before coming by!"

"I'll put in a call to Bob, see where he's at. I could do with a coffee, if you're making some?" He's already moving in my direction and without hesitation, I shut the door in his face and shout loud enough for him to hear me on the other side.

"Absolutely not! *I'll* call Bob. *You* can remove yourself from my property, or I'm calling your dad!"

"Not before I tell him you've slammed the door in my face!"

I can't believe I just did that.

My hands fly to my mouth to suppress my laughter. An old familiar feeling of warmth pings warning signals in my brain. I retreat to my yoga studio. Jimmy Jones might be a safe space or the most dangerous place for someone like me.

HUNTER, AGED 13

Silence would be nice.

Lorraine, the third nanny he's hired, can't stand it. She chatters at me, firing questions about my day as she sets a garden salad in front of me.

"What's this?" my nose wrinkles in distaste.

"It's a healthy option. You eat too much junk food," she chirps, ignoring my disgust.

"I'm not eating this..."

"HUNTER!" Father bellows in a warning tone from the kitchen doorway.

What's he doing out of his office? I scowl in his direction.

"You will not speak to Lorraine that way. Apologize!" he demands.

"It's OK, Alex..." she begins, before quickly correcting herself. "I mean, Mr. Fisher."

Interesting.

Seeing my notice, heat crawls up their necks, coloring their deceitful faces red. He stands tall. His attempt to assert some authority is wasted.

"No, he will show you some respect under this roof!"

"And in the yard?" I snort.

"What about the yard?" he growls.

"Or what about in the car?"

"What are you talking about?"

"Can I tell her to shove her salad when I'm not under this *roof?"*

"Go to your room!" His fists curl into balls at his side. "You'll go hungry for the night, maybe then you'll appreciate the effort made on your behalf."

Unfazed, I push against the table with both hands, putting all my weight into my chair and forcing the legs to scrape loudly against the wooden floor. Yawning, I waltz past them, enjoying how they both stare in disbelief at my cool response.

"I'm sorry, Lorraine, this looks delicious ..." he tells her.

Lying son of a bitch!

Leaving them both in the kitchen, I sneak outside. There's a path running along Quantico Creek. Where it passes behind our house, Mom's friends put her name on a bench that stands in her memory, allowing me to visit every day. I unearth Molly's wooden box from under the wrought iron bench to keep me company. I keep her here as a gift to Mom. On a windy day, as air whips across the creek, I can hear her irritable whistles. It reminds me of Father's suffering and sends a rush of warmth through me. He can't suffer enough for how he's treated us. Lifting the lid, I peak inside. Some feathers remain, but I've taken enough to torture him. Maybe one day, I'll throw the rest of her back into the aviary he still keeps. Feeling more in control, I drop the wooden lid back in place, returning Molly to the ground before climbing back through my bedroom window.

They're still laughing and chatting. They hadn't even noticed I'd left. Heading straight to his office, I rummage through the drawers of his desk. Hidden beneath a stack of files is a new folder. The word survivors *is written across the front in thick red marker. Flipping it open, I lift the first image.*

This is different. She's alive! Smiling and looking into the camera.

Flipping through the photos, I see different faces, all very much alive. Beneath the pile, he's keeping cut-out newspaper articles. I scan the headlines:

Survivor of the "Quantico Killer" Recounts Her Ordeal During Trial.

The Girl that Got Away! City Slayer Leaves Victim Alive.

Hide & Seek Saves Little Girl's Life: Killer Still at Large.

This is new.

Another peal of laughter filters down the hallway and spurs my anger into action. Dropping one of Molly's long black feathers between the manilla sleeves, I take the entire contents of the folder. Finding it should remind him that he can't escape his past. He doesn't get to move on and be happy after our suffering.

HUNTER

Present Day

A smile tugs at the edge of my mouth. I watch her sleep from the end of her bed. Each breath she takes is a gift, given by me, to her. I could take her life right now. Images of driving my knife into her heart; watching the blood pump all over the sheets flood my mind. The ripple of my desire is so strong that she must feel it too: She shudders beneath the thin sheet that covers her shoulders.

MacKenna Arnold. All grown up, but still a frightened little girl.

I've watched her for two days now. I understand her much better than Father ever could. He prefers to talk with his victims, but people only say what they want you to hear, to believe. I prefer to observe, to listen when they think they're alone. I become the fly on the wall many people only wish they could be.

MacKenna pretends to be tough, and yet she sleeps each night with her bedside lamp on. She talks like she has her life all worked out, but her pathetic attempts to protect herself reveal her frailty. It's kept me company the past two nights in the cramped bunker.

I'm comfortable enough in that dark hole. But crawling out of it, getting closer—close enough to smell her fear? That's what feeds my patience. One more day and I can take what I came for. Reclaim time that should have been mine. Not hers. She got so much attention, just because she hid in a hole. Sickening.

I crawl back into the space, sliding the false wall back into place. I spy her through the thin sliver, just before I close it, in time to see her leap upright in her bed.

She feels me. I like that. I might even prolong our time together, tomorrow.

The headline "Hide and Seek Saves Little Girl's Life" flashes in my memory. I can't help but grin now. It feels unnatural, but there's no stopping it. It's almost time to rewrite the story.

CHAPTER 8

DEPUTY JONES

Bob's on his way. Apparently, he tried to phone Mac earlier and got no answer. The sun is sinking below the horizon as I pull into her drive for the second time today. Since this afternoon didn't go as planned, I left her alone, deciding to come back after my shift. I lean against the hood of my black GMC, waiting for Bob to arrive. I glance to an upstairs window. I can't see her, but I feel her eyes on me.

After my conversation with Dad, I felt certain that pushing a little harder and coming back here would show her that I want to help; that she can rely on me to serve and protect not just her but this community. My stomach twists with the realization that it matters that she doubts me. She doubts my capabilities and my ego doesn't like it. Memories of the teenager in me, who worked up the courage to ask her to dance and got a bloody nose for his trouble, doesn't like it either. Mac wears her trauma as well as she wore her pretty pink dress that night. Layers of sparkle and tulle all draped carefully into a bubble around her, soft as air and striking as her demeanor. Beneath all the trappings is that eight-year-old child who witnessed her mom get murdered. As soon as you try to get close, you get hurt. I learned my lesson that night, but this is different. It's about her safety. Once Bob gives her security system the all clear, I'll leave her be.

My phone buzzes in the pocket of my jeans. I pull it out and the caller ID shows Walters's name flashing on the screen.

"I left the report on your desk," I tell him, assuming that's why he's calling.

"I got it. I also just got off the phone with a Ms. MacKenna Arnold. Says you're harassing her. Apparently, you're in her driveway, staring up at her window?" An impatient sigh comes over the line.

What the hell?

"She did *not* call the cops on me!"

"Oh yes, she did. And if you don't get your ass off her property, the next call is going through dispatch, so it *will* be on record. Got it?"

"I was waiting for Bob, he's literally just pulling up now!" I turn, pointing to Bob's car as he parks along the curb.

"The pope could be arriving on scene and you'd still have no business being there! Get your ass back in your truck and drive away, Jones. Do you want to put your degree, your career at risk because your ego took a hit?" His tone is firm, certain and annoyingly persuasive. He's right. I've tried to help Mac, but if she phoned John then I've gone too far.

"I'm already getting back in my truck, but just so you know—"

"I know, Jones. I get it. But we've got people phoning night and day, who *want* our help, who need our help. Saving that girl isn't your job."

His words sober me. "Got it."

"I'll see you tomorrow."

He hangs up. I climb back into my truck, rolling down my window as Bob walks up the drive.

"Thanks again, Bob. I'll catch you back at the station tomorrow." I fasten my seatbelt and reverse out of her drive, glancing up at the second -floor window once more. She was watching all right. Then, and now.

I've been out on patrol all morning and don't get to the station until after two p.m. John's out running down leads on a case he's currently working.

"There you are ..." I look up from my monitor to find Bob perching himself on the edge of my desk. "I've been looking for you all morning!" he says, his small eyes finding mine over the silver rims of his glasses.

"Oh yeah?" I sit back, happy to take a break from typing.

"I ran the security checks on the router like you asked. I was a little perplexed, to be honest." He crosses his arms, his shoulders shrugging. "So I checked the router table and found a list of all the recent IP addresses that attached to it."

I hold my hand up to stop him. "Sorry, Bob. You'll have to dumb this down for me." I've heard the terminology, but really that's as far as my knowledge goes on routers. He smiles brightly, apparently relishing the chance to geek out. Hopping off the edge of my desk, he sits down in my guest chair.

"OK, this is hacking 101. A hacker needs your IP address to gain access to your device; whether that's a phone, laptop, security system or smartwatch. Every one of those devices has its own personal IP address."

"I'm following ... "

"When you pay for Wi-fi at home, your Internet Service Provider, or ISP, will come out and install a router in your home. Every device in that home now has its own personal IP address to that router that never changes. Each device, once logged onto the web, sends requests from its personal IP address and the router sends the answer back to that device only. The IP address protects the individual's privacy, ensuring one user's request is never sent to another's device."

"Right, keep going ..." I nod along.

"In order for a hacker to gain access to your router, he needs to know your IP address, which is so random that most often the hacker will send you a link via email to respond to or social media to follow. If you open that link, you've essentially opened a back door for the hacker to access all your information. From there, they can connect to your router and gain access to every other device connected to that router."

"Is that what happened here?"

He nods. "Yeah. Unfortunately, because Mac is security conscious, she opened a link to supposedly update her firewall on her work laptop three nights ago. Little did she know, she was giving access to the hacker."

"Did they steal any information?"

"I can't see anything, because whoever they are, they deleted all of the logs. I ran security checks and couldn't find any bugs either. We changed the passwords on every device and on the router and rebooted her whole system."

"What about her bank accounts?"

"Nothing. The data seems to be safe ..." He chews the inside of his lip.

"What has you perplexed then?" I wonder. From where I'm sitting this seems like good news.

"I'm wondering: why bother?"

"Maybe he intended to come back later, was holding the door open for future access?" I guess.

"It's possible, but it would be unusual."

"OK. But wouldn't Mac's finances be small change to him?"

"No! I asked about that and apparently your girl is *very* well off!"

Oh. I'd always known that Mac's mom left her some money, but Bob's eyes are widening to suggest Mac is more than just comfortable.

"Then why not just take her money and be done with it?"

"Exactly. Unless he planned on coming and going and taking out funds regularly until she noticed her accounts down and money missing from her bank. He looked at her accounts but that's it. Why bother?" He shrugs again. "Oh, and the email the hacker sent was so specific, it's like he knew her."

"Do you have it?" I ask. I stand to try to ease the uncomfortable knot that's forming in my gut again.

"Yeah, I printed it off. I'll go grab you a copy."

I wonder if there could be another possible motive, other than gathering Mac's information.

"Bob, why else would a hacker get onto a system and not touch anything?"

"He did. He deleted the security footage: that's why I came to you. Why only delete the camera footage?"

My heart pounds in my ears.

"Because there's something on it he doesn't want her to see! Jesus, Bob, you could have opened with that information!"

Someone is watching her.

"I was getting to it!" he fumbles.

"Can we trace him somehow?"

"No. Unfortunately, he used a VPN, which is an encrypted code that prevents me from locating his IP address. I could put a warrant in, requesting Mac's service provider supply more information, but guys like these usually bounce the signal from country to country. I doubt a judge will issue the warrant, seeing that there wasn't any real criminal damage."

"Can't we run a secondary trace, try to pinpoint his location?" I begin to pace.

"I don't have access to a system that would allow me to do that."

"Who would have that access?"

"That would be a job for national or military intelligence, and they would never entertain a case like this. Nothing's been taken."

I stop. "National intelligence, as in CIA, FBI?" *As in, Special Agent Della Perez!*

"Yeah?" He's looking at me like I'm the dumbest cop he's ever come across.

"I'll phone Walters. Can you grab the email?"

"On it," he smiles already heading toward the stairs that will take him to his second-floor office.

HUNTER, AGED 14

*T*he banner above the red brick building in Waynesboro, Virginia reads, "Dedicated to setting your son on the right path."

We walk along the wide corridors in silence, the clicking of the receptionist's heels the only sound as she leads us to the dean's office. Dropping into a chair in front of his desk and ignoring his stern expression, I slouch as he speaks with Father. The arrangements were made two nights ago, my bags were packed yesterday and now here I am. I screwed up, royally. Rage heats my blood just thinking about it.

Lorraine cried she was getting fat, but Father told her she was cute. So not true! When she screamed at him for no reason, he looked concerned, but forgave her quickly. Not even the acne, the moustache or oversleeping turned him away. He was at her side, worried about her, so I upped the dose. Just a little extra, but it sent her into a spasm.

I knew she was weak!

My mother suffered through so much worse than that, but Lorraine was rushed to the hospital, with Father by her side. They ran blood tests, and the jig was up. When Father heard the words "corticosteroid poisoning," he knew. That night, he hit me, for the first time ever.

"Where are they?" he'd screamed, pulling my bedroom apart in search of Mom's old medications. She's been dead for three years and this was the first time he'd wondered about them. I stayed silent, pretending *to be clueless with a simple shoulder shrug. He snapped. His open hand contacted my cheek with full force. It knocked me over.*

"YOU COULD HAVE KILLED LORRAINE! DO YOU UNDERSTAND HOW SERIOUS THIS IS?" he screamed. I lay in the wreckage of my bedroom. Everything I own in this world was strewn across the floor as he continued to search. I didn't bother to deny it.

"If the police found out ..." Breathless, he fell onto the mattress. "First it was Molly and now this. You went too far, Hunter. you leave me with no choice."

Those were the last words he spoke to me.

Today, he left a chubby Lorraine at home to bring me here. I've practically grown up on a military base: why he thinks military school will scare me, I don't know.

CHAPTER 9

AGENT DELLA PEREZ

The hallway leading to the section chief's office is lined with the framed faces of agents who have worked this division since its infancy, in 1984. I come to his photo. The once-youthful Agent Leonard, with eyes full of determination, is a far cry from the overweight section chief he is today. Now he's worn down, by hard years and too much bourbon. His nose and eyes are red, and all his words are cynical.

Lingering in his doorway, I exhale slowly, willing my throbbing heart to ease off the throttle. Agent Leonard worked alongside the first profilers: trailblazers in the field of criminal psychology and the men responsible for the BAU he now oversees. I took this job to soak up his knowledge, to strive to be as good as he is. Unfortunately, with every interaction, his disapproval of my appointment to unit chief reveals itself through a pattern of indirect negative remarks. I curl my shaking fingers into fists and squeeze tightly. My physical reaction to having been summoned tells me that all I've really absorbed is snide comments, detrimental to my confidence. I knock lightly.

He turns from his eighth-floor office window. His bloodshot eyes meet mine from across the room. He moves, dropping his weight into his chair. The wheels squeak in protest.

"Agent Perez, come in."

"You wanted to see me, sir?" I approach his mahogany desk, anxious to get this meeting over with as soon as possible.

"Yes. Do you have an update on those murders?"

"I've been liaising with our teams on the ground, trying to find a link between all the victims. The victimology is completely different, other than the fact that they had all survived previous similar attacks. But I think we're missing something," I confess.

"Victimology aside Perez, why did it take the FBI four months to link these cases?"

"Unfortunately, local law enforcement were slow to input the data from their crime scenes into ViCap. A connection between each murder was only established after the third kill."

He sharpens his tone. "And what are we doing now to progress this case?"

"We've sent the feathers to a forensic ornithologist to identify the species of bird they came from. He found some torn skin and blood on the tips of each feather along with damage to the feathers themselves. It indicates that the feathers were violently plucked from the bird. We're waiting on a full analysis."

"How long does it take to find out the type of bird?"

"He has to compare the feather to over 11,000 different specimens. Hopefully soon."

"Could the blood be human?" he asks.

"No, he has confirmed it is avian blood. Unfortunately, we were unable to date it accurately, which suggests the blood itself is over two years old."

"He's held onto these feathers for more than two years?" his faces creases in disgust.

"Or longer, there's no way to know how long for sure."

"Hmm. He's a strange one. OK, so what's next in your investigation?"

He leans back into his chair, his eyes ablaze with disappointment. I squirm under the heat.

"We've requested interviews with the killers in each of the original cases. No formal consent has yet been received. I've emailed the warden of each prison to see how we might be able to convince the prisoner to meet with me. I'm also compiling a list of potential victims, hoping to pre-empt his—"

"No." His hand slices through the air between us. "We can't waste resources running down hypothetical leads. We're not psychics, Agent Perez, our job is to develop investigative tools for local law enforcement. Get those interviews in place, that's the best next step."

"But surely preventing—"

"Do you know what will happen if news of this killer hits the mainstream media? We will have thousands of survivors terrified of a second attack."

"Shouldn't people be alert?"

His eyes narrow. "Keep focused on your role, Agent Perez." There is no hiding the irritation in his tone now. I mull it over for a moment.

"I am focused, however with each new murder, this killer is crossing state lines, sir, making this a federal crime. And while I don't plan on excluding local law enforcement, we should be present and available and using whatever resources are at hand to track him down."

"When the director hired you, Perez, he was impressed by your work on the Jeffrey Carson case. I'm not convinced that seeing one case to a successful conclusion equates to having the skills necessary to oversee a team of agents."

I knew it!

"With all due respect, sir, I was hired because of my initiative on that investigation. I'm a hard worker and prior to that case, I had seen plenty others to a successful conclusion." I assert myself but find my voice shrinking under his glare.

"Yes, and I value your skill set. Women are naturally more intuitive—"

"And men are more suited to leading a team?" I cut across him and sit up straighter in my chair.

"Sex aside, " he ploughs on, drowning out my interruption, "the media have yet to link these murders. Once that happens, the Bureau will come under intense scrutiny. I need someone who can handle that kind of pressure."

"Have I given you reason to believe that I can't?"

He squints with frustration. If he intends on removing me from this case, I refuse to make it easy for him.

"Frankly, no. But I haven't worked with you long enough to know your capabilities."

"Yet here I am, working in a position given to me by the director. My record should speak for itself until such a time that it doesn't."

"I'm not prepared to sit by while a case like this is mishandled!"

"There is nothing to suggest that I would mess this up."

"It has been noted that you are emotionally invested in this case: staying late, checking in with the victims' families by phone. I find it too personal on such a high-level case."

"Noted? By who?" Heat prickles my skin.

"That's irrelevant," he answers, shrugging.

"I'm building trust with the families of the victims, gathering as much information as I can, to find that common thread that we all agree has not yet been found!" I'm livid.

"I have no doubt you are good at your job, Perez. My concern lies solely in your ability to lead so many teams on the ground. This is a large-scale investigation and unlike anything you've had to take on."

"What are you suggesting?"

"Agent Gary Clark will take over as lead, as of tomorrow morning. He will oversee the teams on the ground and direct the investigation from there."

"I think you are making a mistake. Agent Clark has very little experience in the field of profiling—"

"Agent Clark ran a successful team in the counterterrorism division and comes with years of experience in counterintelligence, analysis, and data collection. His judgment and critical thinking won't be clouded by emotional attachment."

Wow.

His sexist attitude toward women in the field flames my irritation, adding fuel to my already blazing intent to catch this killer. He may be my boss but I work for the victims of these heinous criminals. Nevertheless, if I want to continue working the cases and have any chance at furthering my career, I must remain civil with this man.

"Am I to understand that I have already been replaced by Agent Gary Clark?"

"Yes. I hope you will bring him up to speed and continue to work alongside him."

Anger, disappointment and embarrassment all prickle behind my eyes. I contain myself, unwilling to give him any display of emotion to hold against me. My voice is controlled when I speak.

"Absolutely, I will because I am a professional. However, I will not entertain any insinuation that my emotions have influenced your decision-making. If you question my capabilities, that is one thing, but I have worked this case relentlessly and will not be labeled as "emotional". Your antiquated views of women in the field are not only unfounded but deeply offensive."

His jowls redden. I stand to leave.

"Will that be all?" my tongue is heavy with sarcasm.

"For now. We will meet at oh-eight-hundred hours with Clark to consider the next stage in the investigation. Thank you, Perez." He dismisses me. His move is completely unorthodox and undermines me in front of the entire Bureau.

No! I won't let that happen.

With my shoulders pulled back and a renewed sense of determination in my stride, I return to my office. My anger keeps me out of my chair, pacing back and forth I go over the conversation in my mind.

Who the hell *in my team has been reporting to him? And behind my back!*

Clark's face springs to mind.

He wouldn't. Not after our night together ...

The rattle of my phone vibrating across my desk distracts me. It helps to quieten my mind. I reach for my phone.

John Walters! His name on the screen sends my poor heart racing, all over again.

Now, of all the times, he decides to pick up the phone?

Detective John Walters phoned me. *Why?* Hope springs, sending warmth and longing to my gut.

No. I won't do this to myself.

To speak with him now, to see him, to allow myself to indulge in fantasies of his strength, would be dangerous enough when I'm confident, let alone feeling vulnerable.

Ignoring the call, I focus on my breath, on my next move.

I'm not giving this case up without a fight.

I log onto my computer and access the list of names Agent Ryan compiled for me. It identifies serial killers from across the US and any victims that escaped them.

689 in total.

To narrow down the number, we focused on killers active after 1970.

533 serial killers...

If our unsub follows his current pattern, he will kill next in either Iowa or Wisconsin, which reduces the list drastically.

34 possible killers to emulate from those states.

12 potential victims...

Two victims in Iowa and ten in Wisconsin. I scan the list of victims now.

Faye Anderson!

The name jumps off the screen causing my heart to momentarily shrink in fear.

It seems this killer is working in chronological order. Faye was attacked in December. Fortunately for her, our killer will most likely choose a victim originally attacked in July.

With that in mind, we have been able to reduce the list of victims further.

3 potential victims, all of them living in Wisconsin. The anniversary of one of the original attacks is today. She's in Appleton. My feet itch. The urge to go there to check in, follow this line of inquiry is too strong to ignore. Thoughts of Detective Walters simmer in my

memory, but I set them aside. I have a job to do.

I call Agent Ryan's cell. He picks up straight away.

"Hey, Perez. What's up?"

"I'm just looking over the list of names you gave me. I was hoping for some advice," I confess.

"Go for it," I can picture his smiling face. Then I look up and see it in my doorway. We both grin and hang up as he walks in. He's changed since arriving in Virginia. Gone is the smooth baby face. He now sports a full black beard, that he wears well. The confidence he's gained is a reminder of what I'd hoped to achieve here too. I'm so proud to see him grow as an agent.

"Were you lurking in the hallway?" I laugh.

"I just left Leonard's office." He winces.

"Oh yeah?"

"Yeah. And for what it's worth, I think it's bullshit. Nobody is more capable of catching this guy than you."

His vote of confidence has me looking away to compose myself. "Thanks, Ryan. Did you come to check up on me?"

"That, and to call him a dick." I laugh, the sound filling the room. He grins at my response.

"What advice did you need?"

"I was looking over your list: great work, by the way! All three potential victims are in Wisconsin. As of tomorrow, I'm no longer unit chief on the case …"

I nibble on my bottom lip, holding back for a heartbeat before revealing my intentions.

"I'm flying out to Wisconsin today. I want to make one final call as unit chief before Clark takes over tomorrow."

"Lemme see the list?" He peers over my shoulder at the screen. "The survivors are spread out across the state. One in Eau Claire, another in Appleton, and the third in Phillips. Where *will* you begin?" he says archly. There's no hiding his playful smirk, even behind the thick black beard. Agent Ryan is no fool.

"I'll start with the dates. MacKenna Arnold survived serial killer Thomas Moseley twenty years ago today."

"What was Moseley's MO?"

"He broke into the homes of his victims, raped, beat, and stabbed them to death. He was responsible for the deaths of five women and two children. Julie Arnold, MacKenna's mother, was one of his victims. MacKenna Arnold is the only known survivor. Says here she managed to hide in the home."

I look at my watch. It's almost ten.

"I don't want to create panic on a hunch. If it's not her, there are two other names on that list, the anniversaries happen later in the month. I'll check in with MacKenna Arnold and go from there."

Agent Ryan is already tapping away on his phone.

"You could catch the one p.m. Delta flight out of Reagan and fly into Austin Straubel airport in Green Bay. You'll be there by six."

"OK, book me on that flight." I print off all the information I have in front of me, including my current profile on this killer. "Thank you, Ryan."

I turn to leave, my briefcase jammed with all the documentation I can carry.

"Sure, but Della—" he calls, "What about Clark and Leonard?"

"For the next twenty-two hours, I'm still overseeing this case."

"Should I call ahead and let Detective Walters know you're headed to Appleton?"

I can't deny the prospect of seeing John again fills me with both dread and excitement. Is it fate that brings me back into his orbit for the second time or am I creating a connection to this case that doesn't exist?

NO!

My gut screams in response. Whatever my feelings for Detective John Walters I have a job to do.

"No, I'll call when I touch down. Will you follow up with the prisons? Try to get me an interview with a serial killer. If it's easy enough for Piers Morgan, it should be easy enough for the FBI."

He chuckles at that. "I'm not a big fan, but I'll channel my inner Piers."

"Please, don't do the—"

"*I'll do my bloody best, Della!*" His eyes pop wide in his attempt at an English accent. Chortling together, we walk to the elevators. He wishes me luck as the doors slide closed.

Julie Arnold's killer entered her home between eleven p.m. and midnight. I'll need to figure out how to approach MacKenna Arnold without striking fear into her life again.

HUNTER, AGED 15

*F*or the first few weeks, he called almost every day. That dwindled to once a week, then to hearing from him once a month. If I'm lucky.

He's cast me aside, the scraps of his first marriage, too much trouble to be remembered.

Or loved.

When the dean told me Father was on the phone, I was intrigued. Leaning against the cold brick wall of the empty corridor, I bring the handset to my ear. I listen as he delivers his big news, each word hammering home my worst fears. He's never going to choose me.

"We wanted to invite you to the wedding, but it was all very spur of the moment."

Mom's face flashes in my memory. The grief has numbed over time, but his words elicit a strong physical response within me. Tears blur my vision, emotions tighten my throat and chest, squeezing the last shred of hope from my body. My powerlessness begins to burn, heating my blood and causing it to bubble beneath my skin, pulsating until anger fills me.

"I want to come home," I finally force out, pressing my forehead to the cold wall.

"Hunter ..." a buzzer sounds, then I hear a rattle of keys and the clinking of metal.

"Where are you?" I ask.

"I'm in Philadelphia. Can we talk about this when I get home?"

"You're always too busy! I'm done with this shithole: I'm coming home!" I growl.

"No!" he bursts angrily. "Not until your behavior improves. Lorraine is afraid of you."

I can't stand the pressure radiating throughout my entire body. I slam my head into the wall, over and over.

"Hunter? Hunter?"

I ignore the squawking phone, grunting furiously, spitting, heaving, wanting to feel anything but this hurt.

"Hunter! What's that noise?"

It's the last thing I hear before I black out.

CHAPTER 10

DETECTIVE JOHN WALTERS

Perched on the edge of my desk, I reluctantly call Della again.

Why is it so hot in here?

I unfasten the top button of my shirt, listening as the rings are replaced by her voicemail greeting. The strangest sensation washes over me.

Relief? Disappointment?

Both notions are equally discomforting and intrusive to my workload.

"She's not picking up."

Jones stops pacing to face me. He's been busy wearing himself and my wooden floor out, since his conversation with Bob.

"Should you try again? Or I could send her a text." He reaches into the pocket of his uniform slacks to retrieve his cell.

"Jones, we chase criminals, not FBI agents ..."

"It's Perez!" he interrupts. "She's one of us." As if this is obvious.

Is she?

The last time I laid eyes on Agent Della Perez, we were battling serial killer Jeffery Carson in the woods outside Crivitz. Her delicate hands put life-saving pressure on my gunshot wounds. Her eyes pleaded with me to survive. We had saved each other that night, and thoughts of her since always bring my body to life.

"Look, Jones. Take a seat for a few minutes, let's think this through. Even if Della can help trace the hackers, we still need to figure out if there is a real threat to MacKenna Arnold. She's made it abundantly clear that she doesn't want to deal with you. How do we investigate an unreported crime?" I remind him.

"She will want my help, when she knows she's in danger!"

He drops irritably into the offered seat, his fingers already rapping against his thigh. His apprehension is a palpable thing and gives me cause for concern. He's in danger of becoming too invested in this case. *In Mac.*

"We don't know that for sure, Jones. You can't go over there, guns blazing, and scaring her. We need to look into everything a little further first."

"OK. How do we do that?"

"How would you do it with any other case?"

"Go back to the start?" He sounds unsure.

"Exactly. She received this email three nights ago." Reaching to grab the page from my desk, I glance at the details. Date stamped July 10, 7:15 p.m., it appears to be legitimate. The sender email address is the exact company from which MacKenna purchased her home security system.

"We start there. It may be that this store was the target, and their customer database has been compromised. The hacker could have information on everyone that's ever shopped there. If that's the case, we have more than one victim."

And if that's the case, this investigation is going to the cybercrimes division.

He nods. "You're right. It's just ..." he falters.

"What?"

"This feeling keeps poking my chest. Like, I'm missing something," he admits.

"That comes with the territory. We're not psychics. We don't know the answers until we start looking for them. You've got a hunch; it might lead you somewhere, but cutting corners and rushing to conclusions isn't the answer. In fact, it guarantees that you *will* miss something."

Determination flashes in his eyes. "You're right. Let's go back to the start."

"Fox River Mall it is."

Home Sure is nestled between a *Game Stop* and *LA Wireless* on the first floor of the Fox River Mall. A huge banner hangs over a row of cash registers on the back wall that reads *"Number One for Home Security in Wisconsin."*

Staff members walk the floor wearing blue polo shirts, tending to customers and answering questions on the huge range of security products sold here.

"Jesus, they're selling everything from audio jammers to pepper sprays." Jones picks something up as we make our way to the cashiers. "Look: it's a flashlight with a built-in pepper spray!" He turns it over in his hand.

"Yeah, I've seen it before. Put it back." I scowl.

"I'm buying it," he argues.

"That gun on your hip would do a better job of saving you and save your fifty bucks."

"It's only twenty-five. And besides, it's not for me."

I'm about to ask who it's for but I suspect I already know the answer. The clerk calls our turn just then.

"Good afternoon, gentlemen! Will this be all today?" The pretty brunette smiles between us. When her eyes land on Jones, she blushes. Noticing, he leans casually on the countertop, deepening his smile.

Oh man, here we go.

"Actually, we wondered if you could help us out with some information on your home security systems." He's putting on all the charm now.

"Sure thing. What is it you're looking to know?" She rings up the flashlight, her focus solely on him as she does. Content to let him to take the lead, I lean with my back against the counter, scanning the room. It's a busy store. The staff appear to be young, college-aged men and women. No one stands out as oddly suited for the job.

"Can you tell me a little about your home cameras?" Jones asks.

"Most of our cameras and surveillance devices are wireless and allow people to monitor their homes from anywhere in the world, without the hassle of a security contract." She rhymes off a well-rehearsed script. "We don't offer twenty-four-hour monitoring contracts."

"If I purchase a camera today, do you keep a record of that sale on file?"

Too soon, Jones!

Noting the wary look in her eyes, I explain.

"We're with the Outagamie Sheriff's department, miss. These are just routine questions. Nothing to worry about." Her eyes dart between us and our offered badges. Satisfied that we mean no harm, she continues.

"We do ask for your email address upon purchase. We send out malware updates and special offers, in our newsletter." she reveals hesitantly.

"If we provided an email address, could you check if it's in your system?" Jones asks. She nods and Jones passes her a slip of paper with MacKenna's email address.

"OK, let me see if I can find it. ... Oh." She blinks at the screen before looking back to Jones.

"Everything OK?" I wonder.

She tries some more typing. "Yeah. Um, I've been logged out. My password isn't working. I'll go get a manager." She approaches a man at the opposite end of the counter.

An angry female voice pulls our attention to the line of customers forming behind us.

"What are you doing here?!" Hazel eyes are glaring at Jones.

Pinching the bridge of my nose and inhaling deeply, I prepare myself for *Mac and Jones*, round two.

MAC

Home Sure, my ass!

Three nights ago, I opened an email from the store.

One little click of a mouse and a virtual backdoor opened, welcoming a hacker into my life. He had access to all my home security, my bank details, my personal files, to *me*. Having spent all this morning looking through the information he's perused, the knot in my stomach pulled tight as reality dawned. He used my need to feel safe against me and violated me in ways I hadn't anticipated.

I'm moving to the cash registers at the back of the store when my eyes note the unmistakable shoulders of Jimmy Jones, leaning on the counter and flirting with a sales clerk.

This can hardly be a coincidence.

"What are you doing here?!" My words dislodge the fear that's been sitting heavy in my chest all morning. Exposed, it ricochets between us with an angry thump.

He turns, the orange hues of his amber eyes burning briefly, then simmering down. "I'm buying a flashlight," he says shortly, then returns his attention to the clerk.

Thump.

I stare at his back.

Thump.

My cheeks flaming.

Thump.

A throat clears, pulling my attention to the alert stare of Detective Walters. One dark brow raises over those warm brown eyes that strip me of my armour. It's as though it clatters to the floor with just one knowing look from a stranger.

Thump, thump, thump, thump.

His sympathetic nod is the last straw. My eyes tear up, exposing my fear for everyone to witness.

"Next, please." A clerk calls from a different register. Harnessing every ounce of energy to hold myself together, I stay put. I won't run. I won't break down. Not here, not in front of Jones and Detective Walters.

"Next, please!" she calls again.

Jones looks over his ridiculously wide shoulders, stiffening when he meets my watery gaze. The warmth in his amber eyes reveal too much emotion. It's not sympathy or confusion, but something else. Something like concern, but much deeper and infinitely scarier.

"NEXT. PLEASE."

The clerk's impatient tone jolts my attention away from him and demands that the rest of my self-control return, so I finally move to her till.

Was I targeted, or were the store and its customers the goals?

Explaining the reason for my visit, I demand they remove my information from their system. Pushing the black rims of her glasses up her nose, the clerk stares in bewilderment at her computer screen.

"Hm. I can't seem to gain access to the sales logs. Let me go grab a manager."

She rushes over to the same manager dealing with Jones and Walters's sales clerk. I watch their exchange: the clerks' confusion, the manager's frown as he absorbs the information being relayed to him. It's clear they have no idea what is going on. The manager says something to Jones and Walters before walking to me.

"I'm sorry, ma'am. It appears we're locked out of our back office on the system ..." he begins.

"How did you not notice this sooner?"

"Unfortunately, we don't access the computer's back office for the daily running of our store. It's password protected, and only management have access. There was no issue when I last logged in."

"I don't understand how you could miss this."

"The main system seems unaffected. I would have noticed when I did the weekly reports. I can only apologize, and assure you that gaining access and resolving this matter is now a top priority. If you give me a few hours, I will have some answers before end of day."

He's apologetic and clearly determined to figure this mess out. There is nothing more to do until he investigates it. Trusting that he will, I write down my phone number and hand it over. With my head down, I hurry past Jones and Walters without looking their way. I make it out of the store before a new wave of helplessness takes hold. I suck in a lungful of air and sag against the storefront.

The glint of a shiny penny at my feet brings my mom's face to the forefront of my mind. Dipping to pick it up, I'm distracted by memories from my childhood. I regain some composure over my fears. Turning the coin over in my sweaty palm, I remember tiny snippets of Mom: her dark hair, her wide smile, the shape of her bare feet, and her blue summer dress all flash through my mind. Mom, watching me from the kitchen window as I played in the backyard. My excitement to show her the penny I'd found. Fragmented pieces of the memory float and on my next inhale, I smell her lavender shampoo. She had bent down, the glossy strands of her black hair falling over her chest while she turned the penny over in my hand.

"Wow..." she gushed over my discovery. *"It was made in 1995, just like you! That was the best year of my life, because of you. This is your lucky penny, Mac,"* she told me, curling my chubby fingers around it. *"You keep that safe."*

I wish you were here, Mom.

"What year is on the back of the penny?" I imagine her asking me now.

I lift it to read the four digits. *"2007."*

"Share a memory from 2007 with me." Her words are as clear in my mind as if she was here.

"It was another year without you."

"Come on, now. What else?"

I squeeze the penny, knowing all too well the significance of that year. I want so badly for it to be some kind of sign from heaven. *"It was the year Mr. Jones caught your killer, Mom. It was the year I felt safe falling asleep, for the first time since he killed you."*

I close my eyes to imagine what she might say to make me feel better. Instead, it's Jones's voice that fills my ears next.

"Mac, I'm going to get to the bottom of all this."

My eyes pop open to see him and Detective Walters standing before me. Jimmy's insistence to help, in spite of my reluctance, brings a forgotten warmth that I remember feeling with him. It awakens and floods me on a shaky breath.

"OK." Unable to meet his eyes, I focus my attention on Detective Walters. "Will you call, when you have answers?"

"I'll shoot from the hip here, Ms. Arnold," Walters says. "It looks as though the store has been hacked, which means data containing information on every other customer may also have been compromised. On one hand, that's reassuring, because it makes what happened to you less likely to be targeted. The manager has agreed to run security checks and to inform us what information has been stolen. For now, that's all we can really say on the matter. It is an open investigation."

I'm going to throw up.

I've felt sick for three days, my gut is whispering warnings day and night. Shifting from one foot to the other and unsure how to proceed, I glance over my shoulder, searching the bustling mall for the answer.

I turn to Jones, who is staring down at his feet.

"I—" Clearing my throat, I address Detective Walters again. "Will you phone me if you hear back from the manager before I do? If it's happened to others, I can relax. You see, today is the anniversary of my mom's ..."

"I know." His hand rests on my shoulder. "I'll call you and let you know if there are other victims." This small act manages to reassure me, for now.

"Thank you" I smile, turning my attention back to Jones.

Look at me ...

His chin is dropped, his forearms curling around each other across his chest. I've somehow managed to push this powerful man away. But I don't feel strong. In fact, I've never felt as weak as I do right now.

DEPUTY JONES

Determined to keep a professional distance, I listen as Walters reassures Mac that we will be in touch once we know more. Her haughty attitude has melted away, unmasking her fears and exposing her vulnerable side. It tugs on my natural inclination to comfort her. My arms tingle with the urge to reach out, to gather her up. My fists curl tight, squeezing against that need. I've been respectful, I've tried to be helpful and I'm certainly doing everything within my power to resolve her security breach. While on her side, she's been difficult and defensive, giving nothing but blowback for three days.

For twenty years, more like it!

For a long time, she hid away in her home, acting prickly and sharp to keep people out. Those walls are nothing compared to the fortress she's built around her heart. Her decision to report me to Walters not only embarrassed me but put my career in jeopardy.

"We should get back." My eyes lift from my boots to Walters.

"Jimmy?" Mac croaks. "Can I speak with you for a second?" Her fragile voice forces me to meet her eyes. They are weighted in worry and every ounce of me wants to lighten that load, free her of every fear.

"I'll wait in the car," Walters tells me before turning to Mac. "I'll call you later. Nine times out of ten, these things are just bored kids on the internet."

Still avoiding Mac's gaze, I watch him move through the mall, with his shoulders back and his confident stride. He catches the attention of every female he passes.

"What's up?" When I turn, I see she too is focused on his departure.

"I'm sorry for calling Walters on you last night. It was an overreaction."

"No need to apologize, it won't happen again. I'm hoping to put a pin in this whole thing soon."

"Oh, OK ..." Her eyes fall to the flashlight in my hands. "Nice ploy to get information." She forces a smile.

"It's pretty nifty actually ..."

"What is it?"

"It's a flashlight and pepper spray in one. I got it for you."

She looks up from the gadget. "Why?"

Heat creeps up my neck. Her bewildered expression gnaws at my confidence.

"I don't know, with your home security offline, I just thought you'd feel better, having something to protect yourself with. It was stupid. I'll take it back—"

"No!" She reaches for it. "I want it. I mean ... if you still want me to have it." She clears her throat.

"Yeah, of course! You know, Mac, I just want you to be safe. If I crossed a line coming by last night, it's only because I care," I confess.

She looks down at the flashlight, now in her hand. "Thanks, Jimmy." She nods thoughtfully, transferring her gaze back to mine. "Sailor will be impressed with this."

Man, she's beautiful.

I wonder how many men have spoken those words to her.

Does she know how captivating she is?

Clearing my throat, I sweep away the urge to tell her and keep the conversation focused on the case.

"Where *is* Sailor tonight?"

"He's along the Wolf River, camping out. He can't be in the house this time of year."

"That's understandable. How do you face it?"

"I stopped hiding when I was eight years old."

My heart swells, filled with admiration.

"Maybe this year should be different? With all this going on, it might put your mind at ease."

"Yeah, maybe you're right. I ... " she looks down, the words freezing on her pink lips.

"What?" I push.

"I accused you of thinking I was paranoid when you came by the other day."

"You did." I gently nudge her with my elbow. "I remember it well."

A brittle smile curves her lips. "Today, I feel it. Like I'm going crazy, ya know?"

"You're not paranoid. You have reason for concern, Mac, and truthfully, I'd feel better knowing you were camping with Sailor, until we know for sure the security system is safe."

"I got that system to feel secure and now it has me feeling more vulnerable and afraid than I have in years. Last night I dreamt someone was watching me..."

"If you wanted me to come by, sit with you …"

"NO." her tone is set in determination. "I mean no, it was just a dream. I'll camp out," she corrects herself, softening it.

Her rejection clouds my vision. I have to work to keep my voice steady. "Cool. OK, I gotta get going."

My feet move away from her.

"I'll keep you posted," I say, ignoring how her mouth falls open, her mind scrambling to understand my quick departure.

Mac is haunted by her past. Until now, I hadn't realized the ghosting she dished up at thirteen years of age has haunted me too.

HUNTER, AGED 17

Green Day's "21 Guns" is blasting through my earphones when a gentle tap on my shoulder draws my attention to my left. Standing next to me is the most beautiful girl I've ever seen. Her hair's the color of dark chocolate, so smooth and silky, it falls in waves around her shoulders before coming to rest on her full breasts. I'm struck dumb and held captivated by pink lips that move in silence. Tugging the wire to pull out the earphones, I let them fall onto my lap as I turn my whole body to her. Her eyes are blue, dark like indigo and the rarest shade I've ever seen, striking me like a bolt of lightning, jolting me back to life. Lovestruck, I nearly swallow my tongue.

"I, uh, didn't hear you?"

Her small hands grip the chair next to me, her smile turning into a giggle.

"Is this seat taken?"

"NO, sorry, it's free."

"I'm Hunter..."

"I'm Beth. I like your piercing," *she says, pointing to my eyebrow.*

"Thanks, I just got it done but I gotta take it out next month."

She laughs "Why bother if you're taking it out?"

"School just ended and I'm heading to Military base in Florida... Plus, I really want to relish the look on my dad's face when he sees it."

I tell her honestly. She stares at me for a moment, a look of contemplation and even admiration crossing her eyes before smiling.

"Are you sitting alone?" *I dare to ask.*

"I'm with friends." *She lifts the chair, twisting back to look at a group of girls.* "But I'm always open to making new friends."

"Coffee?"

"Latte."

And just like that, she saved me.

HUNTER, AGED 20

*B*eth sniffles over the phone.
"I miss you."

"I'm coming to visit you next month," I promise.

If military school helped to take the edge off my rage, Beth's sweetness silenced it. She came into my life just as I was about to leave for Florida. Four years of studying computer science through the military while continuing my cadet program has made seeing each other difficult.

"I know you're busy, I just love you so much."

"When I'm done with school, I'll be transferring to Virginia to complete the intelligence officer course. When that's done, I'll be an electronics intelligence officer. We can marry, live on base, and when I become an airman, we'll travel the world, baby ..."

I remind her of our plan. Our life together is mapped out. She's all that matters.

"Hunter, I was offered that job in Seattle ..."

Her words plunge like a knife to the gut and my body tenses against the assault. Please, don't leave me Beth. Please don't give up on me.

"Are you taking it?"

"There's an option to work remotely after two years. Hunter, it's a great salary. I could go while you complete training here in Virginia."

"You can be a financial analyst in Virginia, Beth. Just tell me the *truth: are you breaking up with me?"*

She gasps.

"No! Hunter, no ... I'll never leave you. I'll keep looking for something, in Virginia."

I sigh with relief.

"We'll be fine, Beth. Once we're together, we'll take on the world."

HUNTER, AGED 27

"*Dinner is cold.*" *My distaste coats each word.*

"*I phoned ...*" *she begins, ready to hit me with another onslaught of excuses. "I had to stay late."*

"*You're always staying late. Are you having an affair?" I accuse her.*

Regret races through me as soon as the words leave my mouth. She would never do that to me, to us. Her lips quiver and I rush to her, but she steps away.

"*I'm sorry, baby. I didn't mean that—*"

"*I can't do this, Hunter. I gave up the job in Seattle to support you. I waited four years for you while you were in Florida, and now you want me to give up my career to stay home? I'm not ready to be a mother ..." Tears stream down her cheeks. Her words poke at me. Something dark oozes from the hole, tempting me. I yearn to indulge in it.*

"*You're right, I'll never mention it again.*"

"*I ...*" *she looks away from me to the floor, her arms coming across her front as she fights to spit the words out. "I have to go out of town this weekend on business."*

Quelling every instinct to tell her no, to command she stay, I simply nod. I've lost my adoring wife.

She's just like him!

"*OK, Beth, I know how important your work is to you. I'm going to learn to respect that. You've always supported me, it's time I did that for you."* I lift her hands into mine, satisfied by the tremulous smile spreading across her face.

"I love you, Hunter. Sometimes you're a little controlling, but I'm never leaving."

Considering she is leaving in two days, her words are little comfort. I bend my head, her breath touching my lips before I envelope her in a deep kiss. She opens up for me, allowing me to plunge deeper into her mouth, taking what I can. Her hand slides to my pants, feeling my arousal beneath my camos.

"I want you ..." she moans against my lips.

I dip to her neck, whispering against her throbbing pulse. "First, I'm fixing you a glass of wine—" trailing kisses along her collarbone—"then, I'm running you a bath, before taking you to bed to ravish you for the night."

Standing back, I kiss her lips again. "Go, get into your robe. I'll be up in a minute."

She walks to the foot of the stairs with swollen lips and dazed eyes.

CHAPTER 11

DETECTIVE JOHN WALTERS

We haven't heard back from the manager of *Home Sure,* or Della. It shouldn't surprise me and I certainly have no right to feel this odd twinge of disappointment that's been following me around all afternoon.

She's a busy woman. Give her time.

Leaning back into my office chair and glancing at my wristwatch, I decide to phone MacKenna Arnold, hitting the call button just as Jones pops his head around the door.

"Coffee?" he offers.

I hold up one finger, putting the phone to my ear as it rings. She picks up immediately.

"Mackenna, it's Detective Walters ..."

Jones's fingers curl around the doorframe, his ears perking up at the mention of her name.

"Detective, hi. I was about to call you, actually. Any word?" She sounds hopeful.

"No, nothing yet. I wanted to reassure you that we will be following up with the manager tomorrow but unfortunately without a warrant we can't demand the information."

"OK, " she sighs, "I'm heading home now."

"Has anything else unusual happened today?"

"No, but I've decided to camp out with my uncle anyway."

"That's a good idea. I'll hopefully have an update tomorrow. If it's any consolation, the store was most likely the target. I wouldn't be surprised to hear the person responsible has hacked several customers from their database." Uncertainty creeps into my tone. I'm growing increasingly uncomfortable with this crime. Accessing a home security system is an invasion of privacy. I don't like it. MacKenna was quick witted and noticed immediately that something was wrong, but how many customers are unknowingly being watched in their own home, by the very system they assume is protecting them?

Renewed anger at the manager's lack of communication grumbles in my empty stomach.

"Thank you, Detective. Good night."

"Good night, MacKenna."

I'm about to hang up when she calls out to me again.

"Oh, Detective? Would you thank Jimmy—I mean, Deputy Jones?"

"I'll let him know."

Jones's ears perk up at those words. He's like a puppy dog as he waits for me to reveal the details of the call. I hold back. I know I shouldn't tease him, but I'm hungry and need something to tide me over until I can eat.

"Forget coffee, let's go grab some takeout and bring it back here."

"Cool, let me grab my wallet."

"Nah, it's my treat."

We make it all the way to my car before he asks.

"What did Mac say?"

I could be a bastard and withhold a little longer, but he's suffered enough the past few days.

"Apparently, you're the love of her life," I deadpan.

"*What!?*"

"Jeez, you've got it bad for that girl." I shake my head; this is not good.

"I do not. We got history, is all," he huffs.

"Jones, I'm a detective. You can't fool me. She said to thank you, agrees she might have been a bit quick to doubt you."

A small smile plays on his lips before his penchant for arguing with me takes over.

"First, that's bullshit. You investigate murders, not emotions. And second, if that *was* true, as a budding detective myself, I'd be right in saying that *you've* got it bad for Agent Della Perez!" He smirks. No doubt about it, he's pleased with Mac's message and himself.

"You can't see because I'm driving, but I'm rolling my eyes," I grunt.

"Funny how those eyes spent the day checking your phone!"

"Ah, shit," I curse.

"What?"

"I left my phone on my desk," I huff, pulling into the drive thru.

"As long as you have your wallet. We'll be back at the office in ten minutes."

He's right. Usually being separated from my phone wouldn't bother me, but we're waiting on some important calls. I order us burgers and fries, happy when we're on the road back to the station.

HUNTER

FOUR MONTHS AGO...

I wasn't sure I could go through with it, but somewhere between the trepidation and the act of wrapping my hands around her throat, I felt alive. I'd spent my childhood afraid of the dark, but tonight, being part of it, hiding in it as I followed her, made me feel omnipotent.

As soon as Joanna left my home, I regretted the loss. My afternoon was plagued with 'what ifs' until I found myself turning the ignition of my car and driving to her office. A plan formed in my head, a simple fantasy, nothing more until there she was. Walking, alone, to her car, with nobody around to stop me. I knew enough about her previous attack to make it look like a copycat killer. I knew enough about evidence to get away with it, but I'd known nothing of how conflicted I would feel, until her eyes bulged, capillaries bursting as I squeezed.

"Close your eyes!" I'd screamed. She refused, begging me, each plea infuriating me further. There was no turning back, so I covered her face. I focused on remembering how tortured Father was when Molly disappeared. The thrill returned, empowering me as I clamped harder around her neck. The cover up was easy. LeeRoy Chester isn't the sharpest tool in the box. The police would look at him, his family, his acquain-

tances first.

That night, I looked through the files I'd stolen from Father for the first time in years. I'd tasted revenge, embodied evil and relished every second. There were others out there: people he'd cared more about than his dying wife and son. Beth was the angel on my shoulder for a long time until her whimpering started resembling Molly's squawking. I couldn't quell the desire any longer. It took some time to formulate my plan, but in the end, destroying that final link to my old life became vital. It released me, gave me the freedom to just be ... me.

I retrieved Molly's feathers from the deep freezer and went back to the scene, to leave one with Joanna. She deserved to know whose fault it was. They all do.

CHAPTER 12

AGENT DELLA PEREZ

I touched down in Green Bay to three missed calls. One was from Agent Ryan. He left a voicemail letting me know he'd arranged a rental car but was unable to book a hotel. The second was from Agent Clark, but he didn't leave a message. Nor did the third caller, Detective Walters.

Something must be wrong ...

The thought unsettles me. John has never reached out before; twice in one day is a bad sign. Once on route to the Outagamie sheriff's office, I try calling him. He doesn't pick up and my concern increases with each mile that passes.

Don't allow yourself to become too attached ...

Just as I arrive, I see Detective Walters's car pull into his usual parking spot. He and Jones get out and everything in my periphery fades. Detective John Walters becomes my focus. The advice I gave myself on the way here vanishes when his head falls back in laughter. I don't remember ever seeing John laugh so openly. It makes him even more handsome than I remember.

Although his hair could do with a trim ...

A smile spreads across my face as he strides easily into the station. Excitement pulses throughout my body to be back in Appleton, with John and Jones.

It was silly to worry about him.

I step out of the rental and suck in a lungful of fresh Wisconsin air. My feet move toward the station. Each step leaves behind romantic notions of John and brings me back to the job at hand.

I'm here to catch a serial killer.

DEPUTY JONES

"Damn it, I missed calls from the manager of *Home Sure* and Perez."

Taking his phone in hand, John tosses his food onto his desk as he sits to call them back. Settling across from him, I listen intently.

"Mr. Devine, this is Detective Walt—" The words die on his lips, his eyes frozen on something behind me. I turn to find Agent Odelia Perez standing in his doorway. She doesn't see me even though I'm right in front of her. They each stare at the other, green eyes meeting brown across the room and neither of them breaking the silence.

"Della!" I jump up, forcing her to glance my way.

Jeez, it's good to see her!

"Hola, Jones!" she flashes a full, white smile. She looks good. Scratch that: Della Perez is more beautiful than I remember. She glides toward us in a skirt, silk blouse, and heels. Her outfit suggests she's no longer in the field, but her presence and the heavy briefcase on her shoulder imply otherwise.

"Now, that's how you make an entrance!" I wink back, laughing as she wraps her arms around my back. We've never hugged before, and yet it's the most natural reaction. The sound of Walters clearing his throat has us both pulling back.

"Sorry about that, Mr. Devine. Go on." His eyes turn to his computer screen. He's as shocked as I am but doesn't look as near as happy as I feel.

"We've been waiting all day to hear back from this guy, " I whisper in explanation to Della.

"Of course. Is everything OK?" her dusky Latina voice is like music to my ears.

"An old friend of mine had a bit of trouble a few days ago."

I've no idea why I'm blushing, but the profiler before me misses nothing.

"Friend, huh? Is this a *female* friend?" she teases.

Walters suddenly leaps from his chair. "Christ! Couldn't you have called me earlier?" he hisses down the line. All the blood in my body drains to my feet, rooting me to the spot.

"What is it?"

Walters looks between Della and I, still listening to whatever the store manager is saying. His body angles toward Della, his gaze set on me. My heart pounds and my stomach churns with fear.

"I'll send a deputy over to collect it from the store. Do *not* share this information with anyone." Walters growls out before hanging up the call, but he's deathly calm when he speaks directly to me.

"We need to get over to Mac's. Now."

"What's going on?" Della asks.

"That was the manager of a home security store. They were hacked a few days ago. We thought maybe the hackers wanted access to their customer database and we were right ... " He's moving fast around his desk. "Except." Walters looks me dead in the eyes. "They only took one customer's information."

My limbs tremble, reconnecting my mind to my body. "Mac's." I say, knowing it to be true. He nods.

"Mac?" Della gasps. "Please tell me you're not talking about MacKenna Arnold?"

We both whip around to meet her horrified expression.

"How do you know her name?" The hairs on the back of my neck lift.

"She's the reason I've come to Wisconsin."

"Tell me, in thirty seconds or less. *Why*?" Walters demands.

"We have an active serial killer making his way across America. He seems to be hunting down the surviving victims of previous serial killer attacks and …"

"*And* what?" I bark when she pauses.

"He kills them on the anniversary of their original attack." She swallows.

"Jesus. John, we gotta get to her!" Absolute desperation fills me. I'm already moving at speed through the station. Walters and Della catch up as I burst through the exit, all three of us heading straight to Walters's car.

"How far away is she?" Della asks, jumping into the back seat.

"Her house is a ten-minute drive." I say.

"Call dispatch. See who we have in the area!" Walters demands and I do it, listening as Della fills in more of the gaps.

"He kills them at the exact time of the original attack which means, hopefully, he doesn't plan on striking until eleven p.m." Her words give me some hope.

"She said she was leaving to go camping with her uncle," Walters tells her.

Her face turns ashen.

"If he's watching the house, he might see her preparing to leave and push his timeline forward. I need to phone, try to warn her without spooking her."

Della pulls out her cell. She doesn't ask for Mac's number. The realization that it was already programmed into her phone sends a shiver of this dangerous reality down my spine.

"She has security cameras all over her property, that's how she knew about the hacking. He gained access but she has changed passwords and locked him out," I explain, hoping it's enough to keep her safe until we get there.

"It's ringing. What did he do once he had access to her system?"

"He wiped some security footage."

"Jesus, John ...!" Della gasps, her horror communicating something to Walters.

"Holy fuck!" He gets it, gripping the steering wheel and pressing down harder on the gas. Their intensity sends more adrenaline through my veins. My body is readying itself for action, my heart pounding in trepidation.

What are we walking into?

"She's not answering. I'll try her again" Della continues. Neither of them explains what exactly they've deciphered.

"What the fuck is happening?"

"He's already in the house."

CHAPTER 13

MAC

Silence greets me, like every other day. Except, everything about *this* day will forever feel ominous. Dropping my keys, purse and new flashlight on the stairs, I head straight up to my bedroom, depositing my phone on the bed before hurrying to shower.

Sailor won't be expecting me, but he'll be happy to have me. Jones is right. With everything that's happened over the last few days, it's best to get out of the house for the night.

Turning on the faucet, I step in the shower. As I'm enveloped in steam and the soothing sounds of splashing water, my frazzled mind is calmed, the heat washing away some of my worries. The urgency of getting on the road before dark drains away with the soapy water, until the shrill of my phone demands my attention. I really should get going, I sigh to myself and turn off the water.

Wrapped in a towel and leaving a trail of wet footprints behind me, I pick up the phone just as it clicks to voicemail.

Unknown caller.

Tossing the phone back onto the bed, I rush to ready myself. I quickly dry off before wringing my sopping wet hair in a towel on my head. My thoughts are circling, my movements hurried. Pulling sweatpants and a t-shirt on over my still-damp skin, I'm reaching into the closet for my overnight bag, when the phone shrills again. Remembering it could be the manager of Home Sure, I drop the bag on the floor of my closet and answer.

"Hello?" I'm breathless.

A soft-spoken female voice comes over the line.

"MacKenna, hi! This Special Agent Della Perez with the FBI ..."

My eyes fall to the bag I've just dropped.

"FBI?" I repeat, trying to simultaneously digest her words and the fact that the hatch to the bunker Sailor built me is slightly ajar. Fear, like a dark shadow, cascades down my spine, guiding my body backward and away from the closet, until my back hits the windowsill.

"Listen to me carefully, there are police officers on the way to your home right now—" I twist to quickly scan the street below.

Empty.

"I need you to quickly make your way outside and to a neighbor's house. Can you do that?" The urgency in her words echoes in every fiber of my being.

It's too late.

HUNTER

Three days of listening, waiting for the crucial hour to roll around, wasted! From the dark hole, I watched her strip down, rushing about like she had somewhere else to be until her phone chimed again. Biting down on the simmering rage, I carefully push the drywall hatch aside and emerge on all fours from the darkness.

CHAPTER 14

MAC

A slight noise causes the hairs on my neck to stand. Whipping back around, my eyes round in horror. Emerging from my closet, like a demon from hell, an intruder stands blocking the door out of the room. He's dressed head to toe in black, with his face hidden beneath a mask. Only his onyx eyes are visible, glinting with malicious intent, from beneath bushy eyebrows. His long legs bring him slowly to the foot of my bed. My thoughts skitter from the knife strap on his thigh, to the fact that he is blocking my only escape, to the FBI agent, still calling my name through the phone pinned to my ear.

"He's already here …" My whispered horror is barely audible.

"Who's on the phone, Mac?" his cool tone matches the keen edge of the hunting knife as he slides it from its sheath. The blade is like a magnet to my eyes, transporting me back in time. My mom's killer is stalking toward me. My muscles go rigid. My mind screams but nothing passes my lips.

"WHAT DID THEY SAY?" he demands, his steady advance both menacing and predatory until he has me in his grasp. One large hand wraps around my throat. "Answer me," he snarls, squeezing my neck and cutting off my air. My hands claw at his, the phone dropping at my feet as he turns, walking me backward away from the window.

"HELP!" I squeak, the effort causing my eyes to burn and bulge. His fingers dig deeper into the flesh of my neck, choking me at arm's length before slamming me against the wall. The blow loosens the towel, which falls from my head. Wet hair, nausea, and dizziness swirl around my head.

"I wanted to take my time with you," he growls.

"Ple—ease ..."

"You won't weasel away this time, MacKenna." He ignores my hoarse pleas, towering above me in complete control. The knife appears near my eye.

I can't breathe ...

"How was it he killed her?" The cold tip skims my cheek, a tear from each eye following its path. He nicks my chin as he drags the blade down my body, stopping at my stomach.

"He stabbed her, *twelve times*, before he came looking for you, isn't that right?" His cruel sneer is a mental stab at my past, re-opening wounds that bleed old memories to the forefront of my mind. A little girl with skinny legs running up and punching my mother's killer in the butt.

"Leave my mommy alone!" I'd screamed, trying to save her.

"Run MacKenna, hide!"

The recollection of Mom's spine-chilling cries, her protectiveness and bravery rise within me. The water from my hair causes his grip on my neck to slip. It's all the leverage I need. Mom's voice is replaced by Sailor's.

"Drop your chin."

"Bring your arms over his and come down hard."

"Now, push them aside."

Years of routine and training have become second nature. In three quick steps, I'm free!

"Using the heel of your hand, strike upward with one quick blow to his nose."

I'm on auto-pilot, my body only using part of my mind. With another part, I watch as his eyes water with the pain.

"NOW RUN."

His body stumbles back, creating enough space to get out around him. I flee, barefoot, making it out of the bedroom and heading straight for the stairs. I'm almost at the top when my trailing wet hair is yanked backward, bringing me onto my back with a heavy thud. He's already on me, raising the knife over his head with both hands. I twist sideways just as he brings it down. The blade crashes into the carpet, inches from my face. He pulls the knife up again. Panic thumps in my chest. His eyes blaze with pure rage as he growls furiously.

"You fucking *bitch*! You won't survive this time."

"You keep fighting." Sailor's voice in my head is louder than my fear. *"Slow your mind and focus on his vulnerable areas: eyes, ears, nose and mouth..."*

My eyes close, my mind stills to allow my body to remember my training. He's straddling me, his legs on either side of my body. Bending my knees to his back, my right foot crosses over his ankle, pinning *his* foot against my ass. Looking him dead in the eye, I roar, "want to bet, motherfucker?" before bucking off the floor with my left hip. Adrenaline has turned my body to steel and I manage to pitch him off, flipping him onto his back. In one swift move he's beneath me and now I straddle him. I gouge both his eyes with my thumbs. Nausea roils in my stomach at the feel of the wet, soft tissue pushing in. He screams in pain. Bolstered, I reach for the knife with both hands. Gripping its handle, I try to push it up and out of his. He holds it tightly, releasing one hand to punch me across the cheek. White lights blur my vision as the blow knocks me and the knife into the air. I land next to him. The knife tumbles down the stairs. He's writhing in agony, rubbing his eyes with the balls of his gloved hands. Dizzy, I drag my aching body toward the stairs, the edge of each step whacking against my ribs as I begin to slide downward. His fingers claw at my ankles, his arms reaching for me from the landing. Turning to meet his bloodshot gaze, I kick free, sliding on my back toward the bottom. He leaps forward, rolling with me, the weight of his body crushing me as we land near the foot of the stairs.

Like a wild animal, I push, scratch and kick to free myself. Sheer disgust and unadulterated fury leave his lungs on a hair-raising roar. Trying to wriggle free of his weight, my eyes land on the flashlight Jones bought me, still where I left it on the first step. I reach for it, the tips of my fingers grazing it, but it's not quite close enough. I let out my own frustrated cry. He punches me again, the weight of his fist sliding me closer. My hand wraps around it, my finger pressing down to spray it in his direction in one smooth arc.

Nothing.

A satisfied glint flashes in his eyes before I whack him solidly on the head with it and scoot out from under him once again. My bare feet pound the cold marble tiles with speed toward the kitchen. The heavy fall of his boots sounds behind me.

"There's nowhere for you to go! You forget, you lock yourself in here every night, bitch." His sinister laugh echoes around us, stopping me in the doorway. Blue sand forms stormy waters in the art piece that hangs in the space between us both.

"Come out, you little bitch ..." he spits, repeating the words of my mother's killer, from all those years ago. "Isn't that what he said?" He's closing in on me.

It doesn't bring the paralyzing fear he hopes. I don't run. Instead, my hands grip the corners of the glass frame and yank it from the wall. The tempered glass crashes down, the sharp edges slicing his shoulder before shattering onto the floor. Water, glass and blue sand flood the cream marble tiles. His shocked eyes lift from the blood dripping out from under his black sleeve. One drop lands, diluting to nothing before a steady stream joins it.

Got him!

He came here dressed entirely in black, nothing but evil eyes on display. Now, the deep red of his blood exposes him, leaving him with nowhere to hide.

"The FBI will be here any second, you sick fuck. Looks like I got them some DNA to find you."

"I'm going to make you pay for that," he promises before the sound of screeching tires whips his head toward the front door.

"Not tonight. You're going to prison."

"You'll be seeing me real soon, Mac," he spits.

The minacious words hang in the air as he flees. They squeeze at my lungs, while the adrenaline drains, taking my breath with it. I sink to the watery mess on the floor, my chest heaving for oxygen. An eternity passes before the front door flies open. Jones bursts in to find me.

"MAC! " His gun is raised, his head swiveling to survey the surroundings. He rushes past me, checking the space around us before dropping to a crouch in front of me. "Where is he?" His free hand searches my face, my body for injury. I can't speak. I don't hear the detective and a woman come through the door.

"Where is he?" The female voice blurs.

"Mac, where did he go?" Jones's large hand cups my face. My finger lifts, pointing to the garage door, my chest still silently heaving.

"Stay with her, Jones," Walters says, before disappearing into the garage.

"You did good, Mac, you did good." My eyes dart around the hallway. "Mac, hey, keep your eyes on me. Breathe in and out. You're safe. I've got you, OK?" he repeats it over and over. I push at his chest, needing space, needing air.

"I ...can't ... breathe." I've started crying.

"There's an ambulance on the way. Listen to me, Mac. I'm going to lift you out of this glass ..."

His arms come beneath me and my instinct to push him away sets in, my hands pressing at his chest. "You're safe, Mac," his embrace tightens a fraction, drawing me into his body heat. It melts through the cold and eases my uncontrollable shaking. His familiar scent surrounds me and my fighting becomes a desperation to cling on tighter to him as he cradles me.

"You're OK ... " he repeats again, setting me down on the bottom step, stroking my wet hair from my face. "Imagine that you're on your yoga mat. Close your eyes and breathe in and out, slow and steady. I'm right here next to you." Kneeling before me, he wipes away my tears. Through the trembling and the hysteria, I tune into the sound of his voice.

"Breathe in through your nose, and out through your mouth," he continues soothingly.

"Mac, the ambulance crew and police backup are here. They're going to get you to the hospital, OK?" he eventually says. He stands up to let them in. The disappearing heat of his body brings a new wave of panic and I claw at his shirt.

"No! Jimmy, I can't. You can't leave me."

CHAPTER 15

DEPUTY JONES

"*He's already here ...*"

Della's eyes lift from beneath her dark lashes to me. The phone was on speaker. Walters guns it. The feel of the car accelerating and the utter terror in Mac's cry for help come at the same time. We'll be there in a few minutes.

But all it takes is a few seconds.

I call for backup, giving the address, the situation at hand and requesting an ambulance.

"Walters—" my voice breaks,—"We need to get there!"

"HELP!" Mac's muffled cry comes over the line, rattling me to the core.

"How was it he killed her?" He taunts her, torturing us both as I listen in on the struggle. My eyes squeeze against the thumps and banging. It doesn't help to avoid the truth. Mac is hurt, she's afraid, alone, and fighting for her life. And there is nothing I can do at this moment to help her. My body aches to act, to protect her, to fight with her.

"It sounds like they're moving throughout the house." Della

reaches forward, squeezing my shoulder.

"Jones." Walters's voice is sharp, clear. His eyes are fixed forward, his jaw ticking with determination. "When we get there, the focus is to get Mac out alive. Keep your head on straight, you hear me?"

"I hear you."

We squeal around the corner, taking the curb as we go. Flinging myself out of the car, I don't wait for the others. I sprint toward her, jumping the plants and shrubbery to the path, before kicking her door open in one try.

My heart races to keep up with my legs as I rush to her side. Slumped against the wall, her clothes are soaked in water and blue sand. She's breathing erratically. Dropping to a crouch, I take her in. Eyes, wild with fear, struggle to focus on mine. My hand cups her bruised face. Her cheekbone is already swelling from the blows he administered. Blood trickles from her nose and lip, dripping onto her white t-shirt. My eyes drop lower to see blood floating in the water beneath her.

Scanning her body, I don't find any life-threatening wounds but do notice a nasty bruise already showing itself around her neck, red raw from where he choked her. My stomach turns.

He beat her.

The rage claws up my chest into an angry growl.

"Where is he?"

Walters and Perez run through the door behind me.

"She OK?" Walters calls. They both have their guns raised, eyes searching the house.

"Yeah. Mac, where is he?" I ask her again.

"The—" Her chest rattles, she can't speak. Instead, she points to the garage.

"Stay with her," Walters orders, as he and Della disappear through the door into the garage.

She's sitting in glass.

Telling her what I'm doing, I slide my hand beneath her knees and around her back, lifting her from the mess. She's as light as a feather, looks as delicate as the shattered glass on the floor but she pushes at me, the fight still draining from her body until I squeeze tighter. I'm relieved when she sags against me.

"I got you, Mac. You're OK," I whisper in her ear, carrying her trembling body to the stairs. Settling her down and cupping her face, I catch the silent tears tracking down her cheeks. She tries to speak, her words coming out in heavy sobs.

"I ... He ..."

"It's OK, just breathe, Mac."

I'm checking her pulse, searching her body for any other injuries and repeating words of reassurance as I go. Sirens blare outside. Heavy boots sound on the ground and the urgent voices of men and women arriving on scene approach.

"Mac, the ambulance is here. We need to get you to the hospital, OK?"

"NO! JONES!" she shrieks.

"Mac, I need to find him. You're safe," I repeat, trying to hush her.

A scream, heartfelt and raw, rips free from the very depths of her soul.

"Oh, Jimmy! I can't ..." she sobs, "I—I don't ... want to be alone."

Her slender fingers bunch on my shirt, over my heart, and keep me with her. She needs me: nothing could be strong enough to pull me away.

"OK, Mac. I'm here. I'll stay with you."

She cries even harder against my chest. My arms wrap around her.

Gently kissing the crown of her head, I whisper, "you're safe."

She's safe, I tell myself.

DETECTIVE JOHN WALTERS

The old tightness in my chest flared to life the moment she walked into my office. Those long legs striding toward me, her steady, bottle-green gaze wiped all thought from my brain. I hate surprises but it's rare that someone leaves me speechless. Della did.

The ache intensified on the car ride here. The high speed had my hands squeezing the steering wheel hard enough to whiten my knuckles. My foot on the gas amplifying the panic trying to surface within me. I was head of the homicide division in Madison when my car went off the road during a high-speed chase. For months after anxieties plagued, while I slowly healed my broken ribs and got back on the road. That angst choosing to return at the worst possible time.

MacKenna Arnold was in danger. It was my job to help her, which meant I had to get us there alive. For the first time since moving to Appleton, I doubted myself.

"He can't have gotten far," Della pants next to me as we walk back to the house. Barefoot and breathless from chase, she throws her head back, opening her chest for air.

"This neighborhood is so compact: there's nothing beyond it but fields and brush. He's exposed ..." I look up at the two helicopters hovering above us. "Let's find your shoes."

Somewhere during the chase she kicked them off.

"They were slowing me down," she says, smiling. I'd heard about her promotion; knew she was out of fieldwork and tucked into an office in Quantico. I'd even imagined her there, but my speculations about Perez never included heels. Now I doubt I'll ever imagine her any other way.

I return my attention to the chaos around us. Police cars, ambulances and fire crews all line the street. Officers are knocking on every door, searching every house, questioning everyone who lives here. We reach the Arnold home, Perez re-donning her heels in the drive. My eyes follow her, captivated by the gentle sway of her hips. My unwanted attraction to her is already sinking back to my core, distracting me.

"Are you OK?" She looks at me curiously as she slips them back on.

"Yep. Let's get inside." I nod toward the house, pulling my phone from my pocket when a text message chimes.

"It's Jones: they're at the hospital. She's in shock, but other than some cuts and bruises, she'll be OK. He's going to stay with her," I relay to her.

"Good idea"

We take in the scene. Broken glass, the blue sand, water, and blood have spread across the hallway. Crime scene techs are already carefully collecting what they can. We head straight upstairs.

"What do I need to know about this guy?" I ask as we climb.

"He just made his biggest mistake. He underestimated you guys."

"He underestimated MacKenna. She held her own against this fucker and survived another attempt on her life."

Halfway up the stairs she turns , forcing me to meet her gaze. "I couldn't have put it better myself! She's a fighter. I'm happy she has Jones looking out for her, too."

"He's a great cop. I'm proud of him," I admit.

"Looks like you've found a partner! But ..." she smiles mischievously, "are you up for catching another killer with *me,* Detective?"

"Does that mean you plan on sticking around?"

Her eyes narrow. "I hate to break it to you, but I've been chasing this guy for months. This is my case. Are you in or out?"

If I sounded irritated, it's because I'm having to work double time to stamp out the flames her heated stare ignite within me. But I'm not letting her know that. "Last time I checked, we're still in Appleton. I'm not sitting back while a killer stalks this community."

"Good! let's get to work then."

Her hair whips back, saturating the air with her flowery scent.

At the top, Maria, head of the crime scene forensics unit, calls to us. "You both need to see this."

"What is it?" I ask, as we enter what looks to be MacKenna's room.

"He hid in here." Stepping aside, she points to the closet. Behind a rail of clothes, a cubby hole comes into view. Roughly eight feet wide and four feet high, the bunker that saved MacKenna's life all those years ago is still here, hidden behind a false wall.

"How did he manage that?" Della hunkers down, looking into the small space.

"This piece of drywall slides across, concealing it completely" Maria moves it back into place. To unsuspecting eyes, it looks like the back of any other closet.

Della stands. "Did he leave anything behind?"

"Yeah, this." Maria holds up an evidence bag containing a black feather. Della reaches for it.

"Where was it?"

"Inside the bunker."

"Anything else?" she says, handing the bag to me. I turn it over in my hand.

"No food containers, if he was in there for a few days it suggests that he was using the home amenities while MacKenna was out. We're scouring the house for more evidence. The good news is we have his DNA from the fight," Maria tells her.

"This feather indicates it's definitely your guy," I say as the radio on my hip crackles to life.

"WE HAVE SOMETHING."

"LOOKS LIKE A COMPUTER OF SOME KIND," the female voice continues.

"What's your location?" I call into my radio.

"Back of the house."

"Don't touch it, forensics are on the way," I confirm. Della, Maria and I all head straight outside. Lying on the grass between the house and the landscaping bushes is a pocket-sized computer. I point to the broken branches of the bush.

"He must have dropped it running that way."

"Bag it," Maria directs her techs.

"Maybe he used it to hack her system from inside the home?" Della suggests. "This is good. With some luck he didn't have time to wipe it."

I look around, gnashing my teeth. We ran in the opposite direction looking for him.

I let him escape ...

"We'll head to the hospital. If you find anything else, you can get me on my cell ..." I decide.

"Good idea. Thank you, Maria," Della agrees.

We walk in silence to my car. I take the opportunity to suck in some fresh air and muddle through the shock of Della's reappearance in Appleton. It's been hardly an hour and already I need some distance to clear my mind and untether myself from Special Agent Della Perez.

She's back in Wisconsin.

My chest tightens again. Considering the circumstances that brought her back into my orbit, I'm an asshole for feeling good about it.

Fuck.

Nothing good ever comes from this feeling.

CHAPTER 16

AGENT DELLA PEREZ

My adrenaline dwindles as St. Mark's hospital comes into view. I turn toward John, remembering the blood and the fear that he would die in my arms, out in the Wisconsin woods before he was airlifted to this hospital. "Last time we were here, you had more holes in you than a block of cheese."

"Aren't those the steps where you gave your TV interview about the Bone Breaker killer?" He nods toward the entrance of the hospital. Heat creeps up my neck. I hated giving that interview. It was John's case, and about saving Faye Anderson. It was never about the glory.

"About that ..." My throat constricts.

"Don't apologize. You deserved the credit: your profile was spot on. Hopefully you can do the same with this guy."

"Hopefully *we* can do the same."

"Oh, there's no 'hopefully' about it. I'm catching this guy. But you can come along for the ride if you like." He smirks.

"I'll need to phone my supervisor soon. I haven't had a chance to bring him up to speed on the case yet." The last time we worked together, I made the mistake of not keeping John informed of the

FBI's intentions. I'm not doing that again.

"I expect you to fill me in on everything you have so far. No surprises." His eyes are fixed ahead as we pull into a parking space.

"Mm-hmm, naturally. I have some notes with me but I know this case inside and out. I was unit supervisor on it at Quantico."

"Was?"

Detective John Walters misses nothing.

"Am," I say, through my teeth.

Technically it's not a lie until eight a.m. Which means for the next nine hours, I'm still overseeing this case.

"Hmm ..." His head bobs up and down, a doubtful expression marring his handsome face. "Well either way—" His eyes flick to mine briefly—"As long as I'm kept in the loop this time."

"Still the same cynical cop. Only ..." I pause, examining his side profile. "Older, I see!"

The engine cuts out right before he turns his dark eyes on me.

"Still the same nuisance. Only ..." His eyes search my face, slowly, painfully. "A lot more dangerous, I see," he deadpans.

"Dangerous?" I splutter, surprised.

"Very. Last time you came to Wisconsin, I wound up with more holes than a cheese block, as you so delicately put it."

"That's hardly my fault!"

"I was distracted!" he frowns, holding my gaze. The intensity of his stare sends my heart pounding.

"Oh, really?" My shaking fingers curl into my palms.

"Yeah. The sun was in my eyes."

"It was after midnight!" I laugh.

"It's almost midnight now, and the sun is still in my eyes ..."

Is he .... Is he flirting with me?

"Oh, wow. John, you *must* be exhausted!"

"Yeah, must be ..." His tongue slides along his bottom lip. Swallowing, he says "Sorry. Let's keep our focus on the case."

"Good idea, because this killer is a hell of a lot more dangerous than me."

DEPUTY JONES

The steady ticking of a clock, the stale smell of sweat and disinfectant all hang in the air of the hospital room. Watching Mac sleep does nothing to ease the sick sense of dread knotting in my stomach. Dark eyelashes fan her cheeks, fluttering lightly as her full lips part, allowing her to breathe more easily. My eyes shift from the rise and fall of her chest to the purple marks he left on her neck. Bile rises and burns in my chest. If I hadn't let my bruised ego get in the way, I could have insisted on taking her out to Sailor's.

Two police officers stand guard outside the door, while I sit with her, armed and ready to defend her if the man who just tried to kill her comes back.

She was quiet when we arrived at the hospital. My cop instincts, the urge to hound her with questions, to get as much information about this guy while it was fresh in her mind took over. But one withering look from the nurse tending to her was enough to shut me up.

The door slides open ushering Della and John in.

"How is she doing?" Della asks.

"She's been asleep for about an hour now."

"How are *you* doing?" she keeps her voice low, her warm accent soothing some of my jangled nerves.

"I'd feel better if we found this guy." I stand, my eyes leaving hers to find John's.

"We will." His tone, sure and assertive holds none of Della's softness but comforts me just the same.

"I'm not sitting this one out." My hands come to my hips, glaring at them both. I may be the rookie detective with an 'almost' degree in criminology, but I know Mac's history better than the two of them.

"Good." John doesn't even try to fight me and I'm grateful. "Now, wanna start by filling us in on what you know?"

"She hasn't said much. She was in shock …"

"Not in here. Let's go outside," Della interrupts me, her head nodding toward Mac.

MAC

The three of them move to the door.

"He was tall, at least six foot three, and wore all black …" the words, like tiny blades, scratch and score my throat to a deep rasp. Jimmy turns quickly, his entire body moving to me until my hand comes up, stopping him mid-stride.

"No, please don't touch me …" Disappointment flashes in his eyes. "Not yet. I need to tell you everything I remember and then I need time to process it all. I can't do that with you here, being kind to me. I can't put that on you," I try to explain before turning my focus turns to Walters.

"Detective, he knew about my mother's murder. He said I wouldn't survive this time and threatened to come back and kill me, just before you showed up …" tears fill my eyes, rolling down my cheeks and onto my pillow. By-passing Jimmy and Walters, the female agent comes to the end of my bed.

"MacKenna, I'm FBI Agent Della Perez."

"That was you on the phone?"

She nods. "I'm sorry I couldn't get to you sooner." Her delicate tone fills with regret. "It appears he's been hiding in your home for the last three days. Did you notice anything unusual, or out of place?"

"No, although a client said she heard scratches, like a mouse. It must have been him. I did feel uneasy, but with it being my mom's anniversary and the hacking …"

"Try to remember, MacKenna. Was there anything about him, a scar or an accent, anything that would be a distinguishing feature?" Jimmy steps forward.

"No."

"What about the color of his eyes?"

"Black, maybe dark blue, I don't know."

"Think, Mac, anything you can tell us about him will help," he urges desperately. My head shakes no, my mind flicking between snippets of the attack, each one vanishing before I can capture any detail.

"Jones." Walters cuts him off. His voice, surprisingly soothing, takes over "MacKenna, close your eyes. Try to remember something."

I don't want to recall, but I need this conversation to end, so I close my eyes. My hands come to my ears, my knees to my chest, the tears falling freely while my body trembles.

"Go back to his eyes. What do you see?" Walters continues.

The evil glint of my attacker's eyes returns.

"He had … bushy eyebrows." My eyes squeeze tighter. "And a small scar at the edge of his left eyebrow, the kind a piercing leaves."

"That's good, MacKenna. Anything else?"

"His voice was deep. Nothing stood out about it other than how angry he was."

"Mac, you're safe" Jimmy hushes. My head shakes no.

How can I be safe? How will I ever feel safe again?

"I'm tired, I just want to sleep."

"OK, OK. We're going, MacKenna. There will be officers stationed right outside your door. We'll come back when you're feeling up to it. We're trying to find Sailor for you," Jones promises, before the door shuts behind them. My entire body aches. Unable to fight the pull any longer, I'm sucked down, overcome by the darkness.

DEPUTY JONES

Back at the sheriff's station, we walk the center aisle of the bull pen toward John's office. Della lingers outside his door, making a call to the Bureau. It's after midnight when we all sit down around John's desk. I'm jittery with the need to do something. A deep sigh leaves my body.

"Shouldn't we be out searching for him?"

"Jones, let's remove emotion and focus on catching this guy. You did the right thing coming to me about MacKenna, so any guilt you're feeling? You drop it, now. You have a job to do and it's because of you that this isn't a murder scene." John demands my attention on the case. I set aside my concern for Mac, making the active choice to be present. I nod in agreement.

"OK. What update do you have?" His eyes cut to Della.

"The chief is sending two agents here tomorrow. I've requested Ryan join. Considering this guy knows his way around a computer, we could use Ryan's expertise. From there, the FBI will liaise with the Appleton sheriff's department as an aid to your investigation," she informs us.

"That's good. What about a profile?" I ask.

"I have one drafted, based off the other murders, but I will need to revise it now that we have some more information on how he accesses the home and his interactions with the latest victim.

"Mac," I correct her.

"Mac." She nods in understanding.

"We will need to arrange some kind of safe house for her," John muses.

"I can do that."

His eyes narrow suspiciously at me. "So long as it's not yours!" he warns.

"No!" I scoff. "She'll need twenty-four-hour protection! I can't provide that, but I know someone who can. Someone that she trusts."

He sighs. "We'll come back to that tomorrow. Right now we need to know what information was on that computer. How long before Ryan can get that information?" he asks Della.

"I don't know. It depends on what security this guy has in place on the device. DNA can be processed within a few days. In the meantime, we run down leads, canvas the neighborhood, question Mac again, and check hotels, motels and any vacant properties he could hide in."

"The choppers are still out. With some luck they'll find him tonight," John responds.

"OK, then. Let's get some sleep and reconvene at eight a.m." Della suggests.

We all stand to leave. Walters lingers behind in his office as Della and I make our way back through the bull pen.

"I'm gonna head back over to the hospital," I say. Her small hand catches my forearm, turning me toward her.

"Jones ..." She stops, forcing me to look into her eyes as she speaks. "Mac was a little girl when her mother was murdered, in front of her eyes. She spent hours alone in a dark hole before police found her. She's most likely gone back to that time. She needs that hole and that time, to process what has happened tonight. Don't push her. She came out of it before and she'll come out again. Right now, the best thing you can do is go home and get some sleep. Show up as a police officer tomorrow, not a friend. She needs you to be a cop, because if anyone can catch this guy, it's you and Walters."

I nod and fight the urge to prove her wrong. I decide to skip the hospital and head straight to Mom and Dad's. If I could carry Mac back from the darkness, I'd do it in a heartbeat. But Della is right. I'm her friend, but first I'm a cop. And a damn good one.

HUNTER

I sat for a while, nursing the gash on my shoulder and reassuring myself that I could regain control before fear slithered in, snaking and sinking its fangs into my pounding heart. The useless emotion was wringing me out until the fury fought back. MacKenna Arnold is going to pay. I lost more than my blood and my computer at that house. She took away my pride as she stripped me of my anonymity. It won't be long before they figure it out. Once that happens, Father will know of my final plan.

I'd always accounted for the FBI eventually catching up, but not so soon. I'd be impressed by their work, if I wasn't having to readjust my schedule. Moving things forward is possible but it will mean redirecting their investigation. Getting to MacKenna will be as easy as throwing glitter in the air. While they're dazzled and looking in one direction, I'll be finishing what I started here in Wisconsin. I'm already one step ahead. Once that bitch gets home from the hospital, things will begin to slot back in place.

Chapter 17

AGENT DELLA PEREZ

Walters walks with me to my car.

"Where are you staying?"

"I'll head over to the Holiday Inn, get a room there."

"You're not already booked in?" A line appears between his brows.

"Go home, Walters. Don't worry about me!" My smile is meant to reassure him. Instead, he flicks his wristwatch to check the time before digging into his pocket to retrieve his cell phone. I watch in amused curiosity as he dials a number.

"Marina, it's Detective Walters with the ..." he begins. "That's right. I was wondering if you had any rooms available?" he listens.

"All booked up, huh?" his head shakes in mock dismay toward me. Feeling thoroughly scolded, like a naughty child who forgot to hand in her homework assignment, I cross my arms in frustration.

"Could you call me when the next available room comes up? I'll need at least three, for some out-of-town guests. Thank you, Marina." He hangs up.

"Well, that was completely unnecessary!"

"The Fox City Marathon is on this weekend, Agent. Unless you booked your room months ago, there ain't a hotel room for you in Appleton, until Monday at the earliest." Leaning closer, he reaches behind me to open my car door.

"What are you doing?"

He shoos me aside, popping the trunk without permission.

"I'm tired, I need a shower, and now I need to set up my guest bedroom" he grumbles, walking to the trunk and removing my overnight bag.

"I can't stay with you!"

"Unless you plan on sleeping in your car, I don't see how you've got much choice."

My mouth falls open, watching as he strides to his car, opening his own trunk and dropping my bag inside. My heart debates with my mind. This is not a good idea. The passenger door of his car is open, the invitation too much to resist.

"Thank you."

A smile plays on my lips as I climb in.

"What are colleagues for?" he closes the door. My stomach flutters with excitement before I pull back and remind myself that Detective Walters is off limits. Permanently.

AGENT DELLA PEREZ

My thoughts scattered as we rounded the bend bringing us onto Hawthorne Avenue in Little Chute, Appleton. I took a moment to absorb the wide street bordered by single-family homes. All different sizes and colors, some have basketball nets hanging over double garage doors, others have toys littered around the yard, abandoned after sundown. All properties with well-manicured lawns on this peaceful street. A street for raising a family, and the last place I'd expect a bachelor like John to live.

Swinging right, we pull up outside his single-story ranch home. Holding onto the open car door as I step out, my eyes take in the freshly-painted gray paneling, the white trim and garage doors.

"Wow, your home is beautiful," I say as he moves to the trunk, grabbing my bags and ignoring my surprised tone.

"Do you have everything?"

"Yes, thank you." Closing the car door, we move along a gravel path onto a small porch. Two armchairs sit behind the white wooden rail, a small table between them, looking out onto his lawn. Images of him reading out here on a warm summer evening float to mind.

Does he sit alone?

He steps inside, holding the door for me to enter. I move tentatively past him crossing the threshold into John's private domain.

"I have a guest bedroom in the basement. Hope that's OK?"

"Sure, thank you." I feel his hard body slip past me in the darkness. Bergamot fills my senses, followed by the distinct scents of orange varnish and pine. The heady mixture evokes a warm sentiment, that intensifies with the glow from the table lamps John switches on.

My eyes widen to soak it all in. A brown leather sofa, wide and inviting, faces the exposed brick fireplace, with family photos littering the mantel. Large bookshelves on either side are fully stocked and dust free. Drawn into the space, my feet turn me full circle impressed at how serene it feels. My fingers itch to pick up a black-and-white photo on the mantel. Encased in a mirrored frame, two young boys stand next to each other, both smiling, while one holds a toddler. His arms are wrapped around her chubby belly as he protectively cradles her.

They must be his siblings.

Pointing to the little boy holding the toddler, my lips part in an easy smile.

"Is this you?"

"Yeah. That's my sister, Clara, and my brother, Rob."

There is an edge of unease in his tone that shifts my focus back to him. He's still in the doorway, his body leaning against the frame, an uncomfortable expression on his face.

"I'm sorry! I can be a little nosey. But you were a cute kid." My cheeks burn and I return the frame to its spot. Turning to go, I spot another photo, with a face too familiar to ignore. Embarrassment forgotten, I reach for it.

DETECTIVE JOHN WALTERS

My nerves are pulled tight watching Della's heels step into my home. I held the door open, watching with apprehension as her curious eyes swept the room, gathering every detail and storing it away in her analytical mind.

Unsure if it is Della the profiler or the woman, I remain silent as she moves about, filling my home with her fresh scent and bringing the place to life. Her dainty fingers skim the spines of the books on my bookshelf before those busy hands pick up another photo frame. My pulse flares with the memory of my protests against posing for that photo but the volunteers at the *Fox Cities Victim Crisis Response Team* insisted upon it. Savannah Philips, Faye Anderson and I, stand next to a table of "go bags" we helped to raise funds for. The ladies have really stepped up for their community since Faye's attack.

Della swings around, flipping her long dark hair over her shoulders.

"This must have been recent?"

"Yeah, the ladies are doing great work for victims of crime. I just helped with something …" My throat thickens uncomfortably. "Anyway, your room is this way." My head tilts toward the dark hallway behind me.

"What is in the bags?"

"They're called 'go bags.' They're for victims of domestic violence or violent crimes. Inside are essential supplies to help anyone who needs to flee their situation in a hurry," I explain.

"Where do they distribute them?"

"At the station."

"What an amazing idea! And Faye and Savannah helped to raise funds? How were you involved?"

"I wasn't. Not really …" my hand rubs against the coarse bristles of my five o'clock shadow. "The radio and sheriff's stations held a family fun day last month. We raised funds."

"Who organized it?"

"We all did, OK? This way." thumbing behind me, my shoulder lifts from the doorframe. She doesn't budge. Instead, her full lips part into a wide, open smile that shimmers in the green of her eyes before she places the frame back on the bookshelf, running her finger along its glossy edge.

"I'm impressed, John. Did you paint this yourself?"

"What makes you ask that?"

"I smell Citristrip. My dad is a carpenter," she tosses casually over her shoulder, finally moving away from the bookcase.

"You're very perceptive, Agent Perez."

"It's my job, Detective Walters."

"Well, you're good at your job, Della."

"Hmm …" Her cheeks flush lightly. "Thank you, John." She steps closer, her dusky tone prickling along the back of my neck.

Clearing my throat, I declare, "I need a drink."

"Is the kitchen through here?" She brushes by me, disappearing into the dark hallway toward the kitchen. She pauses in the doorway. I step behind her to reach for the light switch, my hand lightly grazing her shoulder on the way by. She visibly shivers at my feather-light touch. She glances sideways, holding my gaze.

My pulse quickens, thrumming in my ears.

"Is vodka OK?"

"Uh huh …" She drags her bottom lip between her teeth.

Fuck, don't do that!

My heart thrashes against my chest, making it hard to breathe.

"Ice?"

She nods. "It might help to cool me down …"

"In that case, I'll need some too." Before I can stop myself, I smile. It hitches up one side of my face, deepening when her husky laughter echoes around the kitchen, releasing me from under her spell.

"About those drinks." My throat clears. Moving to the cabinet, I make our drinks, in full awareness of Della on the other side of my kitchen island. She examines my current project. Her hand trails across the solid wood nightstand sitting in the middle of my kitchen floor.

Twenty-four hours ago, I'd never have imagined it.

"So, not just the bookshelves. You refurbish old pieces of furniture, huh?"

"Drink's ready," I say, sliding it to her, before leaning back against the counter in silence. She bends low, ignoring the vodka to examine it further.

"It's a beauty. Where did you get it?"

"At a thrift store in town."

"You thrift?"

"More like I look for old, abandoned pieces of furniture and bring them back to life." The words slip from my mouth before I can stop them.

"You spend your days hunting killers and nights saving furniture?" she teases.

"I wouldn't put it quite like that, but it helps to shift my focus from murder to the mundane when I get home."

"You're talented. The bookcases are beautifully done ..." She reaches for her drink. "You continue to surprise me."

I take a long hard sip. The vodka burns away any need to speak.

"Thank you for allowing me to stay here ..." She stares into her glass, dropping it without taking a sip. "I'll get to bed; let you get some sleep."

I nod, picking up her bags and leading her down to the basement. "This way."

She doesn't speak as we navigate the basement to the guest bedroom at the back. I use this space to store pieces of furniture I've already restored. Her eyes round as we pass, but if she likes them, she keeps her thoughts to herself. Opening the sliding glass door that I installed to close off the bedroom, I step aside, handing over her bag.

"You have your own bathroom and shower down here and the bed is pretty comfortable."

Often, after I've spent hours on a piece and can't face dragging my tired limbs back up the stairs, I've crashed here. It's convenient.

"*Gracias*, Walters." the words curl into a beautiful purr that rolls off her tongue.

Fuck! My heart seizes in my chest. Agent Della Perez is breathtaking. And with that, I head straight to bed.

CHAPTER 18

DEPUTY JONES

Fluorescent lights flicker along the empty hospital corridor. With a tray of fresh coffees in hand, I find my way to the high-security ward. Mac has been under armed guard since the attack. The deputies weren't able to locate Sailor's camp last night, but Dad's going up the Wolf River trail to find him this morning. In the meantime, I've got some details to settle with Walters and Perez about Mac's protection once she's discharged. It's best she stays with my folks. Dad won't let anything happen to Mac on his watch.

Deputy Devlin stands outside Mac's room, alone.

Where's the second deputy?

"How is she?" I ask passing him a coffee.

"Thanks …" He tips the cup. "She's been quiet. Nurses checked on her a few times during the night, but nothing out of the ordinary."

"Where's Parker?"

"Toilet break." He rolls his tired eyes up to the ceiling.

It's almost five a.m., the next shift will be here soon to relieve them.

"I'll go on in. Thanks for keeping an eye out."

"Yeah man, no problem …" As I move past him into Mac's room, he pats my shoulder. "We'll keep her safe until we catch this bastard," he promises.

Her bed is empty, the bathroom door closed. Setting the coffees on the bedside table, I call out.

"Mac? It's Jones."

Silence.

"Mac?"

Nothing.

My heartrate picks up as I move to the bathroom door and knock.

"Mac, are you in there?"

I grip the handle, my pulse pounding against my wrist. When she doesn't answer again, I press down on it. The latch releases. My hand goes to the gun at my hip as every worst-case scenario flash through my mind.

"Mac?"

Empty.

Panic bounces around the chambers of my heart. There's a low whimper from behind the closed shower curtain. Whipping it open, I find her curled up in the fetal position on the shower floor, trembling and rocking back and forth, silently weeping.

"Oh, Jesus. Mac, I've got you," I say, lifting her into my arms for the second time in just a few hours. She doesn't put up a fight, doesn't push me away. Instead, her slender fingers grip my brown shirt until we reach the edge of her bed.

"You're not alone, I've got you ..." Wrapping her in the blanket, my hands work to keep her warm, rubbing her arms and back, wiping the hair from her face.

She's been crying alone, afraid ...

Reliving her childhood trauma, just like Perez said she might.

I should have been here.

It's a special kind of torture to witness someone you care about suffer violence once in their lifetime, but twice? She's still shaking when I gently cup her red blotchy face to examine her closely. The brown, green and gold of her hazel eyes are drowning in grief.

"Mac, we need to get you warm."

Lifting her gaze to mine, her fragile control breaks again. On instinct, my arms wrap around her as a new wave of tears rakes her body.

"Jo—ones." She sniffles against my chest.

"It's OK, I got you."

"I—" She speaks through short, shallow gasps. "I'm ... sor—ry."

"Don't say that, Mac. Don't apologize. You haven't done anything wrong."

A tight knot squeezes my vocal cords.

"I'm so tired!"

"Let's get you into bed."

"No, I mean ..." She gulps, still shaking. "I'm tired of being afraid."

Her admission sears through my heart. My arms tighten around her body, her vulnerability. I can't fix the parts of her that are broken, but I can hold her while she tries.

DETECTIVE JOHN WALTERS

He bounds through the hospital doors with the speed of a gazelle.

Sailor Arnold.

I've never met him before, but Jones gave me his description.

"*He* must have gotten some bad news." Della frowns. I'm about to tell her who he is when a familiar voice calls out from behind us.

"Walters!"

Turning, we see Detective James Jones Senior, retired, walking up the path toward us.

"Jim." I smile, extending my hand to shake his. "This is Agent Perez."

"Jim? As in Jones's father?" Her face lights up.

"The one and only. It's nice to finally meet you!"

"The feeling is mutual; Jones has told me so much about you."

There is a familiarity between them, the kind of warmth that is established over time.

"I believe he has you on speed dial. Don't be afraid to ignore him if he's getting to be too much," he chuckles.

"I'm happy to help. He's got a great head for the criminal mind. You must feel very proud."

He never told me that Della was helping him too ...

I'm both impressed and irritated that he managed to keep it to himself.

"I am, thank you, Della." He turns back to me. "Anyway, Walters, I just dropped Sailor Arnold here. Found him fishing over by Wolf River. He was frantic, but calmed down once I assured him Mac was OK. Any leads?"

"It's early yet, but thanks to MacKenna, this guy made a few mistakes."

"Jimmy came out to the farm last night," he tells me.

I don't bother pretending to be shocked. There was no way that Jones would entrust Mac to the care of strangers.

"I had a feeling he would ..." I sigh. "Do you think it's a good idea, for Mac to stay with you? He's emotionally tangled up in this."

"He is. The whole family cares about her."

"That could be a dangerous mix."

"Mac is a tough nut. We'll keep her safe." There's a finality to his words.

"I guess the decision is made."

"I worked her mom's case. You know that, right?"

"Yeah, I read the files."

"Is all this connected?" he asks.

"I …"

"It is." Della cuts across me. I grimace in her direction.

We shouldn't be talking so freely about an open investigation!

"How?"

"We shouldn't—" I begin before she cuts me off again.

"It's obviously not the same guy, but there is some link between the cases. Any information from the original investigation that you can think of would be a great help."

Jim smiles at my obvious reluctance to speak so early on the case.

"I have copies of the old files in my home office. I'll go over them …"

Well that could *help …*

"Walters, Mac will be safe with us. Sailor too. You guys just catch this monster before he hurts someone else."

"We will," Della and I respond in unison, both our tones certain.

"That Jeffrey Carson character you caught was some of the finest police work this town has ever seen. I was so proud my son got to be part of it."

"He's a good cop and he'll be a great detective. Mac is alive because of him," I admit, because quite frankly it's true. Jim has raised a good man who's a great cop.

"I'll let you get back to it. I'm off to install some extra home security measures, old school!"

We watch as he walks back toward the parking lot.

Daylight pours through the glass wall into the waiting area of the hospital lobby. Sailor paces next to the reception area. From a distance he looks fit for a man of his age, sprightly even. But as we near, a lifetime of tragedy is written in the lines of his face. He's dressed in a pair of black shorts and a blue tank top. He turns as we approach, dark green eyes scanning us for potential threats.

"Sailor? I'm Detective John Walters."

"Are you the man in charge of finding this guy?"

Right down to business. I like it.

"I am, along with Agent Perez here."

He nods to her in greeting.

"I'd like to see Mac. The nurse is gone off looking for some kind of authorization."

"It's all in the interest of Mac's safety. But we will get you in soon," I promise.

"Could you answer some questions first? Let us get on our way?" Della's tone is warm, inviting.

"I wasn't there ..." he looks down at his feet. "Again!" he growls.

Sailor was serving his country when his sister was killed. Guilt and shame dwell in his eyes, a heavy burden. Sailor has most likely carried it around for over twenty years.

"Mac fought him off. Do you know how she might have done that?" I ask.

"She's tough, knows how to protect herself."

"Where did she learn those moves?" I push.

"I've been teaching her self-defense since she was a little girl."

"Seems to me you *were* there, all right ..."

His eyes lift from the floor. "I wish I could take credit, but Mac has always been a fighter, just like her momma."

"I'm sure that's true, Mr. Arnold, but she put up a hell of a fight, thanks to your training," Della says.

"Is she OK? Did he ..." He gulps, his hands shaking. It dawns on me. Mac's mother wasn't just badly beaten and stabbed to death. Thomas Moseley raped her. Sailor sat through every minute of the trial, listening to every detail. His mind must be running riot with all the possibilities of Mac's attack.

"No, he didn't get the chance. She kicked the shit out of him."

His chin jerks up. "Good."

Della steps forward. "Mr. Arnold ..."

"Call me Sailor," he tells her.

"Mackenna suffered a similar trauma when she was eight years old. There are some emotional wounds she's working through."

"What does that mean?"

"This morning, Deputy Jones found her curled up and shaking. It's most likely a coping mechanism from her childhood, to help with the fear and shock."

"It is. I often found her in that state."

"Does it happen often?" Della takes lead on the questioning.

"Not in a long time. It was mostly when she was younger, stopped in her early teens."

"Is there anything we can do for her now to help?"

"I would sit with her, wait for it to pass. She'd settle after an hour or two."

I'm relieved to know that she can push through this emotional break.

"That's good. seeing you now might help get her there sooner. How are *you* feeling?" she asks. The compassion in her tone is inspiring, watching it soften the hard edges of Sailor's own trauma is something to behold.

"I did my best, you know …"

"This isn't your fault, Mr. Arnold."

"I've spent twenty years trying to help her feel strong and safe!" He shakes his head in bewilderment. "How can this have happened to us again?"

"This killer carefully selects his victims based on the fact that they have already survived an attack. We're still figuring out why he chose Mac, specifically, but she survived because she fought him off. She survived twice and both times it was because of you."

"No …" A nostalgic smile wobbles across his face as he shakes his head. "It's because of her mother. Mac is just like Julie. They're two strong fighters. People think that because Julie died that night, she lost her fight with the fucker who killed her. They're fools. Julie fought to keep that child alive, and she won.

"I tried to fill Julie's boots. I never wanted to be a father. I couldn't give Mac the kind of affection a child needs, so I did all I could to keep her safe …" His words are soaked in regret. "Right now, she needs someone who can hug her without feeling their body seize up, you know?" He drops his eyes to the floor again.

"Jones is with her now …" I tell him.

"Good. That boy's been in love with her since they were ten years old."

I want to smile. Poor Jones has done a lousy job of hiding his feelings.

"There are other ways to help her. What can you tell us about her father?" reaching for my notepad and pen, I ready myself to take notes.

"Piece-of-shit CEO from New York. Runs some global finance company. Left Julie the day she got pregnant." He spits. A nearby nurse looks horrified.

"Would he have any reason to hurt Mac?"

"Doubt it. That spineless weasel wouldn't have it in him. Never called once after Julie's murder. I have his contact info somewhere: I'll get it for you, but you'd better warn him to stay away!"

"We'll do our best, but we do need to investigate him." I look up from my shorthand.

"I understand. Is this bastard likely to try again?"

"We don't know." Della answers honestly.

"I won't interfere with your investigation but mark my words: if he comes back, he'll meet the end of my knife before he hurts that girl again. Do we understand each other?"

"We do. But trust me, I'll find him long before that can happen."

Flipping my notepad closed, I tuck it into my inside pocket. A cold shiver runs down my spine, calling my attention to the waiting area. A few people sit, most with their heads down and eyes on their phones. All except for one set, that have zeroed in on our group. Dark eyes, with bushy eyebrows, looking too curious for my liking.

"Good. Well, you better get to searching for him ..."

Sailor's voice fades into background noise. Eyes trained on the stranger, my body instinctively turns in time to see him stand. Slowly, with deliberate strides, he walks through the rows of blue plastic chairs. His head is down. Picking up speed, I follow behind.

"Walters?" Della calls.

A nanosecond of distraction is all it takes. In the blink of an eye, he's disappeared.

"Shit."

"What is it?" She runs alongside me now, our eyes searching the empty corridor he escaped onto.

"I think our killer was just here. Tall, black jacket, jeans and hair. Dark eyes, that's all I got. Search every room!" We split up.

I'm speaking into my radio, whipping open blue curtains, startling nurses and doctors while warning the deputies outside Mac's room to be on guard.

Sailor comes up behind me.

"I saw him too. He went left, down this corridor." He runs past me. Sprinting after him, our legs carry us to the end of a hallway. A red exit sign over a door that leads onto the parking lot.

Fuck!

My blood sizzles with frustration as we rush back inside to find Perez.

"We need to get our hands on the surveillance footage," I growl, holstering my gun.

A wide-eyed nurse pokes her head out of a door, her shaking hand to her chest.

"Is everything OK, officer?"

"Yes, ma'am. False alarm."

CHAPTER 19

DEPUTY JONES

Two guards sit monitoring twenty screens, mounted on the wall of the hospital's security office. Walters, Della and I all watch closely as they pull up the footage.

"We have over one hundred cameras in operation. Twenty cover the entrances and exits, including the parking lot. There are five in the main reception area and then three on each floor. They're located on either end of the corridors, with one in the middle. These monitors here rotate between each camera, every twenty seconds." One guard points to the wall of screens. Each one flicks between different wards, and camera angles every few seconds.

"This is your guy arriving—" He zooms in. "Look, he knows where the cameras are. See how he keeps his head down and away?"

"Did he arrive on foot?" Walters asks.

"Let me pull up the lot footage."

We wait. My foot taps impatiently until I see a dark figure walking from the main road into the frame. My heart stops, watching as my dad passes him on the footpath to his truck.

"Your dad turned back ..." Della says absently.

"Shit, he walked here." Walters sighs.

"Can you bring up the waiting room again?" I ask. My eyes are laser focused on the screen, Walters and Della enter, immediately approaching Sailor. Seconds later, and as brazen as they come, I see the motherfucker walk through the main entrance and slink into a seat. No one noticed his arrival.

"Zoom in on his face." I say.

He kept his head down, his face resting in his steepled hands as he watches John and Della.

"He is definitely solely focused on us." Della steps closer behind the guard at the control panel. "Can you zoom in on his feet?"

Her lips purse. "He's wearing boots ..."

"Nothing about them stands out to me ..." John moves closer to the screen. He's been in a bad mood since the slippery fucker got away from him.

"It's July. Everyone else is in sneakers or sandals, except me, you and our killer ..."

"D'you think he's a cop?" My eyes dart from the screen to her.

"I think it's an angle we'll need to explore ..." She trails off. "OK. Watch here: this is where you spot him ..."

Any other cop would have missed him. Not Walters. His observant eyes note him immediately. Detective Walters has the intuition of a fucking psychic. I watch the footage of his entire body turning in the direction of the killer.

"John you're a legend ..." Sheer admiration drives the words from my mouth. We watch as John stalks his prey, subtly picking up his pace until he turns aside for a brief moment. Taking the opportunity, the dark figure slithers sideways down a side corridor. It takes him less than ten seconds to exit the building.

"Jesus Christ, he's fast. Have you ever seen anything like this before?" Walters says.

I shake my head, as does Della. All three of us are dumbfounded.

"Can you get us a copy of this footage, immediately?" He asks the guard, then turns back to us. "OK, let's regroup outside." He leads the way out of the office.

"Jones. CCTV from the surrounding buildings is top priority. I need you on it now."

"You got it. Is Mac safe here?"

"This guy is clever, controlled, and organized. He won't risk coming here again, not today. We'll put an officer on the two-ground floor exits too. The best shot we have of catching him is CCTV. We need to know where he went," Della answers.

"The other FBI agents arrive today. Get whatever you can and come back to the station. Agent Ryan will help you." Walters nods.

"What's the quickest way to get off the streets around here?" Della asks us both.

"The bus station is two blocks from here …"

"I doubt he'll leave town without—" she bites down on her own words.

"Finishing the job?" I finish her sentence.

"He knows we've spotted him; he might feel some pressure to get out of town, regroup," Walters continues. "Jones, we'll head there now and meet you back at the station in an hour?"

"OK, on it."

The clock above their head reads eight a.m.

Daylight had just broken and this fucker was out for blood. My chest once again swells with utter appreciation for Walters.

AGENT DELLA PEREZ

He caught a Greyhound to Milwaukee.

7:00 a.m.: CCTV shows him arriving at the Appleton bus station.

7:04 a.m.: He buys his ticket with cash.

7:10 a.m.: He sits, alone, outside the station, waiting for the bus to arrive.

7:21 a.m.: He boards the bus. We watch as other passengers climb on behind him. He doesn't exit the bus.

7:35 a.m.: The bus leaves the station.

"How long does that bus take to get to Milwaukee?" John looks up from the monitor to the superintendent of Appleton's small bus station.

"Three hours, maybe a little longer, depending on how often it stops."

"How many stops are there, between here and Milwaukee?" I ask.

"I'll need to check the route, but right off my head we got stops in Eau Claire, Menomonie, Stevens Point, Wausau, Marienette ..." she rhymes off several more stops.

He's already had forty-five minutes of travel time.

My stomach flares to life with the need to act. Quickly.

"We have to get on that bus."

"It's covered too much ground for us to catch up."

"How do you want to do this?" I ask him.

"We contact the driver. Tell him to continue as normal, without stopping. Let's find out which sheriff stations are along the route; they can intercept the bus."

Trusting this killer into the hands of other deputies feels like a risk, but we have no choice. I turn back to the superintendent.

"Can you get in touch with the driver?"

"Sure ..." She puts on a headset that was sitting at a control panel in front of her. She makes contact before offering her seat and headset to me.

Walters is on his cell to the sheriff's station, coordinating where we can intercept the bus. Keeping my tone light, I introduce myself to the driver. His name is Trevor. Calmly, I direct him to continue as planned but to reduce his speed.

"Trevor, do you have any lone male passengers on the bus?" I ask.

"There are two or three" his voice wavers.

"Trevor, listen to me. You're safe. This man just wants to get to his destination. I need you to think. Has anyone gotten off the bus since leaving Appleton?"

"Yeah, a few passengers got off in Fond Du Lac, but I didn't pay much attention."

"That's OK. I'm going to stay on the radio with you ..."

John comes to stand next to me, his cell phone to his ear. "We have two highway patrol cars along I41, at Lomira. They're parked at a truck stop next to the McDonald's. Where is he now?"

"Trevor, how close to Lomira are you?"

"Maybe five minutes."

"Do you know the stretch of road by the McDonalds?"

"Yeah, there's an exit there. Should I get off?" his voice wobbles with fear.

"No, stay on the road. Just tell me when you see the McDonald's and I'll direct you from there."

We all wait for what seems an eternity before Trevor speaks again. "OK, I see it," he calls out.

John speaks into his cell again.

"Trevor, you should see two patrol cars soon. When they direct you,

I want you to pull over. Don't do anything other than follow their instructions, OK?"

"They're signaling now," he tells me.

We listen as the officers board the bus.

"OK Trevor, you did great," I say. I hand the headphones back to the superintendent and go to stand next to Walters. His face twists in frustration.

Mierda!

He meets my eye and shakes his head sharply.

"Take their information anyway and let the bus get back on the road," he sighs, hanging up.

"None of them match the description."

"Fuck."

This is the closest to catching him I've been. The disappointment of losing him for the third time in less than twenty-four hours is soul crushing.

"Let's get back to the station." There is no hiding how deflated I feel. We travel in silence back to the Outagamie station.

CHAPTER 20

DETECTIVE JOHN WALTERS

Beyond the confines of the conference room, the hustle and bustle of everyday life in the Outagamie County sheriff's office is amplified tenfold by the presence of the FBI once again. News of a second attack on MacKenna Arnold has traveled through town and the phones have been ringing all morning with concerned citizens jamming up the lines. Jones and I are working on piecing the information we have onto an investigation wall when my phone buzzes. I scribble down the details of the call before hanging up. Turning, I meet Della's eyes across the room.

"That was the Fond Du Lac Sheriff's department. An eyewitness spotted someone matching our killer's description leaving a motel a few hours ago. I'm going to head over there shortly to interview the staff."

"Do we know if he was on foot, or traveling by car?"

"They're reviewing surveillance footage now. I'll let you know more as soon as I do. How are your calls to Minnesota going?"

She's been liaising with the Duluth and St. Cloud sheriff's offices all morning. She brought a list of potential victims that Agent Ryan developed. Two of them live in those Minnesota cities.

"Deputies have been dispatched to each possible victim's home. All we can do for now is to prewarn them, advise them to take extra precautions and have officers patrol their neighborhoods until we know more on where this guy is headed."

"How sure are you that he'll move on to his next victim?" Jones asks.

"Well, he was selecting and killing a new victim each month. We must consider that he will continue with his spree."

"Is he a spree killer?" My brows furrow.

"No, he's classified as a serial, but the only real difference between a spree killer and a serial is the cooling off period."

"And he doesn't cool off?" I'm intrigued.

"Well, there are weeks between each kill. Ordinarily that would be considered his cooling off period. In this case, the date of the victim's original attack dictates when he will kill again. It's a fine line. He doesn't follow standard behavioral patterns." She blows out a heavy breath.

"You already got one step ahead of him. You'll do it again, Chief." My chest swells with pride, then regret. I'd heard about her promotion to unit chief.

I should have reached out.

Our gazes hold, and for the first time since meeting Della, sadness shimmers there. Her mouth is opening to speak just as the conference room door swings opens.

"Well there's a sight for sore eyes!" Tall, broad and very obviously FBI, an agent walks in. He focuses all his attention on Perez. "A heads up you were going out into the field would have been nice," he exclaims.

"Clark." Shocked, she stands to greet him. All the ease is sucked from the air, replaced by the agitation that has Della's fingers twisting around her pen.

She's nervous ...

"Detective Walters, this is Agent Gary Clark. " We nod to each other. "And you know Agent Ryan." The familiar face of Agent Ryan is a welcomed relief. He's carrying three boxes and struggling in. Jones and I move to help him.

"Thanks," he chirps. "Jeez, it's good to see you both again!" He drops his load on the table, turning back to shake our hands. He's grown a beard: thick, black and adding a few years to his baby face. It suits him.

"Good to see you too, man!" Jones shakes his hand, before turning to greet Agent Gary Clark. Following his lead, I offer my hand to the newest addition of Della's team. His grip is unnecessarily tight.

"Nice to meet you. Perez has told me a lot about your small-town sheriff's office." He throws her a conspiratorial smirk before wrinkling his nose in my direction. Shifting my focus to Della, I watch their exchange. Her cheeks are flushing with embarrassment, her lips thinning with disapproval.

"Nice to know she hasn't forgotten about the small folk around here."

I release his grip with a withering glare.

"OK. Let's get down to business. If you guys could get me up to speed, I can establish the best course of action moving forward." His chest puffs out with self-importance.

"Shouldn't Agent Perez be giving the orders?" I ask.

All eyes shift to Della, who is glaring at Clark.

She pulls her shoulders back, throwing a saccharine smile in his direction. "I was removed as unit chief this morning."

Jesus. Della ...

"Sorry, I assumed you'd told ..." He shrugs.

"No, I'm sorry." She glances between Jones and me. "It was the last thing on my mind after the morning we've had. Speaking of which ..." Chief or not, she commands the room. All eyes move to her as she speaks. "Let's go over everything we have. Physical evidence collected at the scene confirms that this unsub is indeed the same man the FBI has been chasing. Like the other murders, he left his signature black feather. We've bagged and tagged it and sent to our forensic ornithologist. Thankfully he's been able to confirm the feathers came from a rare breed of parrot, known as a vasa parrot. He'll run test on the new feather but has established that all the feathers to date came from the same parrot."

"If the parrots are rare that might work in our favor." I say.

"Yes, Ryan is currently running background checks on breeders and aviary specialists. People do keep this type of parrot as pets, so we are hoping they'll know some owners. So far, we've no names."

"What about microchip databases? If he keeps it as a pet, he might have it microchipped."

Ryan lifts his head from his laptop to speak.

"Unfortunately, the personal information on a microchip is stored against a ten-digit code that's scanned. Once we have the bird, it will tell us the owner and their contact information. Great evidence after the fact but nothing that can lead us to him unless we find the bird first."

"Ryan—" Della turns to face him now—"we found a small handheld computer. The killer dropped it fleeing the Arnold home. Use your skills to pull whatever data you can from it. If there's a barcode or anyway that we can track where he purchased it, find it."

"Sure, I'll collect it from Evidence and run some forensic analysis. If he's technically minded, it's most likely encrypted, but with some time I'm sure I can crack it." He rubs his hands together, excited by the challenge.

Della's attention shifts to Jones "Could you take over from Ryan and look into breeders and avian specialists here in Wisconsin? It's a long shot, but we need to rule out a connection to those organizations."

"On it!" he nods.

"Thanks to MacKenna Arnold, we now have a description of our killer. White, over six feet tall, late twenties to early thirties, with dark blue or brown eyes. He has bushy eyebrows and a small scar from a piercing of the left eyebrow. He wore all black, carried a hunter's knife on a thigh strap and for the first time he left his DNA at the scene. It's being processed here in the Appleton lab and will be transferred to the Madison crime lab for testing. It will be a week or two before we know if there is a hit on it. He's moving too fast for us to wait on the results, so for now we keep going."

"What other new information do we have?" Clark straightens next to me, his arms coming across his chest. If he's trying to assert his authority, he's being ignored.

"The question of how he entered our victims' homes undetected and without forced entry has been answered. He hacked the Arnold home security system and entered the house three days before the intended attack. That, coupled with the computer we found, bolsters our initial assessment that our killer is meticulous, and computer minded."

With this in mind, I address Della again. "You mentioned earlier that this unsub doesn't follow normal behavioral patterns. How so?"

She sighs, her shoulder lifting lightly before she resumes her seat "He used a different method of murder on each victim. From strangulation to stabbing, he followed the original killer's method. But unlike the other killers, he didn't rape his victims."

"Why is that important?" Jones wonders.

"I believe he sees giving into the sexual urges as a weakness. He may pride himself on his self-control above all else. Forcing the victims to relive their darkest hours is what turns him on."

"What were the key points of your original profile?" I push.

"Well, the victimology is completely different, other than the obvious connection of having survived a previous attack. They are all of different ages, races, sexual orientations and living in different states. It's unlikely they were known to him personally. But there is anger, rage, and overkill at all of the murders. This suggests it was personal, fueled by some need for revenge against surviving victims. My profile surmises that he is on some mission, a righting of wrongs, so to speak, and he won't stop until he is arrested or killed."

Nodding in agreement, I add, "He showed up at the hospital. That was a bold move."

"I disagree, " Clark pipes up. "Serial killers rarely return for the victims that got away. He was injured in his struggle with MacKenna Arnold, maybe that's why he was at the hospital?"

An interesting theory.

"Isn't hunting down the victims that 'got away' this killer's exact signature?"

"He's killing victims that survived other killers, not his own." Jones interrupts.

"Mac is still Thomas Moseley's victim as much as she is his. He wasn't there to see a doctor, he was there to finish what he started."

Della nods. "I tend to agree with Jones. The profile so far has led us here. Mac's statement reaffirms that this guy is meticulous, organized. But it also highlights that he is much more calculating than we had given him credit for. She survived his attack. A blow to the ego like that could cause him to unravel, potentially make mistakes, take another shot at her."

"Who was his first victim?" My experience has taught me that the first victim is usually known to the killer.

"Joanna Deveraux. Forty-eight-year-old nurse from Quantico, Virginia ..." Della begins to rattle off information from memory while searching for the file in her case. When she finds it, she hands it across for me to look over.

"Tell me about her."

"She survived an abduction and attempted murder by LeeRoy Chester, in 1994. She was nineteen at the time of the original crime. Chester bundled her into his car in broad daylight and took her to a secluded location, where he subjected her to over ten hours of torture, including raping, sodomizing and extreme brutality. She managed to escape by playing dead when he attempted to strangle her. Her description of his car, and the composite sketch drawn up by the police artist working with her led to his arrest. In the trunk of his car they found a tarp, a shovel, and a knife, along with items that were later determined to belong to other victims of his. In all, he'd murdered six women and buried them in shallow graves by a creek in the Wissahickon Valley park. On March 3rd of this year, exactly twenty-five years after her original assault, Joanna Deveraux left her home at the same time she did every morning to go to work. She went out on calls and returned to her office to file that day's reports before heading home. She never made it. Her body was found the next day in Wissahickon Valley park. She was left by the same creek as Chester's other victims. With the exception of sexual assault, the MO was the same. Unlike Chester, and unlike any of the unsub's following victims, he covered her face with a shopping bag, suffocating and strangling her at once."

"Is that telling?" I wonder, considering he is copycatting the original killers.

"It was overkill. There was no need for the bag, considering he was manually strangling her, which suggests there was another reason for it. It was his first kill that we know of. He may not have felt good about it, or perhaps Joanna Deveraux resembled someone in his life. He may have felt shame, or needed to cover it up, stop her dead eyes from accusing him, as he took her life."

"You said she was a nurse? Have we investigated her patients?"

"We did. They came up empty." Clark answers for Perez, as he moves around to stand next to her. Too close for mere colleagues. His eyes roam her body slowly. My chest burns with unwanted jealousy.

"I'm heading to Fond Du Lac now, but when I get back, I'd like to start going over the Deveraux's case, see what I can uncover."

"My dad led the investigation on the Julie Arnold murder. I'll ask if there was a link to the LeeRoy Chester case. Maybe Dad had him on a list of suspects?" Jones turns hopeful eyes to me.

"I'd rather we didn't share information with civilians," Clark barks, his tone too assertive for my liking in *my* conference room in the very sheriff's office he disparaged.

"I'll decide how my team operates, Agent Clarence," I growl.

"It's Clark." A smug smile spreads across his face, growing wider when I glare in his direction.

"Whatever. I'd appreciate it if you could focus on *aiding* this small-town law enforcement office, rather than dictating every course of action."

I remind him of the FBI's role, anger searing through my veins. *How dare he?*

"Jones, we're going. We need to interview the motel staff."

My tone matches my sharp movements, reaching for my jacket, I pull it over my white shirt.

"OK, boss." He follows behind me.

AGENT DELLA PEREZ

John's exit bangs the door closed, rattling the whiteboard.

"Care to tell me what the *fuck* that was about?" I turn to Clark.

He snorts. "What a dick. Talk about an overreaction."

"No, Clark. You acted like a dick. You insulted this office, you're not making our job here any easier!"

He shrugs nonchalantly.

"He's not the kind you want watching your back, Della."

"What exactly *are* you implying?"

"He's a loner. Doesn't know how to work in a team and you'd do well to remember who your team is. We have a job to do. I'd appreciate if you'd get the profile updated."

His curt tone is no doubt meant to remind me that he is head of "my" team now.

"Funny you should mention it, because Leonard had a long list of interesting things to say about my work on this case, as coming from someone on my team! You wouldn't know anything about that, would you?"

He squirms under my heated stare.

Counterintelligence, my ass!

"You ..." Clamping my lips shut, I gather up some files and my laptop and leave before saying something I'll regret.

"Where are you going?"

"I'll be in the building; you can get me on my cell."

"We have too much to go over!" He throws his hands up in the air.

"You can reach me on my cell phone." My tone is final.

I can't believe I've been such a fool.

He used me to get ahead, and I allowed it to happen.

My stomach recoils just thinking about the night we spent together. It was a huge mistake, one we both agreed shouldn't have happened. And then, he'd poked and prodded into my work on the case afterward.

Idiota!

Distracted and weighted by self-loathing thoughts, my head is down as I move through the bullpen. I come to an abrupt stop when I crash into John's back.

"Ah! Mierda," I curse softly, as the files in my hands slide sideways toward the floor. He manages to catch them before they fall. He takes the bundle from my arms.

"I'm sorry." My cheeks flush.

"What are you sorry for, exactly?" He lifts a suspicious brow.

"Clark's behavior, bumping into you just now. Everything."

"It's hardly your fault that your boyfriend is a dick."

"OK! That's my cue to leave: I'll meet you at the car ..." Jones's eyes widen between us both before he escapes.

"He's not my boyfriend."

It's the truth.

Why does it feel like a lie?

My emotions are wound so tightly around this man, my thoughts are completely irrational. There was no betrayal, but those guilty feelings grab hold regardless.

"He is your boss though?"

"I should have told you about the demotion, but ..." I sigh.

"It's only my business when it effects this investigation. I hate looking like a fool and not knowing made me look stupid."

A sharp derisive laugh leaves my lungs on an exhale. "Yeah, because *your* feelings about it are the most important thing!"

"I don't have 'feelings' about it. It's professional courtesy."

"You're right, John. It was unprofessional." I take the files from him. "I have work to do." I've had enough of fragile male egos for one day.

"I'm taking your office," I tell him.

His face is set in stone, but he nods in agreement.

I close the door behind me, leaving him and this morning's events in the hallway. The sight of four plants on his windowsill stops me in my tracks. Green and full of life, they sit in stark contrast to the previous resident, a dead weeping fig. Noticing the little cactus plant I left for him among them sets a flutter of hope stirring in my chest.

No!

There will be no more romanticizing of Walters. These plants are only proof that anything can flourish, if the conditions are right. Detective John Walters restores old furniture, bringing pieces of the past back to life. Those same hands that cuff killers also tend to these plants. He can do anything he sets his mind to, and if his words weren't clear this is evidence enough.

He could *care, but he doesn't want to. He'll never want it, Della. Not with you, not with anyone.*

The conditions will never be right unless he changes his mind.

CHAPTER 21

MAC

According to the hospital psychiatrist, my reaction was a trauma response. This attack triggered memories of Mom's murder and I regressed to a place of safety. It's something that happened often when I was a child. My fear manifested itself as physical pain. It would wrap like vines around my lungs and heart, squeezing tightly, incapacitating me. I'd curl into a ball until it passed.

"As you got older, you didn't react the same way. How did you handle fear as an adult, before this recent attack?" she'd asked. The question forced me to look at my life to this point. The hyper-vigilance, the isolation and worse, my treatment of Jones.

Whenever he's around, I'm terrified. My breathing slows, my heartrate picks up, my palms sweat and my stomach swirls. The first time those feelings crept in was the day I returned from my camping trip at thirteen. The sudden fear of *losing him* became too big, but instead of curling into a ball, I fought back. I started a battle with my best friend, sabotaged our love because losing him on my terms felt like a win.

The realization brought shame, and years of pain rode to the surface on a low guttural scream. The fear temporarily left my body, followed by a wave of emotion and relief. Talking with the psychiatrist opened my eyes to another form of healing. Yoga has brought me so far on my healing journey, but therapy might be what I need to get over the finish line.

Is there ever a finish line?

When she leaves, Sailor's weathered face pokes through the doorway.

"Mac. I'm sorry, I should have been there."

I'm exhausted, but the tears in his eyes have me leaping off the bed.

Sailor doesn't cry.

"You've *been there* my entire life! Without you taking me in as your own, Sailor, God knows where I'd have ended up."

We don't embrace, awkwardly reaching to hold hands instead.

"I've never told you this before …" He sucks in another lungful of air, releasing it on a shaky exhale. "When you saved yourself as a child, you saved me too. I wouldn't have—I came so close—so many times, to …" His confession startles me.

He and Mom were extremely close. We were all he had, until it was just me. He had never married; I don't even remember there ever being a girlfriend in his life.

"It's OK." I try to comfort him.

"No. I was in survival mode, for so many years, just trying to make it through the days. I should have checked in with your …" he sniffles, "feelings. And that."

"We're more alike than you know. I guess it's how we've both gotten through."

"I should have known better …"

"Please, Sailor, don't do this to yourself. Maybe another man would have patted my knee and tucked me into bed, but you trained me to be ready and two nights ago, that's what saved me."

"Do we hug now?" He shifts from one foot to the other.

A flutter of laughter bubbles up in my throat. "We could try."

"OK," he nods.

Closing the gap between us, my arms come around his back. It takes us a couple seconds to relax into it, then the hug we never knew we needed allows years of unshed tears to fall freely, silently between us.

"That wasn't so bad, was it?" I pull back, wiping my tears with the back of my hand.

"It was good." He nudges me with his shoulder. Our watery eyes meet.

"Oh boy, it *was* bad. You're a terrible liar," I sniffle.

He chuckles.

"We'll practice. If we can master the guillotine choke, we can learn how to hug more often."

His eyes light up. "Did you use the guillotine on him?"

"No, but the mount escape came in handy."

"Good girl! I'm so proud of you, you know?"

"I know."

"Your mom watched over you. She's smiling down now, proud too."

"I hope so."

His words bring me a sense of peace.

I hope so

HUNTER

> Mr. Chester,
> How does it feel to know she's gone? Wouldn't it be nice to help me in the same way?
> I believe the FBI want to speak with you, think about it.
> Your friend.

It was too easy to hack the database of Finch & Flood, Attorneys at Law. Their ability to protect their clients' information is about as good as their ability to keep them out of prison. I wasn't sure the effort would pay off, but I hit the jackpot when I read the FBI correspondence with LeeRoy Chester. He's refusing their visit, but I'm hoping to persuade him otherwise. Sending the letter is risky, so I printed it on his attorney's letterhead, folded it into an envelope I designed myself and marked it as a legal document. There's no guarantee the guards will respect client-attorney privilege or that Chester will be interested in fucking with the FBI, but if I can get the big dogs out of town long enough, it will be worth the risk. MacKenna Arnold is still in the hospital, which means I'll need to figure out a plan B if she doesn't go home soon. Dropping the envelope into a mailbox, I climb back into my car. I get back on I94 toward Minnesota.

CHAPTER 22

DEPUTY JONES

Our drive to Fond Du Lac yielded results. The staff at the motel remembered a single Caucasian man checking in a week before the attack. He kept a low profile, paid in cash for a week's stay but hadn't been seen in the few days leading up the attempt on Mac's life. We questioned the housekeeping staff, who all agreed the bed wasn't slept in for three days. There were no personal belongings left in the room. However, his car, a silver Honda Accord, was parked outside for the duration of his stay. It was gone by noon today. CCTV footage at the motel only covers the entrance to the parking lot. It was too grainy to get a plate, but it's enough for us to send out a BOLO to all other law enforcement agencies across America.

"We have a car, this is good." My hands clap together on the drive back to Appleton.

"Yeah, it lines up. It's our first solid lead to tracking him down. If we can find out who owns that car, we have our killer."

"What about toll booths, from Chicago to Wisconsin? Traffic cameras might have caught him coming through. If we go back a week, we might get lucky," I suggest.

"That's a lot of footage, but you may be on to something. Hopefully Ryan was able to pull information from the computer too. Have Deputies Lee and O'Hare compile that list of bird breeders, while you get a start on searching for the car. If we can start narrowing down our search perimeter, we'll have a better chance of catching him before he kills again."

"I'll also liaise with the Fond Du Lac sheriff's department when we get back. I'll see what CCTV they have in a five-block radius of the motel. He turned left out of the parking lot, heading away from Appleton, which is a sign that he might have left Wisconsin."

Walters nods, his finger lightly tapping the steering wheel. There is a far-off, pensive look in his eyes before he speaks.

"I want to look back over the investigation into Joanna Deveraux's murder. You're studying criminology: What's your take on the fact that he put a bag over her head and not the others?" he asks.

"It's like what Della said. The victim represents someone he knows, or he didn't feel good about killing her."

"Let's focus on that for a moment. If he didn't feel good about killing her, why do it at all?"

I consider his question for a minute.

"Stop thinking. What is your gut telling you?"

"He's trying to prove something."

"Go on."

"He's a copycat of sorts. He's finishing what other men failed to do and proving he's better than all of them put together."

Walters pushes me to go on.

"Proving it to whom?"

"I don't know. The world? A role model in his life maybe."

"If you had to guess. Forget the training, use your common sense!"

"His father?"

John smiles.

"Exactly. Look at you: you grew up and followed in your dad's footsteps, right? We need to consider that he's doing the same thing."

"LeeRoy Chester didn't have children."

"Let's look into every girlfriend he ever had, see if there were any children born before his arrest. There may be an ex who didn't want the world to know her child is the son of a serial killer."

"That actually makes a lot of sense. But then, why go on and kill the others?" I throw the question back at him.

"I'll leave the psychology of these sickos to you and Della."

"Give me a break, you're the best detective we've got. What's *your* gut telling you?"

"He likes the thrill of the kill and the games that follow."

"What you make of the feathers?" I wonder now.

"Maybe it's linked to him being a copycat, you know, parroting the original killers."

"That's actually a great theory!"

He groans "You know what they're going to call him, don't you?"

"I hope it's something ridiculous like Parrot Killer."

"I might just grant one interview with the press to drop that title."

We're both smiling at the thought as we head straight to the station. I spend hours going over CCTV footage, while John gets up to speed on all the other murders and investigations. Della's back in the conference room with Clark and Ryan developing the profile. Tomorrow we will all sit around the table again, to outline which lines of investigation should take priority. Leaning back in my hard wooden chair, I try to squeeze the exhaustion from my eyes.

"Go home, Jones!" John yells from his office. The guy misses nothing.

I lean further back, catching his eye through the open door. Sitting at his desk, looking as worn out as I feel, he pushes a page away as he tries to focus on the print.

"Get some glasses, old man!" I call back, then snicker when he rolls his eyes.

"I think I'll head over and check up on Mac. See you back here in the morning." I stand, stretching, and wave him goodnight. I decide against disturbing Della. She's been knee deep in files all afternoon and wants to have her profile ready to go for tomorrow's meeting.

"Good night." He waves back. I head out.

MAC

I was eight when I first met Deputy James Jones Junior. He was watching cartoons and eating cereal, sitting on his living room floor. I remember his folks whispering in the kitchen and the strange look on his face when I sat down next to him. Guilt seized me whenever I thought about that day. My mom's body was still lying cold in her bed while I was laughing and building pillow forts with Jimmy Jones.

He arrived a few minutes ago, sat in the chair next to the hospital bed. My back is to him, he hasn't checked to see if I'm sleeping.

"Did you come here to stare at my back?"

"You're awake!" He sounds surprised.

Smiling, I turn to face him.

"You didn't think to check?"

"I didn't want to wake you," he whispers, shrugging. "How you feeling?"

"Why are you whispering?"

He scrunches his face. "It's late."

"There's no one else in here, we're not disturbing anyone."

"Yeah, but it feels weird to disturb the silence."

"You didn't mind disturbing me, coming here in your heavy boots, handcuffs rattling." I look to the belt around his waist.

"Shit, sorry. Did I wake you?"

"No, I can't sleep. I'm sorry about ..." Heat creeps up my neck. "All that stuff, earlier."

"You *should* be sorry! You scared me half to death." His nose wrinkles in mock disgust.

",But seriously, how *are* you feeling?" His tone settles into one of concern. It pokes at my natural inclination to appear strong, but I think about my discussion with the psychiatrist.

Don't push him away.

"Like I want to get back on my yoga mat" I try for honesty.

"I've never done yoga before, you know."

"I charge sixty dollars for a one-on-one session. You can book through my website," I tease.

"Sixty bucks to twist myself into a pretzel?" he gasps, clearly shocked by my prices.

"You wish! It would take a lot more than sixty dollars to get you that flexible. Although ..." I look into his eyes, allowing the mischief he's inciting within me to take over. "You'd make a great downward dog."

He laughs, flushing a deep shade of red.

"Isn't there a child's position I could get into?" he teases back. I'm shocked and thrilled that he went there, so soon after today's incident. I'm grateful he's making light of it, allowing me to move through the shame it stirs within. Reaching for my pillow, I throw it playfully in his direction.

"You're an asshole, Deputy Jones," I laugh.

"Yeah, well you're not exactly a pleasure to deal with, yourself."

His amber eyes swim with relief. I've made his job difficult.

"I'm sorry. I know you only wanted to help. I just ..."

"It's *OK*." The sincerity in his tone holds my gaze, until I see the impish glint return. "You're just a pain in the ass. I understand." He laughs, throwing the pillow back at me.

"I should have reported you when I had the chance!"

"Don't lose hope yet. You haven't heard where you'll be staying until we catch this guy."

Actually, Sailor told me this afternoon. Initially, I was against the idea, terrified by how much my past trauma was colliding with the present. The Joneses exude love, warmth, and safety. For someone like me, that's a scary place to try to exist. The very idea felt like I was letting my guard down until I realized those defenses had collapsed the moment Jones plucked me up from the shower basin this morning. With Sailor close by, there really is nowhere else I'd rather go.

"I've heard. Is it OK with your mom and dad?"

"Yeah, Dad's itching to be of use since he retired and Mom will revel in having more people to feed."

I do a quick scan of his toned body. Her cooking clearly hasn't had any adverse effects, pressing my lips together to suppress my smile, I tease him anyway.

"Hmm. You *are* a little round for an officer of the law."

"Careful, next you'll be calling me a pig!"

"Pay me sixty bucks an hour and I'll trim that fat in no time."

Laughter breaks the tension between us before we settle into a comfortable silence. I don't remember falling asleep, but when I wake up the sun is beaming through the window and Deputy Jones is gone.

CHAPTER 23

AGENT DELLA PEREZ

There was no way to have known, to have physically prepared. Obviously, showing up at John's home this late in the evening was unorthodox, bordering on unprofessional. Driving here, I knew I should just phone him, confess that I felt like a fool for keeping my demotion from him, but somehow that felt cowardly.

I was surprised to hear music filtering onto the porch and considered getting back into my car until the music cut off and a flood light came on. He knew someone was at his door. Within seconds it swung open and Detective John Walters stood before me.

Molten brown eyes meet mine, and I've lost the apology I was still formulating. This is the first time I've seen him out of work attire, and I'm unable to think of anything but his bare chest and denim-clad legs. I swallow hard, clearing my throat when a bead of sweat rolls from his neck down onto his hard pecs. I don't dare follow its decent to his stomach.

"Did the hotel cancel your room?" he asks, understandably confused by my arrival at his door. I lift my eyes from his bare feet to the bottle of beer in his hand. My stomach sinks as reality dawns. There was music playing. John is half naked.

"Oh, shit. I'm sorry! you have a guest ..." My hand flies to my mouth. Mortified and suddenly too queasy to think straight, I turn to flee.

"Della," he growls, "there's nobody else here." His brow gathers in further confusion. "Are you all right?"

"I, um—" Clearing my throat, I try again. "It's stupid, really ..." I comb my fingers through my hair. It's after dark, but I'm sweltering under John's heated gaze.

"Do you want a beer?" He smiles, taking pity on me.

"I could do with a glass of water," I admit. He steps aside, opening the door wider for me to enter. It's only once I'm inside that I notice the gun he was holding behind the door.

"Do you always answer the door with your gun in hand?" My brows arch upward.

"I don't get many visitors, especially this time of night."

I find it hard to believe that a man like John spends his nights alone very often. That suspicion deepens as he leads the way into the kitchen. My attention is drawn to the waistband of his tight-fitting jeans as he tucks the gun firmly into it. I swallow back my thought that I'm surprised there was room for anything in there but the hard muscle of his ass. I forcibly look everywhere else but at him. I see, from the sawdust floating in the air and coating the floor, John must be restoring the small cabinet here.

"I've disturbed you ..."

"You tend to do that a lot."

His words surprise me. Leaning against the kitchen counter, as cool as the beer bottle next to him, he reaches for a black t-shirt. He pulls it over his head, the silvery glint of his scars winking at me before he hides them underneath the thin material. Reaching into the fridge, he pops the lid off a fresh bottle of beer and extends his hand.

"I shouldn't. I'm driving—"

"It's late. Have a beer, you can take the guest bedroom again."

With a small nod, I step forward and take the beer from his hand before slipping my heels off my tired feet. His eyes fall from mine to my lips before dropping to my black toe polish.

"Do you mind?" I ask.

On a deep inhale he shakes his head no, breathing out slowly before taking a swig of his beer. Suddenly, being barefoot in his presence feels intimate. And dangerous. Parched, I sip the beer, my chin forced to tilt up. I meet his gaze.

"Is that a gun in your pants, or are you happy to see me?"

"It's both." His lips curve. Removing the gun from his waistband, he sets it down on the counter with a gentle thud, before leaning closer. "Are you trying to disarm me, Della?"

I throw my head back with a laugh of pure pleasure. John is a good flirt.

"I think I might enjoy trying ..."

His deep growl sends a delicious shiver across my skin. "You won't have to try too hard, if you keep looking at me with those eyes ..." He picks up his beer. "Come on, you can help me with this." Taking my hand in his, he pulls me to the cabinet he was working on. We both kneel next to it.

"What were you listening to when I arrived?" I ask, rolling up the sleeves of my silk blouse.

"Guns N' Roses."

"Oh. It didn't sound like rock."

He leans over toward a large black stereo.

"Is that a tape?" My eyes widen with surprise.

"Yep." He hits the rewind button, then presses down, hard, on the stop button. "It jams sometimes," he explains, pressing play. The song I'd heard when I first arrived begins. Soft guitar and whistling drifts from the old speakers.

"What song is this?" I wonder. The sad, melodic voice not what I expected to hear.

"It's called 'Patience.'" He lifts a piece of sandpaper and begins to work on the cabinet. I watch in comfortable silence, mesmerized by the steady strokes as his hand lightly removes the old varnish. The next song begins, bringing with it hard rock and heavy drumbeats. I smile.

"Pass me a sheet of sandpaper."

He obliges.

"Don't stay in one spot too long. Keep it moving, but go easy, otherwise it will be uneven." He guides my hand.

"Yes, yes, I know."

When he doesn't release my hand, I look directly at him. "You ready to tell me why you're here yet?" he asks.

I nod. He gives me some space, both of us focusing on the sanding as I speak.

"I wanted to apologize. In person. You know ... for keeping the fact that I was demoted from you. I was embarrassed."

"You don't owe me an apology."

"No?"

"No. But if it's worth anything, I think it's a bullshit decision."

I smile.

"What makes you so sure I didn't deserve to lose the position?"

"You were replaced by *Clark*," he snorts. "I suspect that whatever the reason, it wasn't because of your capabilities. You're a great agent."

"*Gracias.*"

"I just call it how I see it."

"Oh, really? I'm curious what else you can see." I laugh softly.

A fire lights in his eyes. The prolonged stare scorches me with its intensity.

"I thought we weren't doing this, Della." He leans back, the hard lines of his body stretching beneath his black t-shirt. Dropping the sandpaper, I stand, rubbing hands sticky with sweat and sawdust on my skirt.

"I ... You're right, this was a bad idea."

He moves to stand.

"No, no. Don't get up," I beg. "I shouldn't have come." I try to pass him but his large hand seizes my ankle, stopping me.

"Why did you?" His expression reveals an internal battle in every crease and line of his face. All the while, his hand is sliding slowly upward, dragging grainy pieces of sawdust with it. My body quivers against his touch, buckling when he reaches behind my knee to pull me down. Holding me above him, he asks again.

"Why did you come here, tonight?"

"I don't know—" I can't think straight. "John ..." His name passes my lips on shallow breaths. I don't resist as he moves me over his lap, my skirt riding up as I straddle him. One look into his eyes seals my fate. My tongue darts out, wetting my lips.

"Mmm. You smell so good." He inhales sharply, hesitation tensing every muscle of his body. *He's still deciding*.

"Tell me what you see, John?" I ask again, bolstered by this new position on his lap.

Long black lashes fan his cheeks as he heaves a deep sigh. Gone is the hard detective's glare.

"I see a nuisance." The corner of his mouth twitches.

"Not just any nuisance, if I remember correctly." I lean closer.

"A prolific one!" His fingers slide into my long brown hair, pulling my lips to his. There is nothing tender as he swallows my gasp of pleasure. I melt into him. Our lips part and his tongue meets mine in slow, hot kisses. My hands grip his t-shirt, tearing it up his back. White lights burst behind my eyelids when a deep groan vibrates down my throat.

"Jesus, Della!" He sits up straight. I dispose of his shirt, showering us both in saw dust. I barely have time to react before his body is lifting mine easily as he rises from the floor. I expect him to turn me away. Instead, he sets me down on my feet and begins to slowly unbutton my blouse. My chest heaves with pleasure, my mind blank as he takes charge. It is both intimidating and the sexiest thing I've ever experienced.

I don't miss his short intake of breath as he exposes my breasts. My hard nipples tease us both as they graze against the black lace. His mouth finds one, his wet tongue not bothering to remove my bra.

"Bedroom. Now," he growls. Lifting me in his arms, he carries me down the hallway. I find his mouth, sucking on the bottom lip before taking his tongue in my mouth and gently sucking again.

"Fuck me, do that again!" he begs.

I give him what he asks, dragging my fingernails up his neck and burying them in his hair. He sets me down. We're standing nose to nose, eyes locked. He brushes a strand of hair from my face with one finger.

"Are you sure?" he asks tenderly. My nod is all he needs before his warm lips find mine again, the gentle pressure, kissing away all tenderness. His tongue slides against mine as our lips fuse together in a frenzy of hot, passionate kisses that burn straight to my core. He deftly removes my blouse and bra, before tucking his thumbs into the waistband of my skirt and yanking it down my legs. Kicking it off, I walk him to the bed, my trembling fingers unbuttoning his jeans, working them down his legs. Our moans turn to gasps as we fall onto the bed. He rolls me onto my back, his lips leaving mine to journey down my neck and onto my hardened nipples. My body checks in as my mind checks out. He tortures me with languid strokes before sucking hard.

"John!" I scream before inhaling a lungful of thick, balmy air. Laden with passion, it fuels my body. My hips thrust upward, my legs wrapping around his back as he returns his attention to my neck. He gives a low, deep groan next to my ear in response.

"Condom." He nibbles my bottom lip before sitting up. My eyes drag across his broad shoulders, and down his strong back. I hear the rustling of plastic and smile. *God, he's so sexy!* I've been aroused before, turned on by men, but never like this. I'm surprised when he stands. Feeling suddenly exposed, I bring my knees together. His dark eyes journey up my legs. As he slows his sweeping gaze, my heartrate increases until it hammers against my chest. He smoothly slides a leg between mine, and one at a time he parts them.

"Della?" his gravelly voice sends scores of goosepimples across my heated skin. The tips of his fingers follow their path straight to my core. He looks me in the eye as his fingers work my body. His eyes shoot a whole different kind of pleasure to my heart. I take him in, tall, toned, and bulging before my eyes. I try to sit up, reaching for him, needing to touch him before he enters me. He's quick though, and pins me back onto the bed.

"I really want to taste you." He swallows, his eyes swimming with vulnerability. An act so intimate has him fighting his baser instincts.

"I really want you to," I admit, already feeling the pool of pleasure weeping between my legs.

Without further delay, he drops his head between my legs. His tongue separates the folds in one long stroke. My head lolls sideways in pleasure, one fist gripping the bed sheet. He's done asking. He takes me with his mouth, demands my body respond. I buck beneath him.

"JOHN!" I pant. "I'm ... going ... to—!" My words come out as short rapid breaths right before my muscles clench, releasing waves of pleasure. Lights burst behind my eyes, blinding me temporarily.

He's fast, already above me and thrusting forward. He enters hard. Setting a rhythm, he fucks me unapologetically. The bed rocks beneath us as he leans back. He grabs my knee for purchase, then adjusts himself to thrust faster, deeper. I scream in pleasure, my thoughts only on his hard cock inside me and the sweat that glistens on his perfect body. Seeing his face crumple in pleasure draws another wave from my core.

"Let me get on top," I beg, needing some control, wanting to straddle him. He rolls onto his back, bringing me with him. I rest my hands on his chest, my hips rolling slowly as I find that sweet spot and drive deeper onto him, grinding faster. I lean more heavily on his chest, surprised when his groan turns to one of pain. Gently, he lifts my hand and holds it in his.

"Sorry!" I whisper.

"It's OK, don't stop," he urges me. He takes my other hand in his, allowing me to lean into his strength as I push forward. I'm dizzy with pleasure, aroused even further when he cries out.

"Don't ... stop, Della ... fuuuuuuck!" his eyes squeeze shut, his body tensing before going limp beneath me. I watch him, naked and exposed as he cums inside me and my body quivers, before exploding around him again. I fall onto his chest, panting, gasping for air. He rolls me sideways, his fingers brushing the hair from my eyes.

"Sorry I hurt you" I tell him.

"You didn't hurt me." He sighs.

"Are you sure?"

He nods. He turns to face the ceiling and inhales deeply, filling his lungs. I rub my hand over his ribcage, surprised when his hand comes over mine, stopping my caress.

"I'm sure," he whispers, pressing his lips to mine as he wraps me in his arms.

DETECTIVE JOHN WALTERS

Her mass of brown hair tickles my nose, the curve of her warm body nestled into mine as she sleeps. Her scent is dizzying, her soft skin begging me to touch, to taste her again. Gently, I tug on the sheet, exposing her shoulder and feel myself growing hard at once.

"Someone is happy this morning ..." her husky morning voice must be the sexiest thing I've ever heard because I'm like a madman, turning her in my arms and hovering over her in an instant. She is even more breathtaking after a night of lovemaking.

"Very ..." I smile down into her green eyes.

"Oh wow, John, are you feeling OK?" she teases me. I can't help but laugh.

"Yes, Odelia, I'm feeling very perky, as you can tell."

She whips back the sheet. "Let me get a closer look. We need to be certain." She winks before pushing me onto my back. Her lips connect with mine.

    Both our cell phones blare.

    "Shit," we growl in unison.

CHAPTER 24

DEPUTY JONES

There's been a break in the case. When John phoned, I came straight in. The sun is barely awake in the sky and save for the voices coming from the conference room, the station is eerily still. Pushing through the wooden gates of the bull pen, I bypass my desk heading straight there.

John, Della, Ryan and Clark have all congregated around the large oval table at the centre of the room. Four indomitable sets of eyes cut to me as I enter, although the conversation continues without pause as I pull up a seat and listen. Ryan is talking.

"The computer was encrypted, heavily. Whoever this guy is, he's highly sophisticated when it comes to cyber security. Everything was wiped clean except for a list of names."

John leans forward in his seat while Clark leans back. Della stands, moving to the investigation wall. Lifting a black marker, she turns to Ryan.

"OK, give me the names."

"He has the original killer and their surviving victims. The list is in order of the date of each attack. You have LeeRoy Chester and in brackets next to his name is Joanna Deveraux. It's the same with Paul Earls and Michelle Curtis; Dillon Newsum and Laura Jarvis; Robert Driver and Gloria Kirkland; Thomas Moseley and MacKenna Arnold, and finally one last name stands alone: Nessa," he finishes.

"This is his kill list …" Della points to the board. One half is made up the names of the serial killers. The other, their victims, and one singular name.

"Our focus needs to be finding out who Nessa is. She is most likely someone our killer knows personally."

"I could look up surviving victims with that name or variations of it, like Janessa, Vanessa and so on," Ryan offers.

"Good idea …" Della circles the name on her board in red marker. "Every victim on this board was carefully selected. He compiled a list and traveled, state to state, waiting calmly to exact his maniacal rage on them. This unsub is cruel, meticulous, and unwavering in his determination to complete his task. He showed up at the hospital, brazen and cocksure. Make no mistake, each one of these victims was chosen for a reason that goes beyond having survived an attempt on their life. It's our job to figure out what they mean to him, and what Nessa means to him, before he unravels further."

Walters stands with his hands on his hips and eyes narrowed on the list of names. He moves closer to Della at the board. Taking the marker from her, he draws a straight line down the center of the board, separating the list of killers from the list of victims.

"We've spent so much time trying to figure out what connects the victims. Maybe we should be asking, what connects the killers?"

Della's eyes widen. Leaning back on her heels, she examines the board carefully.

"What could possibly connect the killers?" she wonders.

"Well, right now, *we* all do." John's words weren't meant to shock but we are. A pin could drop before Della breaks the silence.

"Law enforcement. Ryan, get me a list of every law enforcement officer that worked each case. Include detectives, crime scene techs, FBI, first responding officers, county coroners. If they were involved in any of these investigations, they make the list. Once you have it, cross reference and see if a name pops out."

"Now, hold on a minute. We can't lose sight of other possibilities …" Clark finally joins the conversation.

"We're not. We're simply broadening our suspect pool to include law enforcement," John counters.

"Shouldn't our focus be on finding Nessa?"

"It is. No stone will remain unturned. What else could potentially connect these killers?" Della says.

"Maybe he's the child of one of the original killers, and Nessa is the surviving victim that led to his father's capture?" I suggest.

Clark interjects. "We looked into that. Every known child of the original killers has been interviewed and alibied out."

"What about the unknown children?" John says.

"There aren't any!" Clark harrumphs.

"Actually, you're wrong." John walks to where he was sitting and picks up a photo. Walking back to the investigation wall he pins it up. "This is Paul Chandler, son of Noreen Chandler and LeeRoy Chester. He works as a human rights lawyer out of Texas …"

"How did you find him?" Clark sounds dumbfounded.

"I came across her name in the original casefile on LeeRoy Chester. She moved out of Virginia one month after he was arrested. Gave birth six months later, in Texas. Turns out, Chester has been keeping tabs on him."

"Is he our guy?" I ask, my eyes studying the photo on the board. He's young enough to match the description, but his eyes are a pale shade of blue and not at all like what Mac described.

"No. I was on the phone with Justin Police Department last night. At my request, they interviewed him and he has an alibi for all of the murders. He's not our killer, but we need to investigate other possible unknown children."

"Great work! Maybe we can use this information as leverage to get an interview with Chester in prison." Della smiles, delighted with the update.

Ryan gawps. "Imagine finding out your dad was a serial killer, learning your whole life is a lie? That could trigger anyone to go on a killing spree."

"This kind of emotional dysfunction would have developed over time, most likely from childhood. It would take more than that to trigger this kind of violent outburst." Agent Clark says and I have to agree with him.

Della ponders this for a moment before speaking. "Basic human psychology shows us that these murders are acts of anger. Anger stems from hurt. Hurt stems from not having your psychological needs met. Now apply that to criminals. People don't just wake up one day and decide to murder a list of people. Four months ago, this killer set out to do just that. My professional opinion would be that Nessa represents his deep-seated anger toward women, society, or a role model in his life. He believes that he is better than they are, that he is the real killer or the real survivor."

"OK. What psychological need was lacking, for him to feel like he has something to prove?" John pushes.

"A lack of belonging, of feeling safe and secure. We know our killer to be strategic, intelligent. Maybe an event from his childhood is repeating itself in his adult life. Something he had no control over, something he suffered because of and was never given any credit for having overcome it. He wants to tarnish their status as survivors and return them to victims."

"His first victim, Joanna Deveraux, was a nurse …" John's eyes light up. "Maybe he was sick as a child? Maybe he crossed paths with her as an adult, and it triggered all of those wounds," he suggests.

"It is more likely that he grew up in a home with a sick parent. That kind of strain on his childhood may have forced him into an early role as caregiver. The parent may have been too ill to attend to his needs, which could have led to him resent peers or people in authority. If now a girlfriend or child has become sick, it may have triggered a loss of identity, or of feeling trapped at having to care for others."

"Joanna Deveraux worked for Adult Protective Services before her death. She was visiting the homes of adults at risk. Maybe she uncovered something she shouldn't have on one of her visits?"

"We did look into all of her reports leading up to her death. Nothing stood out, but a fresh set of eyes could help."

John locks eyes with Della. "On it," he smiles.

"Virginia is home to the FBI headquarters, and several military bases …" I muse.

"Twenty-seven, to be exact." Ryan puts in.

"Mac described our unsub as wearing all black, with a thigh strap for a hunter's knife. Ryan, can you get me images of military tactical gear to show her, see if she recognizes it?"

"Sure …" Ryan is already typing furiously.

"Great thinking, Jones," Walters says, before addressing Clark.

"We know he has skills in cybersecurity, so he could very well work for the military. We also know that FBI agents cross state lines to work different cases. So our guy could be FBI."

"Now hold on a damn minute!" Clark stands, his cheeks flushing a deep shade of red.

Unfazed, John continues. "This is a murder investigation. Everyone is a suspect until we rule them out. Law enforcement, reporters, their family members and the family members of every killer. No stone will be left unturned."

"Or, he could work for a private security company, or any company that deals with technology, for that matter!" Clark smarts.

"True. Let's add that to our list of leads to run down." John's stoic expression only further deepens Clark's anger. Della chooses this moment to step forward.

"OK, everyone calm down ..."

"Della, you've already been demoted. Are you sure you want to start poking into the lives of our colleagues? Investigating their children? Do you realize how fucked up that is?" Clark growls at her.

"HEY!" John's voice takes on an edge I've never heard before. "This is a *murder* investigation. We are here to catch a killer, not to protect the ego of the FBI, or anyone else for that matter. We do our job and if that means ruffling a few feathers, then so be it!"

"Oh, that reminds me ..." Ignoring the mounting tension between John and Clark, Della turns to Ryan. "Look into the family pets of everyone on the list. And Jones, where are we on those avian specialists?"

"Can you believe there are *thirty* bird clubs in Wisconsin alone?" I blow out a breath. "I phoned them all: no new members, no member owns a vasa parrot that they could tell me of, and they haven't had anyone looking for information on one."

"And Virginia?"

"They've got over fifty bird clubs. I'm still working through that list."

"Work with Ryan on this. Moving on, what about the toll booths?" she pushes.

"Still going through them. I'll keep you updated."

"OK. Walters, I'll get that list of patients ready for you. Clark and I will look deeper into possible connections between the killers …" She checks the time on her wristwatch. "Let's all reconvene in three hours?" she looks around the room.

Walters nods, already reaching for his jacket. "Jones and I will head to the hospital now. Ryan, can you forward us those images?"

"Will do," Ryan says.

Standing, I follow, like always, behind Walters.

MAC

The hospital is discharging me today. The plan is for Sailor and me to stay with Jones's parents until the investigation is complete, or at least until the threat to my life is gone.

"Are you ready to go?"

I turn from the bed to find Sailor standing in the doorway. He hasn't left the hospital these past three days. If I wasn't used to him looking disheveled, I might be worried about how tired he looks.

I nod. "Let's go." I grab the plastic bag holding the few belongings Sailor brought to the hospital for me.

"I need to get some stuff from home," I tell him. My heart stirs at the thought of walking across the threshold of our home. *Home?* I'm not even sure what that is anymore.

"Let's just go to the mall, girly ..." He takes a hesitant step closer, his fingers running through his unruly hair.

I shake my head. "I need to get my yoga mat and my music, and there's a photo of Mom I keep by my bed and my necklace. I took it off to shower ..." My hand comes to my chest at the bare space my necklace normally rests over my heart.

"I'll go ..."

"No." I shake my head adamantly. "I can't let this get on top of me, Sailor. I can't start another chapter of my life in fear. I don't want to ..."

"OK, girly. We'll go. But young Jimmy called: he's on his way here. We should wait for him."

"OK."

We head to the hospital cafeteria. A deputy is always close by as we sit, sipping coffee. It's early. The July sun, beaming bright through the window, lights up the space.

It's not long before the automatic doors from the entrance part, admitting Jones and Detective Walters. Unable to tear my eyes away, I watch them both stride confidently toward me. Tall and broad, Jones holds his own next to the formidable Detective Walters. There is a sharpness to Walter's expression, a stoic look in his eyes that he wears everywhere. Next to him, Jones's eyes swirl with optimism and warmth. A bright smile lights up his face when he meets my gaze.

"Hey, Mac! You feeling better?" He sits next to me. There's so much familiarity in his movements. I try to ignore how close he is, but I'm also trying to recall when his scent became so intoxicating.

My eyes drop to the cup in my hand. "I'm good, I just want to get back to normal."

"One day at a time ..." Detective Walters slides into a seat across from us, nodding in greeting to Sailor as he takes a notepad and pen from inside his jacket pocket. "I have some follow-up questions for you, and then we'll get you out of here."

I nod.

"You said the intruder wore all black. Is there anything else you can remember about his clothing?" he asks.

"Take your time, Mac. If it's too much to remember, don't force it." The low and mellow sound of Jones's voice distracts me from my fears.

"OK. I'll try." I look up into his eyes again. "It was hard. When I pushed at him, it felt tougher than latex." I set the coffee cup down, rubbing my hands on my thighs to erase the sensation.

"What about the knife? Was he holding it in his hand the whole time?"

I want to say yes. My head begins to nod in that direction.

"Take your time," Walters insists.

I close my eyes, bringing myself back to three nights ago, when I turned around and found a stranger standing in my bedroom. My skin crawls thinking of how he hid there, spying on me while I dressed and slept. He hid in the very space that had saved me all those years ago. Slithering from it, as if a figment of my imagination, my worst nightmare coming to life. All the fears I'd buried resurrecting themselves, in flesh and blood before my very eyes. I was frozen in a state of shock. My eyes absorbed his eyes, his bushy eyebrows, and the knife in his hand. It dangled at his side.

"He'd removed it from a strap on his thigh." My eyes pop open. I'd forgotten that.

"That's great, MacKenna. Anything else you can tell us will help."

I squeeze my trembling fingers into fists on my lap. I'm surprised when Jones's large hand comes to rest on mine. With reassuring pressure, he motions for me to continue at my own pace.

"He was quiet. I didn't hear him sliding the door aside. He moved with …" I pause, looking for the right word.

"Stealth?" Walters suggests.

"Exactly!"

"Is he military?" Sailor sits forward now.

Detective Walters's phone pings. He lifts it from the table and nods to himself. "I have some photos for you to look through. Tell me if any of the attire looks familiar." He hands me the phone. I scroll through it, Sailor peering over my shoulder.

"Is this guy a member of the defense forces?" Sailor says again looking to Walters.

"It's something we're considering," he admits.

I stop scrolling at a photo of a man all in black. The tight-fitting suit looks ribbed and hard, just like I remember. The man in this photo wearing a leg strap and a holster too.

"That one is almost identical. I can't be sure, but the hood is the same. His nose and mouth were covered just like that and the knee strap is the same." I hand back the phone.

Detective Walters looks at the photo I stopped at, then to Jones, giving him a slight nod. It's clear that they're following some line of inquiry. Sailor's eyes widen.

"I don't like this. If this psycho is military and he sees this as a mission, he won't stop until he completes it!" I can hear the fear in every word that leaves his mouth.

"It's too early to know for sure, but keeping Mac safe and catching this guy are our top priorities," Jones asserts in absolute certainty. When Mom was murdered, I remember how frustrating it was for

Sailor to be always wondering what the police were doing. He phoned every day looking for updates and most of the time he was told nothing.

"Promise you'll keep us updated," I plead.

"We can't—" Walters begins.

"No. I promise, Mac ..." Jones looks from me to Sailor. "I promise to keep you both in the loop, as I much as I can. But I need you to trust us to do our job."

Sailor must see the same sincerity in his eyes that I do because he nods, accepting the terms.

"I trust you both." I look to Walters, whose glare is drilling holes into the back of Jones's head. He smiles at me politely.

"Let's get you out of here." He stands, ending the conversation.

Sailor cleaned up. The pungent smell of bleach still lingers in the hallway as we enter. At a glance it looks untouched by his violence. The eyes of a stranger would never know the horror that thickens the air between these walls. If they looked closely, they might see the outline of the missing art piece on the wall, or the remnants of blood lodged in the new cracks on the tiled flooring. Walter and Jones hang back inside the door. Sailor's hand comes to rest between my shoulder blades as he walks with me to the foot of the stairs.

The unexpected touch has me jerking away. " Sorry. I'm a little rattled."

"I'll come up with you. Let's not hang around." He moves to pass me.

I catch his forearm, slowing his forward motion. "I'll go, I'll be fine," I promise.

He throws a hesitant glance over his shoulder to Jones and Walters. Both men remain silent. I'm relieved when Sailor steps back.

Climbing the stairs, my mind retraces the events of just three nights ago. The struggle at the top, the clambering to get away. The fear, the urgency to survive all lodging itself in my chest and leaving my lungs on a deep exhale. At the top, the carpet is stained brown, though I can tell Sailor tried to scrub the blood out. Queasy at the sight of it, I hurry to my bedroom. The door to my closet is wide open. A flashback of him crawling toward me sends my breathing into violent heaves that rake through my body. I look for anything to distract me. Seeing Mom's photo on the bedside table draws me away from the closet.

Trembling, I take the silver photo frame into my hands. I hug it tightly, crushing it to my chest. The constant teetering between survivor's guilt and a determination to keep going rarely leaves enough energy for me to grieve. My very existence is a constant reminder that she's no longer here. She died saving me and the weight of that reality is exhausting. The pressure to live a full life is maddening, especially on the days that I want to curl up and cry. Today, my threshold for being strong is at its lowest. Taking the photo with me, I sink onto my mattress and allow. I allow the grief to consume me. I allow the fear to pulsate throughout my body and hot, angry tears to fill my eyes before unleashing it all in a muffled groan into my pillow.

"Mac?" Jones's deep voice calls from the doorway.

"I'll be down now ..." I don't look up.

"It's too soon for you to be here, alone ..." he begins.

"I've been alone here all my life," I sniffle, lifting my swollen eyes to face him.

He nods in agreement.

"True but you're not alone now."

Wiping my tears, I sit up. "I chose to be alone," I confess.

"Can I ask why?"

"It was too hard pretending that I was OK. I was never OK." My lip quivers.

I hate that he keeps his tone soft, hate that he moves easily toward me.

"Mac, you never have to pretend with me."

"You're the only person ..." I look away and down at my mom's photo. "I didn't with you."

"Why were you crying when I came in?"

His question is asking me to be vulnerable. To stop hiding, to trust him again.

"She was mutilated trying to save me. I have no choice but to live. Everyday I'm trying to do just that, but it's so goddamn hard, Jimmy." My voice breaks, tears wetting my cheeks and lips.

He sits next to me. He doesn't speak, instead he gently nudges closer, until my head falls against his shoulder.

"Mac, you've pushed through this feeling for twenty years now. Day after day, you proved that she didn't die in vain. You survived this guy on your own. Now, it's time to live for *you*. You're strong enough to overcome anything. You're the strongest person I know."

I turn my face to look at him through blurry eyes. "I'm a blubbering mess."

"You're a beautiful blubbering mess." He smiles.

"Jeez, Jimmy ..." A watery smile creeps over my face. "Are you hitting on me right now?"

Leaning against my shoulder, he softly tucks my tear-soaked hair behind my ears. "Believe me, MacKenna. If I was flirting with you,

you'd know it."

"Oh."

He stands briskly, stretching out his hand for me to take. "Come on, let's grab your things and get out of here."

I place my palm in his, allowing him to pull me from the bed.

"I don't need much. Just my yoga mat, some changes of clothes and my purse."

"I'll stay with you while you pack."

His calm presence reinforces the idea that having someone to cry with isn't as scary a notion as I once believed.

HUNTER

Sailor. Jimmy. Detective Walters.

The three of them surround her, their muffled voices reassuring her that where they're taking her, she will be safe. My eyes lift to the mirror of my visor and grin to myself. Putting the car into gear, I listen on as I continue with phase two of my plan.

It's all coming together.

It always does when you plan for every eventuality.

CHAPTER 25

DETECTIVE JOHN WALTERS

We're leaving Silentwind Lane when my cell phone vibrates against my thigh.

"It's Perez," I tell Jones before answering.

"Hey ..." she croons, "we just got approval to interview LeeRoy Chester. Clark and I are heading to Virginia tonight. Ryan will stay here to run down leads on the car. How did your follow-up interview go with Mac?"

She keeps her tone professional, but my mind races with images of her and Clark spending the night in a hotel together. I turn away from the others waiting for me to join them.

"I'd like to be part of that interview."

"I thought you might. We leave tonight: can you and Jones get back in the next hour?"

"We'll be there." I pause for a beat. "Della, about last—"

She cuts me off. "Great! We'll update you then." I blow out a surprised breath as the call ends, disappointment lancing through me. Maybe she was with someone ...

Pulling Jones aside, I fill him in while ignoring the angry glare Sailor

Arnold throws me for not including him.

"I think I should stay here," Jones is quick to say.

"I agree. You need to be close to Mac and keep going through the surveillance and police reports."

Agreed of the best path forward, we head out to the Joneses' farm.

MAC

Jones and Detective Walters headed back to the Outagamie sheriff's department as soon as Ruby Jones wrapped me in a welcoming hug. Mr Jones took his turn to hug me, before heading outside to chat with the deputies in the patrol car. Both deputies are staying here until we know more about the killers' movements. Sailor is already walking the perimeter, checking for the best place to set up camp. He refused the spare bedroom, preferring to camp along the treeline. I begged him to stay indoors until they catch the killer, but he refused. His plan is to guard the property from a distance.

"I spent my youth as a Navy SEAL, girly. If I can't use those skills to help keep you safe, what good am I?" he asked. When Mom died, his sole purpose became protecting me, training me to protect myself and rearing me to be strong. Just like her. Until now, I never realized how much of his own self-worth was tied to that role, how he needed me as much as I need him. So I nodded, not wanting to deny him the opportunity to rewrite the past. His biggest regret was not being there for Mom. I won't let him carry that regret twice.

When we are alone Mrs Jones picks up my bag and heads to the foot of the stairs of their two-story farmhouse. Next to her husband and son, Mrs. Jones always seemed small and petite. It's been a few years since I last saw her, but compared to me now, she is a tall, slender woman and just as warm as I remember. There was always a sturdiness to her, a confidence in her stride that still exists.

"Let's get you settled."

"Thank you again for having me."

"It's so good to have you back with us. We've missed you. Especially Jimmy!"

"I'm sorry I've stayed away so long."

"You're always welcome here, we won't let you get away again." My cheeks flush and just like when I was a little girl, she pinches one and begins to ascend the stairs. The house itself is old, the furnishings all in keeping with farmhouse living. The smell of fresh bread perfumes the air.

"Do you still bake?" I wonder, following behind.

"Everyday! Since Jim retired he's hungrier than ever, drives me crazy under my feet all day but it's an excuse to bake."

"He looks great, you both do."

She looks back over her shoulder, her silky gray hair falling down her back as she flashes me a smile.

"You too MacKenna, you've grown into a beautiful woman. Your mom would be so proud."

"Thank you Mrs Jones...

"Ruby"

"Ruby..." I concede before changing the subject ",I love your new home."

"We moved out here a few years back. We love it..."

She continues her march on up the narrow staircase. The wooden stairs creak reassuringly loudly. It would be impossible to creep up them without alerting the whole house.

",I'll set you up in Jimmy's room."

"Oh no! I don't want to put anyone out,"

"Nonsense. This room faces east: it will be the perfect place for your morning yoga."

"That's so thoughtful. Thank you."

"You might show me one or two stretches while you're here. My hips aren't what they used to be."

"Of course! I'd be happy to." My mood picks up. The possibility of teaching yoga while I'm here will be the perfect distraction.

"Great, this way."

She opens a door on our left and steps inside, opening her arms for me to come in. Her eyes, the exact same shade of brown as Jones's, fill with the same warmth and charm I've seen in his. "I have a feeling I'll be seeing my boy more often with you around." She winks.

"He's a great cop," I tell her.

"Just like his dad. I've known since he was four years old, he'd be following in his father's footsteps. Had me playing cops and robbers morning, noon, and night."

"Isn't it a constant worry, that he's in such a dangerous job?"

"I used to lie awake at night before James became a homicide detective. My imagination ran wild. I was a newlywed, married to a cop. I was terrified he'd be hurt or worse. When I got pregnant, my focus shifted to young Jimmy. I began to appreciate that his dad was out there keeping the streets safe for *him*, and those fears somehow transformed into an acceptance that nothing was in my control."

"I've spent what feels like my entire life trying to prevent what happened three nights ago. And if anything, I'm learning exactly that," I sigh, moving to the window. I look down at the yard, where Mr. Jones laughs with the two deputies by their patrol car, to the long dirt lane leading from the road. Wide, green fields flank the lane, hidden from the road by tall bushes.

"Give yourself some time to rest now. Lean on us and let young Jimmy do his job. He'll catch this guy and then you can start to heal again."

I turn back and nod. Her kindness has brought tears to my eyes.

"Let's put some food in that belly." She shoos me out of the room and back down the stairs. I'm excited to taste whatever the hell smells so good.

DEPUTY JONES

This killer is determined to exact some kind of revenge and Mac's life is in jeopardy until we catch him or until he completes his mission. A shiver of dread crawls up my spine at that unthinkable outcome. Walters, Perez and Clark all left for Virginia two hours ago, leaving me and Agent Ryan to go through mountains of paperwork. Walters asked me to look through Joanna Deveraux's file again. He believes that somewhere among the hundreds of manila folders, there is a link to these crimes and I want to be the one to find it. I've spent the day scrupulously wading through her patient reports. Most of them outline concern for adults in the care for others. I'm running background searches, pulling up drivers licenses, looking into the cars they drive, but so far, I haven't found anything solid.

We've also determined that the FBI did in fact develop profiles on all these killers. However, the profiles were developed by different agents, and the field agents were different on each case. Another dead end.

Sitting back in my chair, I rub my tired eyes before glancing at the clock. It's after nine p.m. I phoned Dad an hour ago. All is quiet out at the farm, but I've decided to sleep there regardless.

"I'm going to head out. I'll take these with me ..." I stand, replacing the lid on the box of files I'm currently working through. "Do you need anything else?" Ryan sits back, looking as equally deflated.

"No, I'm good. I've come up empty." He pulls his hands behind his head as he stretches out his back.

"No Nessas coming up on your list of surviving victims?" I wonder.

"No Nessas, Vanessas, Janessas, Anessas, and I've a pain-in-my-ass-as, tryna find her." We laugh, enjoying the sensation it brings before he delves back into his workload.

"What about the car?"

"I've gone through hours of surveillance of toll bridges along I94. Apparently, everyone and their mother drives a silver Honda Accord. I'm running plates, but nothing stands out."

"How are you whittling them down?"

"I'm checking the plates, running the license of the owner. I'm discounting any males that don't match Mac's physical description or age."

"What about female car owners?"

"I'll get on those next and investigate husbands or sons that might match the profile. I'll be here for a few more hours yet."

"Whew. Let me know if you come up with anything, I'll keep working this angle, and meet you back here in the morning. I'll be on my cell if you need me," I tell him. Heaving up the box with both hands, I head to my car. Turning right out of the parking lot, I drive straight to the farm.

Mom and Dad are sitting at the kitchen table when I walk in.

"I told you he'd be staying!" Mom jumps up, smacking Dad's shoulder as she crosses to kiss my cheek. Delighted with herself, she waltzes across the kitchen. I smile as she slips on her oven mitts before pulling open the shiny red door to her cherished wood stove.

"I kept you a plate." She whips out a cellophane covered plate. "Had it keeping warm in the oven: it's lasagna." She grins, delighted to be feeding me.

"Thanks Mom." Dropping the box of files on the floor next to the kitchen door, I walk over and sit across from Dad. "How're Mac and Sailor?"

"Sailor just left. He wants to sleep outside, we didn't argue with him," Dad begins. I notice for the first time that his shotgun is on the floor next to him. The gravity of the potential danger I've put my family in hits me. My eyes widen in horror. He immediately understands my concerns.

"Now, don't you start feeling guilty, son. You've got a job to do, and thanks to you and that Detective Walters, I've got one too. Mom and I are happy to be helping little Mac."

They're the strongest people I know. My entire life, Mom has been volunteering with the Outagamie sheriff's department and the community. Whether it was organizing family fun days to raise money for victims of crime or petitioning local councillors to invest in their local law enforcement facilities, she was right in there. While Dad was running down leads and catching killers, she was baking cookies and making sure he had the best resources available to help him do it.

"I should have thought a little harder about how much danger I'm putting you guys in." I sigh, dropping my eyes to the mouth-watering plate that Mom sets down in front of me.

"Eat up, Jimmy, then you and me are gonna go through that box of files, and get this case wrapped up before that man gets anywhere near Mac again."

Mom stands behind him, her hand resting on his shoulder with confidence. All the reasons why I thought this would be the safest place for Mac return. I nod. The stairs creak, and all our heads turn toward them. In the silence we hear the sound of Mac's bedroom door closing. She just heard me questioning her staying here! I curse under my breath.

"I'll go check on her," Mom offers.

"It's OK. Keep my plate warm?" I stand. Both loving sets of eyes follow me as I climb the stairs to the room where I usually sleep when I stay over. I knock twice on the door.

"Who's there?" Mac calls out, which reminds me of the *knock-knock* jokes.

"Knock, knock," I say. I'm met with silence.

"Knock, knock?" I say again.

"Who's there?" She relents and a wide grin stretches my face from ear to ear.

"Jimmy."

"Jimmy who?" I can just imagine her rolling her eyes on the other side of the door.

"Jimmy back my bed!" I laugh lightly, amused by myself.

She pulls open the door, her lips pressed tightly together as she tries not to smile.

"That was lame." Her words disrupt her attempt to hide the smile that finally escapes, lighting up her beautiful face. We both giggle and my chest fills with a weird sense of achievement.

"I'm sorry you heard that, down there." I lean against the doorjamb.

"Don't be. I didn't mean to eavesdrop. I was coming down to say goodnight and I heard voices."

"How are you settling in?"

"Your parents are great, Jones, you know?"

"Yeah, I do. They'll be watching out for you and Sailor when I'm not around."

"I'm sorry I put you, and them, in this position ..." Her slender arms fold over her chest, her eyes dropping to her bare feet.

"You didn't. The bastard we're hunting for did this. I don't want you thinking you're not welcome here. You got it?" I'm adamant in my tone.

"Got it!"

She looks up, smiling again. "Knock, knock?"

I smile. "Who's there?"

"Mac." She grins now and I can't help the stupid laugh it elicits from me.

"Mac who?"

"Mac on my feet and ready for action!" She winks.

"Wow. That was awful!"

When we're all laughed out, she wipes her eyes. "Goodnight, Jones."

"Goodnight, Mac." I step back, allowing her to close the door, before heading back to the kitchen.

Do not *tell Walters you did that knock-knock joke!*

Dad has already got his paws on the box of files and is organizing them into neat piles on the table.

"You eat up and then tell me, what are we looking for in all this?"

I nod, happy to see him in his element. His expression is one of curiosity and determination, a look I haven't seen him wear in a while. His detective's cap is well and truly on and I can use the extra set of eyes on this case.

CHAPTER 26

DETECTIVE JOHN WALTERS

Today Perez, Clark, and I will interview LeeRoy Chester. Last night, Della described his childhood and violent history in detail over dinner.

Chester grew up in Richmond, Virginia, raised by an alcoholic father and an abusive mother. He was beaten daily throughout his formative years. One such left him in hospital with a concussion and broken ribs. School teachers, neighbors, nurses and doctors all reported the maltreatment to social services, one doctor describing extreme malnourishment, and the worst case of neglect he'd ever witnessed. But, despite the documented abuse, the social services failed to remove him from the home. That inaction was the first of many by the system. At sixteen, LeeRoy was arrested for petty theft, walking free from the court with a slap on the wrist and a smile on his face. He quickly advanced to house burglaries then to the world of grand theft auto. By the age of eighteen, he was a drug addict with a penchant for violent outbursts directed toward his then girlfriend. During one of those assaults, he strangled her with a pair of nylons, not stopping until she fell unconscious. She pressed charges and he was sent to prison. He served eight of the fifteen years he'd been sentenced. Released at the age of twenty-eight, he began working nights at the Richmond Steel Company, only a few blocks from the children's hospital he'd visited so often in childhood. He committed his first murder six months later. His MO involved following young nurses walking home after their long shifts. He abducted them and took them to a secluded location, where he raped and tortured them for hours, before finally murdering them. Wrapping the victim's own pantyhose around her neck, he strangled them to death. This became his signature. Joanna Deveraux was *his* surviving victim, and her testimony sent him here, forty-five minutes north of Richmond, to the Greensville Correctional Centre.

A mile off I95 and standing on a 1,105-acre plot of land, the once-maximum security prison still houses the execution chamber used to carry out capital punishments. In 2021, six months before LeeRoy's scheduled execution date, Virginia abolished the death penalty.

Behind the thick walls, razor wire and six, 52-foot-high guard towers, are four pod-style buildings, arranged within the hexagonal grounds. LeeRoy Chester is confined to his cell for twenty-three hours a day. His small, 13x7 foot sweatbox is in cellblock G of building four. It's his permanent home.

The warden sets us up in large interview room. I've been allotted a chair in the corner, across from Perez and Clark, who sit at a steel table in the middle of the room. Leaning back against the cold, white walls, my eyebrows draw together at the sight of Della's exposed legs. She wore a skirt and pantyhose into an all-male prison, full of not only murderers, but sexual predators too. My throat constricts against the urge to air my concerns.

"I'll develop a rapport with him ..." She's outlining her hopes for the interview.

"Does he know that a female agent is interviewing him?" I interrupt her.

"I believe so ..."

"Do you think that's why he agreed to be interviewed?" My unease reveals itself.

"Maybe, maybe not." She shrugs. "But we do know that criminals like LeeRoy Chester rarely do anything for the greater good. He could want some privileges, or he could be bored ..." She pauses, then posits another theory. "He could also be using this opportunity to relive his crimes, or gloat over the murder of Joanna Deveraux. It won't take long for him to reveal his true motive, but in the meantime, I want to get as much information from him as possible."

The heavy metal door opens. Cold air seeps into the room, followed by three prison guards and LeeRoy Chester. Hunched forward, with cuffed hands and feet, the chains clank as he shuffles in. Dressed in a red prison jumpsuit and white slippers, his wrinkled and weathered face is a far cry from the mugshot photo pinned to our investigation wall. Gone is the fresh face of a thirty-year-old killer. Now fifty-four, with a wiry beard, and greasy, straggly hair, he trudges to the table. I note the bulkier frame and new tattoos. My eyes narrow when he zeros in on Della. Prison has done nothing to erase the sinister intent flaring in his eyes as he follows her every move. Standing and moving around the table, she stretches out her hand with a broad smile.

"Mr. Chester. Thank you for agreeing to meet with us. I'm FBI Special Agent Odelia Perez, and these are my colleagues, Agent Clark and Detective Walters."

"Pleasure's mine, Odelia." A wolfish grin creases his face as his eyes drop to her legs. My gut rolls with disgust as I sit still, forced to watch him salivate over them.

"You can uncuff him," Perez directs the guards as they sit.

My eyes widen, my pulse quickening. *We didn't discuss this!*

His tattoo-covered arms plop onto the table, the hands responsible for killing so many women inches from Della. It unnerves me, challenges me to gather enough willpower to remain in my seat.

Finally, he turns to meet my hard stare. "Got yourself some bodyguards," he says, shifting to look at Clark, who is seated next to Della.

"These guys?" She laughs. "They're sitting in for educational purposes. We're hoping to learn from you today."

"Best tell me what it is you wanted then."

Della takes her time. Keeping her questions light, she begins by asking after his treatment in prison. She commiserates with him when he explains that he has exhausted all his appeals and will spend the rest of his life here. She bolsters his ego, feeding his sense of the grandiose, until he relaxes. I'm impressed when the distant look in his eyes and guarded behavior drains away. At that exact moment, she crosses and uncrosses her legs. His eyes follow her every move, while she turns up the heat on her questioning.

"Do you remember Joanna Deveraux?"

"I remember Joanna well. She was a beautiful woman." He moistens his lips.

"So you know she has been murdered?"

His eyes darken. "I heard. My sister wrote me."

"How does knowing she's dead make you feel?"

When he speaks, each word is coated in undisguised rage. "I feel nothing. She couldn't escape her fate any more than I can escape the prison she put me in."

"So you blame her, for how your life turned out?" Della leans closer to him. My pulse skyrockets.

"There's a long list of folk to blame, O-deliaaa," he drawls.

"What do you remember about Joanna Deveraux?" Perez redirects the conversation again.

His chest puffs with pride. "She was a feisty one. Caught my eye straight away. Wore white pantyhose under that sexy nurse's uniform."

"Why did you choose her?"

"I'd seen her a few times, always walking down Brook Street. But that night she was alone, and the street was empty. I wanted her, so ..."

"You took her." Della finishes his sentence.

His tongue slowly slides across his top teeth before he answers. "Yes."

"Why do you think this killer chose her?"

Great segway!

"I've had some boys tell me they appreciated my work. There's no one I can think of is clever enough to pull it off." He shrugs. "I figure, he's a sick pervert, obsessed with me."

"Do you ever get fan mail?"

"None."

"That's a surprise, I'd have thought folk would want to know about you." Perez leans back into her chair. I breathe a little easier until he inches closer to her.

"Let me ask you this?" he says, leaning his chest into the table. "Why'd you think I killed those women?"

Perez warned us that he might ask such a question. Criminals like LeeRoy Chester spend their entire life trying to understand themselves. Having someone else analyze his crimes, his behavior, feeds his sense of self-importance.

"I think you grew up believing that you were unlovable. I think you have a deep self-loathing and feeling of inadequacy. That inferiority complex manifested itself into a rage you couldn't control, combined with a sense of entitlement. You said it yourself; you saw them and you wanted them. So you took, because you could. Because you're a predator," she finishes.

"I like that word ... predator. Tell me, Odelia, do you really think my nephew is capable of being a predator?"

"He's a suspect, for sure."

"That sniveling fool can hardly tie his shoelaces, let alone commit a murder!" he growls, affronted by the very idea.

"What about your son?" Clark interjects and Chester's eyes turn glacial. The cool air shifts to icy cold.

"You leave my boy out of this. He's about the only good thing to ever come from my miserable existence." He stands to leave.

Perez jumps up. "Hold on. We're not here to meddle in anyone's life. If you say so, we will leave him alone. Sit back down, let us understand you a little more." She plays on his ego again and like a shark to blood he bites. He throws Clark a dirty look before resuming his seat.

"I'd appreciate that. It don't matter much, being that my son or nephew had nothing to do with that murder."

"How can you be so sure?"

"Well, my nephew is a few cent short of a dollar, and my son ain't nothing like me."

"Do you know who *would* want to kill her?"

He shrugs "*I've* killed her, a million times over, up here ..." He taps his temple. "I fantasized about murdering for years you know. I was always too wasted to remember how it felt during the actual act, except with Joanna. She survived, but I remember how powerful it felt to wrap those pretty white pantyhose around her neck. Watching the nylon sink into her skin as I squeezed tighter ..." His eyes roll, relishing the memory, reliving it in front of us. "I can't say I'm sorry she's dead, but I'm grateful to her for those memories."

Tired of listening to this sick bastard rehash his glory days, I growl out, "Is there anything you can tell us to help catch her killer?"

Della's eyes flick to me, full of disappointment at my interruption.

"I've been rotting away behind these bars for over twenty years now. It'd be nice if someone wrote me, admired me even, but unfortunately there's no one."

"Thank you for your help, Mr. Chester, but we're done here today," Della says abruptly.

"If they let me out today, " he tsks, dropping his eyes to her legs again. "I'd wrap those pantyhose around that pretty neck of yours."

"I guess you'll be fantasizing about it until the day you die." She allows a full, daring smile to spread across her face as she stands. My composure begins to slip, anger sizzling as I reluctantly stand too. I've been patient, allowed Della to take the lead, watched as she dangled herself like a slab of meat in front of a lion, and all for nothing.

Turning to Clark and me she announces. "We're done here. He doesn't know anything." Both she and Clark are already making their way out of the interview room when LeeRoy calls out.

"You know, there was one guy, wanting to write a book about me ..."

"Oh yeah?" My tone warns him not to play with me. Disinterested in staying silent for another second, I step closer.

"Yeah. Said he was writing about men like me ..." He looks over my shoulder to where Della and Clark linger in the doorway. "Predators, as you said."

"What was his name?" I ask.

"I don't remember it, exactly. It was a long time ago ... Might be, some extra yard time and snacks would jog my memory," he drawls lazily.

"We'll get you that," Perez promises. She had already agreed in advance with the warden that if Chester could provide information pertinent to this case, the prison would allow him extra yard time and commissaries.

She returns, whipping out the document already drawn up and signed by the warden. LeeRoy looks it over, slowly. Perez and Clark sit back down, across the table from him. With a deep inhale, I follow suit. One leg resting on my knee, my fingers impatiently tap my thigh as I wait.

"This all looks good." He looks to them both again. "Like I said, it was a few years ago now. You'll have to look through the visitation logs for his name, but I do remember that he was *FBI*." He grins.

Fuck me! The realization that FBI might actually be involved just made this case a whole lot more complicated. Clark and Perez squirm under his sleazy glare, both obviously uncomfortable by this revelation too. Relieving them of further questioning, I speak up.

"What did he say about writing a book?"

"Oh, he wanted to explore the whys and the hows of the predator and their survivors."

Della turns ashen.

"Did you hear from him again?" I ask.

"He interviewed me three times. I was happy enough to get out of my cell for the day, but after that? No, he never did get in touch and my sissy says there ain't no book on my crimes available. I had her check the bookstores a few times. I thought maybe he died."

"How long ago was it?" Perez clears her throat.

"I can't say for sure, a few years."

"Guess," I growl, ready to take those extra privileges and tear them up.

"I'd say, maybe seven or eight years ago."

"How old was he?" Perez speaks again.

"I'd say he was in his fifties."

Our killer is in his thirties. This doesn't rule out the mystery FBI visitor, but makes it more likely that the actual murderer is someone he knows.

"Thank you for your help. We'll get this to the warden." Perez stands, reaching for the signed documents.

Without warning, LeeRoy Chester lunges across the table. His thick fingers wrap around her throat, pulling her onto the table within seconds. His lecherous face contorts with both unbridled rage and pleasure as he holds her down. Fury blurs my periphery, my sole focus to help her. I leap to his side in an instant. I catch a glimpse of her red face and watery eyes as she fights to get him off before my fist connects with his jaw. The force is enough to knock him sideways and off Della, before he rounds on me. He fights Clark, me, and the prison guards with unmerciful strength. Della gasps desperately for breath. Just as his clenched fist finds my jaw, I feel nothing in the fight to contain him. Two more guards enter the room at a run, batons in hand. They strike him until he goes down. Satisfied that the threat to Della is over, I seek her out. Clark is next to her, his hand cupping her face. Adrenaline continues to surge around my body, leaving me breathless. I step back and away from them both, ensuring the guards cuff him before stepping out of the room.

Clark comes out moments later, his arm wrapped around Della's shoulder. Pacing back toward them, my frustration and concern comes out as a bark.

"Are you OK?"

"I'm good. Your lip is bleeding." Her voice shakes. Huskier from her injury, it sends a residue of fear skittering down my spine. My head shakes at the sight of her, the imprint of his hands red raw around her neck,

"Jesus Christ. He could have killed you!"

"He didn't." Her weak response only infuriates me more.

"He had no fucking cuffs on! What the hell was that?"

"We had to gain his trust, make him feel comfortable enough to open up to us." Perez is defending what I consider to be the most foolish thing I've ever witnessed.

"You made him comfortable all right. Comfortable enough to try and get one last kill in!" Turning my back on them, I storm down the hallway.

She could have been seriously hurt or killed. My chest tightens as I find the exit. I need fresh air and space to sort through my frenzied thoughts.

It's over an hour before Clark and Perez finally follow me out to the parking lot. Leaning against the hood, I remain silent, allowing the earlier animosity to thicken around us.

"What took you both so long?" I finally grumble.

"We had to write a report for the warden on what happened. You'll be happy to know his privileges were removed for that stunt. Looks like his arm and some ribs could be fractured from the scuffle, too." Perez's flat tone grates on me.

"What about the visitor logs? Did you get a look at them?"

"No—" Clark begins.

"What? Why?" I snap.

"Shut up a second and let me speak!" he demands, glaring at me as I stand off the car.

"*Now* you want to speak? You kept pretty quiet during that shitshow in there!" My finger points toward the prison.

"Oh, and other than your ego, what did you bring in there?" Clark glowers.

"Can you two please stop! this is not helpful …" Perez roars, her voice breaking with the effort as she stands between Clark and me. "The visitor logs were all computerized about ten years ago, they're backed up by an outside IT company that monitors their computer system. The warden put in a request for the information, and he will have it within a few hours," she explains.

My eyes stay locked in battle with Clark. Neither of us speak until Della croaks, "Please, I'm tired."

Clark shakes his head and moves to the driver door. "Let's get out of here." Della follows into the front passenger seat. Looking to the skyline, I inhale deeply before pulling open the car door, dropping into the backseat in silence.

"We're staying in Virginia until that list comes through. You can head back to Wisconsin if you prefer." Perez's casual dismissal cuts deep. My eyes slice to the rearview mirror hoping to find hers there. Instead, she faces out her window with closed eyes. I say nothing for the entire car ride back to the hotel.

CHAPTER 27

MAC

I slept with my curtains open. The morning sun is my silent alarm clock; my body's call to rise and yoga. The house is quiet as I creep out onto the landing, careful not to wake everyone as I sneak down for some water before beginning. Mrs. Jones asked to join me, but we never actually set a time and I don't want to wake her. I'll ask her later this morning if she'd like to do some stretches, or maybe even some poses, if she's up for it. Being here under their feet is a huge inconvenience. If I can help her get stronger and healthier during that time, well then, I'll have been somewhat useful.

I make it to the bottom of the stairs, thrilled as I tiptoe past Jones, who is snoring louder than the creaking floorboards. His brown hair is ruffled with sleep, his mouth hanging open. I smile toward him, pausing to note how tiny the couch is in comparison to his large body. It reminds me again that I've commandeered his bed, and my stomach twitches with anxiety. If there is no movement on the case in a few days, I'll need to figure out another place to stay. I can't expect them to live like this for long.

Now past him, I make it to the kitchen. With the stealth of a ninja,

I take a glass from the cabinet and make it to the sink without so much as a peep. Dipping the glass into the rough marble butler sink, I twist on the faucet, cursing when a loud grinding and crunching of metal sound rings out around me.

"Fuck," I hiss, as it splutters and spits out two violent sprays of water, drenching my t-shirt before settling into a steady flow.

A soft laugh behind me has me jumping around.

"Shit, sorry." Jones's sleepy eyes widen in concern.

"It's OK," I whisper, turning off the faucet. I whip back around to him. "I woke you, I was trying to be quiet."

"I was awake," he lies. My lips spread into a wide smile.

"You were out cold when I passed you in the living room, mouth catching flies and snoring louder than a heavy truck," I tease.

"I was not!"

"Shh!" I bring my finger to my lips, trying to contain my own laughter. "You'll wake your folks."

"They'll be up soon ..." He checks the time on his watch before stretching his arms above his head. "What has you up so early?"

I watch as his white t-shirt lifts with his arms. My gaze fixes on the hard edges of his toned body, in contrast with the smooth-acting Deputy Jones. My mouth waters, my throat dries, I swallow past the confusion lodging itself in my chest. *I don't even like him! Why did I stop liking him again?*

"Earth to Mac," he calls softly and I wrest my eyes from the sharp V disappearing into his pajama bottoms.

"YOGA!" I say. "I'm about to do some yoga. Anyway, I better get started." I move toward him. He doesn't budge from his position in the doorway. His mischievous eyes dare me to bypass him.

"Excuse me."

"Isn't that stretching and balancing?"

"Yep!" I take a sip of the water in my hand.

"Maybe I could join in?" he asks, his brown eyes swirling with trouble. Somewhere between hating Jones and needing him, I've started to enjoy having him around. It scares me. It can only mean trouble.

"Um, your mom is going to, and I don't have an extra mat …"

"Actually …" A voice from behind Jones has us both jumping like school children. Ruby shoos her son aside, coming into the kitchen. "If it's OK with you, I was thinking I'd start tomorrow. Jimmy, you can take my mat: it's under the stairs." She's smiling broadly as I scramble to get out of it.

"There's not enough room … in the … bedroom …"

"Oh, no problem, we can use the barn!" Jones chirps. "Give me five. I'll be right down." He gallops up the stairs, taking them two at a time. I turn to find Ruby Jones grinning. She shrugs unapologetically.

"He's really keen to learn."

"Uh-huh." I narrow my eyes suspiciously as she moves around the kitchen, pulling out pots and pans, setting them on the stove.

"I'm going to cook breakfast. It'll be ready when you two are finished."

The barn is as modern as they come. Beneath the rafters, an orange Allis-Chalmers tractor sits in its center with the hood up and a toolbox sitting next to it. My hand glides along its sleek body as we pass.

"WOW, this takes me back."

"You like it?" Jones says, his tone full of pride as we climb a sturdy set of stairs to the loft.

"Do you compete?"

"Yeah, I drive, Dad's the mechanic."

"OH..." my chest squeezes with regret, I've missed out on so much ",Maybe I could come to your next meet?"

He stops on the final step, turning back to me with a wide grin on his face.

"I'm gonna hold you to that. Wait until you see what mom has up here," he moves again, and I follow him across to a cosy corner of the loft where a small blue couch with a woolly cream throw sit. Positioned in front of a large window, it overlooks a field of wildflowers and a treeline stretching into the distance. Next to it, a three-legged table stands with an open book lying face down and a carefully placed photo frame beside it. Jones picks up the frame and hands it to me. My eyes water immediately at the nostalgic photo in my hands, a snapshot of ten-year-old Jones and me. We're perched on the hood of an Allis Chalmers, with one arm casually draped around the other's shoulder and grinning into the camera. We look so happy.

"Mom comes here to read while Dad works on the tractor" he explains.

"I can't believe she still has this."

"She says it's one of favorite photos."

"I remember posing for it."

"Do you remember pushing me off the hood when we were done taking it?"

He nudges my shoulder, pulling my attention from his boyish grin to the one he wears now as a man. A knot of unspoken feelings and emotions that time could not erase, tighten my stomach.

"I was always pushing you away." I admit. My throat constricts with regret. Jones must notice, gently he takes the frame from my hand and places it back on the table.

"Well today you're twisting me into a pretzel" he winks before rolling out his mat to face the window.

"OK. Yoga me."

Happy to shake out of this melancholy, I walk from the couch and roll my mat out next to his. He's changed into gray track pants and a fresh white t-shirt. Noticing his white socks inside black flip flops.

"Hmm. Stylish but socks off." I say.

"Hey, I wasn't sure if I should go barefoot or not."

"Sure you're not hiding some fugly toes?"

He bursts out laughing. "Wow. Way to put me at ease!"

"You nervous about yoga?" I laugh along.

"Not necessarily yoga, but *you* make me uneasy!" he admits. People have felt uncomfortable around me my whole life. Being the daughter of a murdered woman in a small town brings a certain notoriety, that was heightened by the fact that she was the victim of a serial killer. People are either intrigued or unsure how to behave around me. When the intrigue wears off, all they can see is the damage such a crime creates.

"I'm sorry about that, I do that to a lot of people, actually."

"I didn't mean it like that ..."

I wave away his explanation. "Let's bring ourselves to our mats." I say lowering myself to my pink mat.

He nods, coming to join me. We both face forward, our legs crossed.

"Sitting up straight, pull your shoulders back and away from your ears. With your spine straight, rest your hands on your knees, your palms facing up and allow your eyes to close. We'll start with some deep breathing ..." Jones follows my instructions and after three deep breaths I feel my insecurities drift away. We move through a few different poses. He's surprisingly good.

"Lift your hips higher," I tell him as we come back into another downward dog. "And really push into the palms of your hands. You'll feel that stretch in your hamstrings, calves and ankles."

"Oh, yep! Got it," he groans as his hips lift higher. My lips roll together, trapping the smile begging to free itself.

"When you're ready, come down into your plank pose." I continue to direct him, noticing how his eyes find my body, mimicking my movements with an ease no first timer should have. We both settle in plank pose.

"OK, let's try a side plank. Keeping your hands firm on the mat. Begin to twist your feet to the right, until both feet are resting sideways on the mat. Good ... Now, really leaning into that right palm, find balance, before lifting your left hand up, in line with your shoulders."

I scan his body. His biceps are bulging and trembling under his weight as he holds the pose. His feet are off the mat, his body too long to fit it.

"OK, and back down. We're going to do that on the other side." I continue to talk him through each pose. I'm impressed as he glides along with ease. We spend forty-five minutes, moving through one of the set programs I developed for my students.

"Let's finish with five minutes of silence on our mat," I tell him. "Get comfortable and allow yourself to breathe easy, leaving any stress or concern about the day ahead on the mat." We lie next to each other in silence, our breath settling as our bodies relax further. The July sun beams in on us, licking our already heated skin.

"When you're ready, we'll come back into a seated position, facing each other on our mats. Hands in prayer, at heart center. Thank you for joining me today, namaste."

"Namaste," he repeats, bowing forward with me. Our eyes pop open at the same time. A bright smile lights up his face. "That was great!" he chirps.

"Thanks." I push the strands of wet hair off my face, suddenly conscious of my sweaty appearance.

"You're really good, your voice is so soothing ..." he begins, my face burning under his compliments. "Maybe we could do it again during the week if I can find the time?" he asks, still facing me, with his legs crossed, his hands wrapping around his ankles. Sweat glistens across his skin, mixing with his spicy scent. Its heady combination steals my focus and stirs my defenses, my self-protective barriers rattle to be heard.

"I hope not! I don't want to be here that long," I say, too abruptly.

"Oh." His face falls. Releasing his feet, he stands up. "It was just a thought." He shrugs, before bending to roll up his mat. I join him in rolling up my mat, avoiding his eyes.

"I'm sorry, I didn't mean it like that! I just don't like to be under your mom and dad's feet. Or yours: I'm staying in your bed ..."

He waits for me to finish. With his mat tucked under his arm, he stares intently into my eyes.

"Why are you always apologizing for being ..."

"Being what?" my brow furrows in confusion.

"For just *being*, Mac. Being here, being the victim of a crime, being alive!" He sighs, roughly.

"I'm not ..." I lie, hating how my eyes sting. "It's not fair to expect you guys to house me," I reason with him.

"No one is putting themselves out. We like you Mac. We care about you, always have, but you've been too pig headed to see it," He huffs.

"Pig-headed? Oh, I'm sorry if my childhood trauma blinded me to the notion that people might care about me! I was busy surviving. I'd already disrupted Sailor's life. He was *forced* to take care of me. I don't want to put people out!"

"Bullshit!" he snorts, his tone shifting to anger. "You don't want to risk losing people, Mac. It's not about surviving: you survived! It's about letting people in, knowing full well that you have no control over whether or not they leave, or are taken from you!"

"*You* can leave. I never asked anyone to stay!" I hiss.

"Exactly. You didn't ask and you didn't allow. I've been tryna be your friend for as long as I can remember. I got a bloody nose when I asked you to dance, for Christ's sake!"

"You startled me! You crept up on me, Jimmy Jones, and I got a fright. I just ..."

"You just what?" He steps closer to me.

"Reacted, OK?" I look away from his piercing stare.

He stands close in front of me, forcing my neck back. My eyes meet his in a battle of wills.

"You're a chicken, MacKenna Arnold." He grins.

"You're giving me whiplash, Jimmy. Two seconds ago I was a pig, and now I'm a chicken? Make up your mind. And stop looking at me like that!" I growl.

"You're a pig-headed chicken." his grin stretches wider. He's enjoying how riled up he's made me.

"And what, exactly, am I afraid of?"

"Me!" His grin turns wolfish, like he's ready to eat the chicken for dinner, as he dips his face closer to mine.

"You must like having a bloody nose," I threaten. He just smiles, dipping closer still until his nose touches mine. My breath hitches, just as his hands snake around my body. Our yoga mats fall, rolling out onto the floor around us.

"Jimmy!" I gasp, my body trembling with fear and desire as he lifts me off my feet. He holds me in his arms, my feet dangling as he crushes me to his chest, locking my gaze with a heated stare.

"I've wanted to kiss you my whole life, MacKenna Arnold. Trying to was worth getting a bloody nose then, and if you give me one today, it'll have been worth it now too."

My eyes fall to his lips and back to his amber eyes. With all my heart I want to be kissed. Instead he waits for me to take charge.

"You make me sound so violent," I whisper , with a swallow. He shakes his head.

"No, you've had enough of that in your life. I want to show you everything but violence, Mac."

The allure of him seeing past my defenses draws my lips to his. Hesitantly, I apply a gentle pressure, tasting, testing out this hidden urge to kiss Jimmy Jones. Once, twice … His arms tighten around my body, our torsos hard against each other as he holds stock still. My heart throbs in my ears, until I can't take it any longer. Like a baby koala, I wrap my legs around his waist, my arms around his neck as my mouth crashes against his with the same violence as my fist did, all those years ago. His lips part, his tongue gliding against mine as he groans into my throat. The vibrations send delicious shivers down my sweaty back. As if I'm floating on air, he carries me to the small sofa, and drops into it. I find myself straddling him, my back to a field of flowers as wild as I feel as I run my fingers through his hair. His hands slide up my body, resting on either side of my face as he holds me still. Pulling back, he looks into my eyes.

"You take my breath away, Mac." He says it so earnestly, I can't help the bubble of laughter that escapes me.

"Whatever you do, don't die," I say.

"You're such a smart ass!" he laughs. His thumb running along my bottom lip catches my breath, then and in one swift movement he gently brings his lips back to mine. There is no urgency in his movements. Instead, he teases me with tender kisses along the edges of my mouth. My stomach is whirling with pleasure. I moan, craving more of him. My fingers digging into his shoulders as he continues his trail of kisses along my neck. He squirms beneath me, his arousal pressing into my core.

"I thought you said you wanted to show me everything but violence,"

"I'm going as gently as I can, Mac."

"This is torture." I grip his t-shirt, pulling him closer.

"I can't have that …" His wicked smile disappears as his lips find mine again, with an even deeper kiss. I grind against him, ready to rip his clothes off here and now, until Mrs. Jones yells out in the barn below.

"Breakfast is ready!"

I pull away, jumping off him like a teenager up to no good. I look toward the stairs, relieved that she hasn't come up while I was joy riding her son. My hand finds my swollen lips, still tasting a cocky-looking Jones there. He stretches his arms across the back of the sofa.

"I think I like yoga, a *lot*!" He smiles.

"Your mom almost caught us!" I gawk at him, horrified at the thoughts of it as I rush to the mats, rolling them up again. His eyes follow me about, amusement lighting up his face.

"Well? Let's go!" I demand when he remains seated.

"I should probably wait a minute …" His eyes drop to his groin.

"You're trouble, you know that?"

"You go on in. I'll need a minute to calm down. And looking at you all flustered isn't helping." I walk over, slowly swaying my hips as I lean down toward him. Pressing my nose to his I whisper against his lips "You look hungry, Jones."

"I am." He swallows.

"*I'm* famished …" I lick my lips and walk away. "See you inside!"

"Tease!" he calls after me.

"Sucker!" I call back over my shoulder, before heading to the house. Smiling all the way.

DEPUTY JONES

I've had an unquenchable thirst all morning since leaving the barn. We ate breakfast with my mom and dad, wide smiles breaking across our faces whenever our eyes met across the table. A cold shower might have eased some of the fire simmering beneath my skin but I chose the comfort of hot water before getting dressed for work. With still-wet hair, and running later than I intended, I rush around the house, fastening my belt as I come down the stairs. Mac is in the kitchen chatting with Mom. Her eyes find me as I enter.

"Gotta go, I'll come by again this evening," I tell Mom, my eyes drifting to Mac's.

"Should I keep you a plate?"

"I don't know how late I'll be …" I drag my attention back to her.

"OK, son. Stay safe." She walks over, reaching up to ruffle my wet hair before leaving the kitchen. I glance over my shoulder, watching her climb the stairs. Once she's out of sight, I don't hesitate in moving to Mac, bending to capture her mouth in a quick kiss.

"I'll see you tonight. Stay here, and don't wander the property without Dad or one of the officers."

She nods, her nose grazing mine as she does. I give her another kiss, growling as I pull myself away. I grab my keys from the counter and back out of the kitchen.

"See you later, chicken!" I wink before turning. My gun and holster sit on the coffee table. Reaching them, I wave at Dad who is sitting in his armchair, his shot gun sitting next to him as he watches some morning show.

"I'll check in later," I tell him.

"Sorry we didn't find anything of use in those files, son. Bring home more this evening: we'll whittle it down." His tone full of certainty.

"Will do. Sorry I haven't been helping out on the tractor. Hopefully I'll get some free time this weekend!"

"Just get to work and worry about that later!" he yells back, his voice following me as I rush to my patrol car. I wave at the boys watching over our house and Mac. They changed shift an hour ago. I'm happy there are fresh eyes on all the people I care about most.

CHAPTER 28

DEPUTY JONES

Ryan looks like hell. Seeing him, my brows pinch at the same wrinkled blue shirt he was wearing yesterday and the dark circles under his eyes.

"You look like you haven't slept a wink!" I say as I walk into the conference room. He doesn't look at me, instead turning hurriedly toward the printer. He ignores my comment, offering me the printout.

"I've got good news: we found a car matching the description!"

I snatch it out of his hand. "Why didn't you call me?"

"It literally just came in. It was found abandoned in Minneapolis this morning." We had a BOLO out for silver Honda Accords. "I just got off the phone with Minneapolis PD. They emailed this over."

"This is great. Does John know?"

"I've tried to get through to them, but I doubt they can bring their phones into the interview."

I nod. It makes sense. "What's next?"

"Minneapolis PD have sealed off the area and are treating it as a crime scene. The car was found under a bridge with the plates removed. The VIN number was scratched from the chassis and the

GPS system is gone from the panel under the steering wheel. They're dusting for prints as we speak."

"Great work, man! " I pat his shoulder. "So he's in Minnesota." My shoulders sag with relief. Minnesota is five hundred miles from Mac.

"Police there are still monitoring the potential victims, but the dates of their original attacks aren't for a week or two yet."

"Do you think we should head there?" I wonder.

"If he's escalating or unraveling, the dates could become less important, but until we get through to Perez and Clark, we sit tight."

"OK. With some luck, he'll have left his prints in the car. Until then, I'll keep going through Joanna Deveraux's list of clients. Might be a good idea to look into the vehicles driven by them?"

"Hand over the names you got, and I'll get started." He sounds a lot more optimistic than he looks.

"*Did* you sleep?" I ask him.

"Don't ask me. The cleaning lady woke me a 6 a.m. God love her, she almost had a heart attack when she came in here and found me sprawled out on my laptop."

"No wonder you look like shit!"

"And here I thought I did a good job of hiding my rough night."

"Let's hope you're better at uncovering than concealing!" I joke, pulling a different box of old case files from across the table toward me. Lifting the lid, I begin to rifle through them, eager for Walters to call so we can update him.

DETECTIVE JOHN WALTERS

We part ways in the hotel lobby, agreeing to meet up again within the hour. My fingers twitch. The adrenaline is finally exiting my body as the urge to comfort Della, and myself, makes itself felt. She turns from me, walking away without looking back.

"You're a fool," Clark says, shaking his head as he follows her. I don't argue with him. Instead, my hands curl into the pockets of my black slacks, my eyes, heavy with exhaustion, watch my feet. I'm focused on them, one foot in front of the other, until I reach my room. I'm just in the door when my phone shrills.

"What's the update?" I ask, knowing Jones must have one if he's calling.

"They found a car matching the description of our BOLO in Minnesota. Should I head there? Get started on looking into it?" He's diving straight in.

"Let local PD handle it until we get official confirmation it's our perp's car. I'm heading back to Appleton today."

"Oh, so soon?"

"Perez and Clark will most likely follow up on other leads here. I'll be more useful in Appleton." My chest squeezes at the admission.

"OK. Where do you want me in the meantime?"

We confer for a few minutes more, agreeing to sit tight on the car and to keep our focus on other leads before ending the call. I'm mulling over why this killer would leave the car out in the open, so easy for law enforcement to find, while I pack. There's a sharp rap on my door.

"John?" Della's voice is hoarse as she calls out, knocking again. I rush to the door, pulling it open to find green eyes full of emotion staring back at me.

"What is it? Is everything OK?" I look up and down the hallway behind her before finding her eyes again. As I watch the watery emotion turns to fire.

"You're a real asshole, do you know that?" In her anger, her beautiful accent is more pronounced than I've ever heard it. Stepping aside, I gesture her in. I want to argue with her, want to reach out and grab her hand and pull her into my room. But more than anything, I want to make sure she's OK. She pauses in the doorway, her eyes falling to the bag on my bed.

"Running away, John?"

I consider her question, knowing full well the insinuation.

"I'm heading back to Appleton. There's a new lead on the car."

"Bullshit. You're running away!"

"Jesus, I'm doing my job!"

"Like I was today? You ran away then too!"

Heat rises up my neck. I pull at my collar, shifting my weight from one foot to the other. I try to regain some control over the conversation.

"Perez, what's this all about?"

"Oh, it's back to Agent Perez, is it? Fine, Walters—"

"That's not what I meant …"

She holds her hand up, tears pricking the corner of her eyes when she speaks again.

"We got the list of names. The FBI agent that visited with LeeRoy Chester was Alex Fisher. Clark and I are heading there now." She takes one tentative step back. My body leans closer.

"Della …"

"No, Walters. This is business. Wheels up in one hour. We'll get to Quantico close to when you arrive in Appleton. I'll keep you posted on our interview."

She begins to walk away, still dressed in the same heels and pantyhose she wore to the prison.

"Do you know him?" I call after her. She turns back slightly.

"He is one of the first ever FBI profilers; plays golf with my section chief on the weekend."

"Do you think he's good for it?"

"He doesn't fit the age profile. He had a son who passed away a few years ago. Ryan is working on other relatives."

"We're still working the Joanna Deveraux angle. We're getting close to him."

She offers a curt nod but doesn't look up before walking away. Regret lances through me. Emotions are tricky, sticky bastards, and I knew better. Years of practice at stowing mine away evaporated into thin air when Della resurfaced in Appleton. My attraction to her spilled over into the case and made a huge mess, one I've no experience in cleaning up.

I finish packing my bag and head for the airport.

HUNTER

There was always another interview, another victim to console, another plane ride away from his responsibilities to us. He'd come home bragging about how brave *they* were, about all the good work he was doing for everyone else. Not us, not his wife and child. *We* were struggling to keep our heads above water every fucking day!

My fingers grip the steering wheel, my molars grinding with the memory of it. I did everything the right way. I was a son to be proud of! But where was he on my wedding day? *Interviewing a serial killer.*

That was the first time I thought, as an adult, that I'd see him more if I was a killer. I used to fantasize about being the villain he hunted. Of removing my mask and watching his face crumple with despair. I've grown out of such fanciful imaginings. As a teenage boy it had been the ultimate revenge story. Now, as a grown man, it grew into a compulsion. Not a daydream, but something to be seriously and meticulously strategized.

Not that I plan on ever getting caught. No, he can live out his days knowing I'm out there, knowing that I took everything from him. I'll take each victim he adored and then I'll take *her!* My blood boils just thinking about his *second* wife, his *second* child, his chance at a second life. His weekends are spent at dance recitals and pretending to the world that he's a good father! His life is about to implode. I've already created so much havoc he won't know what hit him when it comes to light.

I log into his home security system through a program I coded and installed on my phone. I have to swallow back the bile as I watch him kiss Lorraine at her car, hugging Nessa before bundling them into their SUV. Must be nice to feel that love!

My fingers tremble with rage as I close the app.

Pressing my earpiece into my ear, I strain to listen to the conversation out at the farmhouse. Another low thrum of anger begins to simmer under the surface. There's no way for me to gain access to the home prior, so I'll be going in blind. I need to know how many cops they have guarding her. In the forces, it was my job to identify threats, to understand any capabilities or vulnerabilities of the adversary and to exploit them to complete any given mission with optimal results.

I'm used to working in the shadows; I've been doing it my entire life. But this is different. There is no room for a second failure. Finding a motel on the opposite side of town, I check in and hunker down. I've been driving for hours and checking in with Father always wrings me out emotionally, even while reminding me of the reason I began this journey in the first place.

Some rest and food will help to revitalize me.

CHAPTER 29

DETECTIVE JOHN WALTERS

It's almost eight p.m. when I finally push through the doors of the conference room. Jones and Agent Ryan both turn from the investigation wall when I enter. Dropping my leather carryall by the door, I head straight to where they stand. My eyes scan the wall, seeing the photos of two men pinned there.

"Man, am I glad to see you!" Jones greets me.

"What am I looking at?"

"We went back over Joanna Deveraux's list of clients and looked at any vehicles registered in their name. We came across one patient, an Elizabeth Fisher—"

"As in, relative of retired FBI Agent Alex Fisher?" I interrupt him.

"Yeah, she showed up in the emergency room of the Inova Fairfax Hospital three days before Joanna's murder, with severe vomiting and dehydration. Doctors ran tests but couldn't determine her prognosis. Her husband, one Hunter Fisher, son of Alex Fisher, refused to leave her in the hospital for monitoring. The next morning Adult Protective Services paid a visit—"

"I thought the son was dead?" My feet move closer to the board.

"He is. Death cert says he died three weeks ago in a car accident with his wife Elizabeth," Ryan says.

I lean closer to his photo, my eyes scanning his dark eyebrows. "What's that?" I point to a small scar on the corner of his right eye.

"Looks like a piercing scar," Jones agrees.

"Ryan, how easy would it be for him to falsify a death cert?"

I swing around, pacing back and forth.

"He grew up the son of an FBI profiler. He was working as an intelligence officer for the Air Force, has a degree in computer science. The guy worked hacking into the lives of people for a living. So yeah, falsifying a death certificate would be as easy as pie for him."

"Here's the thing: we looked into the original investigators on Joanna Deveraux's attempted murder and Alex Fisher was not part of that investigation. There's nothing to link Fisher and Deveraux together," Jones tells me.

"Do we have the report she filed after visiting the home? Maybe she saw something she wasn't supposed to."

"She reported nothing unusual or out of place during her house call and suggested that Hunter Fisher was a caring husband, worried for his wife's wellbeing."

"How long after that report was she murdered?"

"It was her last official report. She left her office and was never seen alive again." Jones tells me.

"Ryan, what else have we got on him?" I stop pacing, turning to face them again.

"His mother died when he was thirteen. A year later he was sent to military school. While he was there, his father married the nanny, Lorraine Lefrey. They're still married and have a thirteen-year-old daughter."

"What's the daughter's name?" I chew my lip.

"Theresa."

"Shit, who's Nessa? Did we find a connection to that name?"

"Not yet, we're still looking. Hoping that Perez and Clark will have some luck with the dad on that angle."

"Where are they now?" I ask.

"They're in an SUV on the way to the house now, should be arriving there any minute." He checks his watch.

I turn my attention to Jones. "OK, we need to get clear on the information we have. Tell me about Alex Fisher's wife's condition."

"She was diagnosed with MS when Hunter was a little boy. School reports show that from the age of ten, Hunter exhibited behavioral problems."

My eyes snap to Ryan. "Where was Alex Fisher during those years?"

He's typing away, reading at the same time. "Alex Fisher never took sick leave during those years. In fact, his case load increased ..." He frowns in confusion. "Looks like he requested the overtime."

"So, mother is sick, dad is away by choice. He's acting out in school, coming home and caring for his mother. ... Why start killing now?"

We look to Jones, who inhales deeply before addressing Ryan.

"Ryan, tell me about Hunter's wife again."

"They met at seventeen. He moved to Florida to finish his army training. She stayed in Virginia. She was a successful financial adviser, had just been promoted when she got sick ..."

He pinches his chin in deep concentration. "Was she traveling with work?"

"Yeah. Until she became too sick to hold onto her position."

He looks to me. "Walters, I'm not a profiler, but his mother was sick and relied on him as a child while his father abandoned them.

His wife's success, especially the need to travel, may have felt like a threat, triggered him on some level. Reminded him of his father's abandonment."

"What's the Joanna Deveraux connection?" I push.

"The doctors sent Adult Protective Services out to the home. They suspected Elizabeth Fisher was at some risk in the home. Could he have been poisoning her?" Ryan suggests.

My head nods with Jones's.

"That's it." He clicks his fingers. "He wanted her to need him. With APS arriving on his doorstep, he may have felt the net closing in and snapped."

"Ryan, we need something else to give to Perez. What else do we know about Alex Fisher? How does he and his visit to LeeRoy Chester eight years ago tie into all of this?"

"He worked for the BAU for over thirty years. Retired about eight years ago and has since written two books: "Basic Killer Psychology," and "Mind Over Motive." We checked up on the visitor logs for all five original killers and he visited with them all over the course of eight months."

"He didn't publish the book?" I wonder.

"No," Jones answers.

"Any idea why not?"

"No, Perez might be able to answer that for us."

"OK, what else?" I unbutton my shirt sleeves, rolling them up to my elbows as I drop into a seat across from him.

"Oh, shit …" Ryan's eyes widen at his screen.

"What?" Jones and I say in unison, Jones leaning over me at the table toward him.

"His wedding day—" Ryan fumbles over his words. "To Elizabeth.

Hunter's wedding ..."

"Spit it out!" I almost growl.

"Alex Fisher was visiting with LeeRoy Chester on the date of his only son's wedding."

"That's it! Get this information to Perez. We need her to tread carefully here and figure out how the hell this son of a bitch managed to fake his own death three weeks ago. Tell them to be careful, we don't know that the father isn't involved. He could be in on it all somehow."

Now Jones begins to pace. I draw his attention while Ryan makes the call.

"Any updates on the car?" I ask, hoping to refocus his thoughts.

"He wiped it clean, no prints."

"OK. We need to think like this guy for a minute. Why abandon that car?" I've been asking myself this question since finding it.

"He may have seen the BOLO, knew it was hot."

"Possible but he left it in plain sight. Why?"

"He wants us to find it?"

"This guy is always one step ahead. He knows police procedures, he wanted us to find the car and we need to figure out why."

"Maybe he wants us to believe he's in Minnesota and not here in Wisconsin or hunting down his final name on the list."

I nod along in agreement.

"Until we know who Nessa is, our focus stays on MacKenna. What did she take with her to your folks' home?" I ask him.

"She grabbed her purse, yoga mat, laptop, iPod and a couple changes of clothes," he's listing when Ryan interrupts us. With the phone still to his ear, he covers the speaker.

"Perez is coming up to the gated community where Alex Fisher lives now. Is there anything else you want me to relay?"

"We need to know about the black feathers. Find out if the family owned a vasa parrot at any point. See if we can we get a sample of Agent Fisher's DNA to compare too." I say, my mind scrambling to remember every other piece of information collected.

"Jones, phone your dad. Check in with Mac, make sure she hasn't used her devices and tell her to stay off them until we know more about this guy's skills."

As Ryan hangs up the phone, Jones is already reaching for his to call his dad.

"Ryan, we know that he has computer know-how. Let's use that to our advantage. Anything at all you can think of to use those skills against him, do it!"

He's scanning his resources. "This guy is a ghost! At least virtually, and possibly literally if we're on the wrong track!"

"Maybe, but if anyone can outsmart him, it's you!" I stand up, stretching out my back.

"Where are you going?" Ryan asks.

"We need coffee. We're in for a long night" I tell him.

MAC

I pad barefoot across the wide wooden floors down to the kitchen. Mr. and Mrs. Jones and Sailor are all playing cards around the kitchen table. It's a cacophony of laughter and arguments as Sailor pulls a few dollars from the center of the table toward him. If not for the shotgun resting between them, it would be a wholesome sight.

"Hey, girly! Feel like giving these two a run for their money with me?" Sailor grins happily toward me.

"It's only round one, don't get ahead of yourself…" Ruby bustles to the oven. I've quickly learned that she loves to feed anyone who enters her kitchen. If she's not baking fresh bread, she has cinnamon rolls or cookies on the go. I'm surprised that the Jones men have managed to stay so trim all these years. "I made pizza!" she announces, pulling it from the oven.

"I'm still digesting dinner!" I laugh.

"I'll have a slice …" Sailor's chin tilts back, eyeing it over the top of Mr. Jones's head. "Looks good, Ruby. I might even let you take a round or two," he jokes. He won't. He's the most competitive man I know. Her amber eyes fill with fire.

"Don't bother, Sailor Arnold. We might look soft, but me and Jimmy are gonna show you just how merciless we can be!"

I chime in "Dream on, Joneses!" and sit down next to Sailor as Ruby leans over her husband's shoulder, setting the pizza in the middle of the table.

"Make sure to leave some room." She pins us with a fighting stare before an evil grin crosses her face. "Because you'll be eating your words, soon enough!"

"Oh, it's on!"

"They don't say 'keepin' up with the Joneses' for nothing," Mr. Jones quips, sitting up tall. The air is rife with competition and I'm loving it. An hour later, the pizza has been devoured. A few uneaten crusts harden on the plate. It's neck and neck. Sailor and I have never come up against such stiff competition in a game of Texas Hold'em.

The phone rings in the hallway.

"No cheating!" Ruby jumps up, running to pick up the landline. Mr. Jones straightens in his seat, eyeing us suspiciously. He needn't look so worried. We are many things, but the Arnolds are not cheaters.

"Jim, it's your son." Ruby comes back to the table. My blood heats, rushing through my veins and sending my pulse racing at the mere mention of Jones. Ruby takes her husband's post, her eyes taking on his warning glint. My ears perk up, trying to hear the exchange between Jones and his dad but it's fruitless. A few minutes later Mr. Jones returns.

"MacKenna? Jimmy wants a word."

I hop out of my seat, and three sets of curious eyes all smile at my eagerness.

"What?"

"Nothing," they say in unison. I walk out, leaving them to snicker like children.

"Hey," I say putting the handset to my ear.

"Hey ..." his voice is smooth and soft. "How are you?"

"I'm great. Your mom and dad are taking good care of us out here. Any news on the investigation?"

"We're following up on a few leads. I'll need you to stay off your laptop and any other smart devices you brought with you. Just for a day or so."

"Yeah, no problem. Are you close to catching him?" A wave of anxiety settles in my stomach, the anticipation of his response churning away in my gut.

"I think so, but you need to stay alert. You're in safe hands with Dad and Sailor, and the patrol unit is gonna camp out front again tonight." He reassures me.

"OK, I'll stay off my devices. Call me if there's news?"

"I will." He's silent for a moment. "Are you OK?"

A soft laugh escapes my lips. "You asked that already," I remind him.

"I mean ... since this morning."

My cheeks flush remembering our kiss. It was the hottest moment of my life, enough to make me forget the impending doom on my doorstep. So yeah, I'm OK.

"I won't be reporting you to your superior, if that's what you're asking." I've lowered my voice, aware that all chatter from the kitchen has ceased since my departure.

"I'm pretty sure I broke a few rules, all right ..." there's a note of disappointment in his tone.

"Oh," my flirtation ebbs, replaced to instant self-doubt.

"I'm also sure I'd like to break a few more," he finishes, and my heart soars again.

"I'm hoping you do."

"First, I need to catch this guy. Don't do anything to put yourself in harm's way, OK?"

"OK," I promise. I'm too tired to take on this fight alone and relieved to realize that there are people, wonderful people, willing to stand beside me until this killer is behind bars.

"I'll call the house after I'm done here but it will be late so don't wait up."

"I won't. I'll try not to wake you in the morning."

"You'd better!"

I laugh again. "OK, yoga at sunrise." I smile, hanging up the phone. When I return to the kitchen all three of them are smiling along with me. I'm in serious danger of falling for the Joneses and I think Sailor might be too.

CHAPTER 30

AGENT DELLA PEREZ

Former FBI Agent Alex Fisher lives in Elmwood Estates, a subdivision in Fairfax County in Virginia, just minutes from downtown McLean. We pull up in front of the gated community. After we've shown our badges to the security guard, he makes the call. Agent Fisher has already agreed to meet with us, so the call won't come as a surprise.

I feel sick thinking about the line of questioning we are about to start. I read over his file on the plane ride here. He, like the current chief, was one of the first men to work for the BAU. I recognize his face from the hall of fame leading to the unit chief's office. I recognized his name the moment Agent Ryan said it over the phone this afternoon. His reputation is impeccable, his input invaluable in developing the techniques and tools we still use today while profiling.

Through the gates, we've been directed to follow a road to the other end of the estate. The winding road is flanked on either side by landscaped grounds teeming with specimen trees and elegant driveways leading to million-dollar homes. Located at the end of the drive, Agent Fisher's is the only home fenced in. The gate's already open to admit us. Clark drives up the graveled drive, both our eyes widening as the French château style home comes into view.

"That's it, I'm writing a book." Clark's mouth sags. I laugh. It feels good, even if the vibration hurts my throat. My hand comes to my neck, gently caressing the area that LeeRoy Chester bruised this morning. We're only hours from the prison but this morning's events feel like a world away.

Clark and I disembark, tiny stones crunching beneath our feet as we make our way to the flagstone terrace. This house was not bought on an FBI salary, that's for sure. The door swings open and we are met by a wide grin and gray eyes. Standing over six feet tall, with gray hair and a ruddy complexion, Agent Fisher looks relaxed and happy in knee-length shorts and a white linen shirt.

"Agent Fisher ..." I step forward about to introduce myself.

"You must be Agent Perez." His eyes drift behind me. "And Agent Clark?"

I smile "Yes, thank you for agreeing to meet with us." I clasp his outstretched hand to shake.

"My wife just left for her sister's for the weekend. She'd kill me if she knew I was working again ... come on in. " He waves us through the door. My eyes note the security cameras above the door as we enter.

"Have you had those long?" I ask, pointing.

"My son installed them a few years ago ..." He sighs. "Insisted on the things."

Clark and I eye each other cautiously, I take the opportunity to probe further about his son. "You must miss him."

A somber expression crosses his face as we enter a large living room. Shaking his head with regret he walks to the center of the room where two large sofas face each other. Throwing his phone onto the coffee table between them, he sits, offering the sofa opposite for Clark and me. We accept, sitting across from him.

"At times, but life is hectic ... you know how it is," he replies, swiftly changing the subject. "Tell me: what is it I can help with? Are you working the Joanna Deveraux case?"

I'm not surprised that he's heard about her death. Not wanting to implicate his son too soon, I allow the conversation to flow in this direction for now.

"Yes. We found a link between her death and three other murders over the past few months. We think you might have information pertinent to catching her killer."

"Oh? I've been out of the game a few years now, but whatever I can do to help the families."

"Since Ms. Deveraux's death, there have been three other murders and one attempted murder that we believe to have been committed by the same man." I list them, watching him pale as I recite each victim's name. If the killer is indeed connected to Agent Fisher, his reaction tells me that he will be just as shocked to learn it as we are.

"A serial killer on a spree kill." He sits forward, eyes alight with professional interest. "This is most unusual. He's seeking out victims that have already survived such an attack. Do you know why?"

This is the hard part. "We think these crimes are somehow linked to the book research you carried out a few years back. Is there anything about the time you spent with each killer that stands out in your memory?" I'm easing into my questioning.

"Other than the fact that they were all twisted serial killers, I'm afraid not. Each one was driven by a different motivation. The purpose of the book was to examine the interactions between the killers and their victims. To understand how these women survived and the subsequent impact it had on the killers' psyches."

"Can you elaborate?" Clark asks.

"The women showed great courage in the face of pure evil. They all managed, in one way or another, to escape these vicious and deadly men. Men who thrive on power and control. They lost both to their surviving victims, many of whom put them behind bars. It was an area of profiling I wanted to explore further. They are predators and their prey escaped. It intrigued me to understand how they felt in the minutes, hours, days, and months after. We know that men like this rarely return to attack a survivor, and I wanted to know why." He explains. My stomach twists with how much this lines up with our killer's behavior.

"Why did you stop work on the book?" I ask.

"My conversations with the killers didn't reveal anything that would add value above what we can already ascertain from our initial assessment of any crime scene and the killer's psychological history. The killer's motive always begins and ends with some sexual deviancy, a sense of entitlement and a deep self-loathing that is most often linked to childhood. Their reasoning for not returning seemed to be a cut-and-dry unwillingness to risk being caught. Most enjoyed the idea of their victim living in fear of their return. They garnered some sense of power knowing they had ruined their lives in many ways." I nod along. This information is indeed already well established within our field, but I admire his attempt to dissect the psychology even further.

"Why did you select these killers in particular?"

He shrugs. "Their signatures were each completely different. The signature tells us so much about the needs being satisfied by each killer. I was intrigued by how different the signatures were and yet the killers, as men, had so many similarities in contrast. I'd hoped there might be some missing link that we had failed to recognize between killers. But alas, we were too good at our jobs in the '70s!" He chuckles.

"Agent Fisher ..."

"Call me Alex," he insists.

"Alex." I correct myself, inching closer to the edge of the sofa as I speak. "We came to the same conclusion. We examined the victimology carefully, and the only similarity between each victim was having survived the original attack and ..." I pause, swallowing against my raw tonsils. "You," I finally say.

His eyes darken in realization. "You think it's me?" he blurts out, followed by a deep rumbling laugh. "That's absurd!" He relaxes back into the sofa again.

"No, not you. Luckily, MacKenna Arnold managed to fight off her attacker and gave us a description of him. We wondered if there was anyone in your life with some kind of vendetta against you. Who might want to damage your reputation somehow?"

"Absolutely not."

"The killer is adept when it comes to cyber security," I begin, getting to the crux of our visit. "He's tall, over six feet, and lean, with dark eyes, blue maybe brown, with a piercing scar over his right eyebrow. He most likely has a military background and some knowledge when it comes to law enforcement. He is strong, intelligent and he's killing the victims of the serial killers that you interviewed. ... Can you tell us about your son's death?"

"Death? What are you talking about?" he chokes out.

"We have a report that he died alongside his wife, three weeks ago." John's suspicions that the son faked his own death to cover up these murders may have some merit, judging by Agent Fisher's shocked expression.

"You'd better get your facts straight, Agent Perez. Hunter and Beth are very much alive! God love her, she's very sick right now and is suffering, both of them are. Why on earth would you think they are dead?" he spits angrily. His patience is running thin.

Clark and I exchange wide-eyed glances. I hope he keeps his temper under control long enough to give me the information we need.

"When did you last speak with him?"

"A few weeks ago …" He pales again. "You need to leave. I need to…" he stands his words trailing off.

"Agent Fisher, we need you to cooperate with us. If your son is in fact alive, he is most likely unraveling. We found a list of names. Does the name 'Nessa' mean anything to you?"

He freezes, all the blood draining from his face. His mouth falls open before quickly closing again. He drops back into his seat. I give him a moment, careful not to push him.

"My phone!" He leaps for the phone on the table, his chubby fingers swiping with urgency.

"Alex—" I begin to speak, but he holds up a hand.

"Lorraine? Where are you?" he speaks hurriedly. "Is Tessa with you? Can you *see* her?" He snaps at his wife. "Stay where you are. Don't move and don't leave the house. I'm on the way! No, everything is not OK. You need to keep Tessa with you until I can get there." Tears well in his eyes as he meets mine across the table. "It's Hunter. He's done something terrible, Lorraine."

Clark and I watch as Special Agent Alex Fisher, once head of the violent crimes unit and renowned for his work in the field of criminal psychology, grapples with the concept that his own son is a serial killer.

"I'll be there soon," he promises, before hanging up the phone. He looks at us again, calling out the location and address of his wife and child. "Get police there, immediately," he demands. Clark pulls out his phone to make the call.

"Why are we sending protection to your wife and child?" I ask.

"My daughter was christened Theresa, after my wife's deceased mother. We've called her 'Tessa' since the day she was born …" He swallows against the lump in his throat. "She would call herself 'Nessa' as a toddler. Hunter is the only one who still calls her that."

"What about his wife Beth? Where is she?"

"She's home, I'm sure of it! We need to go check on her. She'll be devastated if this is true."

"Do they live far from here?"

"They're only ten minutes away. Where is *he* now?" He struggles to keep up as his world crumbles around him.

"We don't know. We suspect in Wisconsin. Alex …" I keep my tone as gentle as I can. "Can you think of why your son would do this? Use your training: there is no one more qualified to piece this together than you."

He shakes his head, pacing back and forth, as he no doubt scrolls through a lifetime of memories, trying to find the signs he missed along the way.

"His mom." His eyes sharpen in my direction: he's moved into investigator mode. "She was ill. Hunter was home alone a lot while I was on the road. Camilla, my first wife, was diagnosed with MS when Hunter was just a boy. Her health deteriorated quickly. By the time he was twelve years old, she was in a wheelchair. Her speech was severely impeded. She died when he was thirteen. I knew he resented me for not being there more, but my work was important. In hindsight, I've come to accept that I used it as an excuse to avoid my own feelings. I couldn't watch the woman I loved, the mother of my child, disappear in front of my eyes. Oh God. I *left* him. This is my fault ..."

"Alex, you mentioned Beth is ill too. Hunter may have resented taking care of another woman in his life. Would he harm—"

"No!" he barks. "Absolutely not. Hunter adores Beth: he's been a devoted husband, refused any help with caring for her. Lorraine and I offered to move them here while she was unwell, but Hunter said no."

"The killings began four months ago. Was there a trigger, anything that happened that might have caused him to snap?"

He continues to rack his brains. "There was some investigation. Adult Protective Services became involved ... But Hunter assured me he wouldn't do it again ..."

"Do what?"

"Oh, no. No, no, no ..." He drops into the sofa, his elbows coming to his knees as he grips his hair in both hands. "When he was a boy ... He was just a boy. No he can't have ..."

"What did he do as a boy?"

"He was jealous. He poisoned Lorraine. But military school changed him; set him on the right path! He went to therapy twice a week until he met Beth. He's been a model citizen since then." Large, guilt-filled tears stream down his face.

"Do you know why he would leave a black feather at the crime scene?"

"Oh Lord, forgive me!" He breaks down completely. "Molly. She was my pet parrot. Hunter killed her. He used to leave feathers in my office."

This information connects the final dot. We have a name for our killer.

"Alex, we need to check on Beth. When did you last speak with Hunter?" I gently coax him from his turmoil.

"He left a voicemail last week, saying he was taking Beth to Texas to visit with her folks. There's just no way he'd harm a hair on her head."

"We don't want to startle him. Is there any way we can get in touch with Beth without Hunter finding out?" Clark asks.

"I could phone her dad. He'll help."

We nod for him to go ahead, although Clark and I both fear the possibility that he will alert his son.

"Larry? Hi." We're both grateful that he puts the call on speaker. "I was trying to get in touch with Beth and Hunter ..." he begins.

"That's strange, we've been calling the house all day, and no answer."

"I've tried a few times myself. I thought maybe they'd decided to visit with you guys?" Fisher hedges.

"I haven't heard from them for a while. I'm a little worried, actually."

The air around us thickens. *If Hunter didn't take Beth to Texas like he said, then where is she?*

"I'm sure everything is all right, but I'll drive over there to check in with them. I'll call you back in a little bit, try not to worry." Alex hangs up and looks directly at me. "Agent Perez, we need to go. Right now," he insists.

He, Clark and I all pile into our black SUV. Along the drive, we watch as the cheerful man from only minutes ago wars with Alex Fisher the FBI Agent and Alex Fisher the father. The profiler in him is putting the pieces together while the protective parent tears them apart: reasoning, rationalizing and then spiraling into self-blame and self-deprecation before coming back to disbelief and anger at the very suggestion that his son could be responsible for such heinous crimes. As we drive down Hampton Roads Avenue, he points to the Victorian style home on the corner. The sun has sunk below the horizon, illuminating the sky in a last glow before nightfall. Warm light floods from the houses along the street. The home of Beth and Hunter Fisher sits in darkness.

"They're not home …" Fisher's voice regains some hope. "There has to be some reasonable explanation for all of this."

He fumbles with the car door handle. Turning in my seat, I face him.

"Agent Fisher, you'll need to wait in the car," I tell him.

"Absolutely not!" He jumps straight out. Clark and I follow as he hurries up the drive and onto the wooden porch. A wheelchair ramp has been recently added to one side of the wrap porch. Alex points it out.

"Would a man about to go on a killing spree build his wife a wheelchair ramp?" he reasons. He's fully entered the denial stage. We reach the door and Clark and I immediately spot the security cameras and motion detectors.

"Well, any chance of catching him off guard is out the window," Clark grumbles next to me, as Agent Fisher bangs on the door. When there is no answer, he pulls out a bunch of keys from the pocket of his navy shorts.

"I have a key, in case of emergency." He inserts the key, turning to us as he enters. "Come in but don't touch anything. I'm pretty sure we can find some indication of where they've gone off to."

We follow, each of us drawing our guns from their holsters. We move cautiously into the home. With the shades drawn, it's dark until Alex flips the light switch in the hallway.

"That's strange," he says. Our eyes follow the path of his gaze to a wheelchair at the bottom of the stairs. "That's Beth's chair. She's been deteriorating, uses it to get around the house when Hunter's at work." As we step closer to the stairs, the pungent smell of death tickles our noses. The foul odor stings our eyes, and we instinctively turn back toward the fresh air wafting in from the door behind us.

"Hunter!" The distraught father runs up the stairs, calling out hysterically. "BETH!" Clark and I race after him. He makes it to the landing before Clark manages to pin him against a wall. preventing him from reaching the stench's source. The acrid waft catches in my throat. Still holding my gun, I shield my nose and mouth with my forearm.

"I'll check the rooms," I gasp, trying to suppress a dry heave. Clark, afraid to breathe let alone speak, simply nods. Agent Fisher, a man long accustomed to the psychology of murder, knows when he is in the presence of just that. He whimpers, the assurances that kept him hoping gone. His son is becoming the very monster he spent his life hunting. The irony of his namesake has not been lost on me.

"Maybe they're both dead. He could be a victim in all of this, too ..." His words, a last-ditch attempt at defending his son, are a sledgehammer to my heart. It breaks for him.

I push open each door, quickly examining each room. Two bedrooms and one bathroom, all empty. I inch closer to the biting stench. The principal bedroom door is slightly ajar. I push it open with my foot and use the sleeve of my blouse to flip on the light switch. From the hallway I can still hear Fisher's muffled sobs, and Clark calling for back up. From the doorway, I see the outline of a body beneath a white bedsheet. A pillow has been placed over its head. The decomposition has been seeping into the mattress and sheets. I quickly check the closet to confirm that there is no other body or person in the room. My bet is that beneath the pillow, I will find Beth Fisher. I don't want to disturb the scene. I snap a quick photo of how I found it before lifting the pillow enough to see long brown hair. It's not official confirmation, but all signs indicate that Hunter Fisher has killed his wife. Dropping the pillow back in place, I move back out into the hall. Clark helps a devastated Alex Fisher from the house. Once outside, we all gasp for air. I leave Fisher with Clark and climb straight into the SUV. Once the door is closed, I phone Ryan.

"It's Perez. I can confirm our killer's name is Hunter Fisher. John was right, he staged his death."

"Where is he now?"

"We don't know. He has a state-of-the-art home security system and motion detectors. He must know that we're onto him at this point."

"Do we know who Nessa is?" Walters calls out.

"Nessa is one Theresa Fisher, his thirteen-year-old sister. She is currently under FBI protection and will be removed to a safe house until we can apprehend the suspect."

"If he knows we're on to him, he may escalate." Jones's voice comes over the line.

The smell of death lingers in my nostrils and my stomach rolls with disgust.

"Going after MacKenna now would be a huge risk. He knows the FBI are on to him, he might run but we can't take that risk."

"What do you suggest?" Walters asks. His trust stops me. John is never one to take direction, especially where his investigations are involved. I sigh. I'm unsure of how to proceed. This guy has so many skills at his disposal.

"He killed his wife. According to his father, the very idea was absurd. That tells me that he has nothing to lose. He has removed all the bargaining chips; he isn't looking to play it safe or loose. He'll know we have Nessa safe, so he will refocus all his rage and double down on his efforts to find Mac. Clark and I will be on the next flight back to Wisconsin. We need to use his knowledge, his thirst for revenge against him. Until then, keep Mac alive."

"OK, we'll do our bit here in Wisconsin. If you need me—" He clears his throat. "Call." His last words are just audible. I hate that my anger for him wavers at this slightest display of vulnerability. I sign off. There's no time to ponder what, if anything, he means. When I exit the car, Agent Fisher approaches me. He's more in control of himself than when I last saw him.

"Agent Perez. He'll go after the last victim, the girl that survived. We need to get her under protection." I can see he is drawing on his years in the service to make it through what must be his darkest hour.

"We have. Theresa and Lorraine are safe too. We are going to take you to them now. Hunter may very well come after you if he can't get to MacKenna Arnold." I warn him.

"No." He shakes his adamantly. "Hunter has spoken far too often about how easy it would be for him to walk into the woods and never be seen again. He has the training, the capabilities, to do just that. He will disappear before you can catch him and I will spend my life looking over my shoulder. Tessa will always be in danger and if his hatred for me runs this deep ..." He points behind him, toward the window of the room where his daughter-in-law's body lies. "If he could do *that*, to beautiful Beth—" His voice catches, the words breaking apart as he tries to maintain his composure. He clears his throat again, wiping again at the new tears forming. "He will run if you make it too difficult for him to get to her."

"What do you suggest?" I'm listening, warily. I by no means undervalue the opinion of the person who knows Hunter Fisher best, better than anyone else. However, he is also the father of a serial killer on the loose. It is impossible for him to be impartial.

"I come with you to Wisconsin. That's your next step, am I right?"

I nod.

"Hunter is angry at *me*. I am the fountain of his rage. If he sees me there, he'll leave her alone. He'll make me his main target. We can use that to our advantage."

I shake my head no.

"I agree," Clark chimes in. My eyes widen in disbelief.

"We can't do that! We'd be offering you up on a plate. It would foolish—"

"I'm in charge, Agent Perez, and with Hunter Fisher being a trained air force intelligence officer who has been three steps ahead of us this entire time, we need to think strategically, just like him," Clark insists. Not broaching any argument, he pulls out his phone to call the chief for approval.

Once he's out of earshot, I try one last time to reason with Agent Fisher.

"Alex, why do you think Hunter is killing?"

"Because he feels abandoned. He thinks that I chose my work, these victims, over him."

"Your family is afraid. They're waiting for you to go to them, right now."

His eyes cloud over as reality dawns. "I'm doing it again, aren't I?" he sniffles.

"You want to stop him. I understand that, but you know how this works. It's not a good idea, Mr. Fisher."

There is no opportunity for me to elaborate further as Clark walks back into the conversation. "I just got off the phone with Chief

Leonard. The jet is fueled up and already on the runway. We'll be in Wisconsin before sunup."

Fisher looks at me, his chin quivering, before turning to Clark.

"I'm staying in Virginia. My wife and child need me."

HUNTER

"*Hunter, no matter what you become, I know you'll make me proud.*"

My eyes fly open, my body bolting upright on the motel bed. Rubbing the sleep from my eyes, I look around the dark room. Other than a sliver of evening sun filtering through the tiny gap in the curtains, it is pitch black. I check the time on the clock radio. It's almost seven p.m.

"Fuck," I hiss, my hand running over my coarse five o'clock shadow before flopping back onto my pillow. When I focus, I recall that my dream was of my childhood. Feelings I'd long forgotten are choosing this time to resurface. It amuses me somewhat, but only solidifies how much he deserves everything coming his way.

I grew up the son of an FBI agent, a man admired by everyone he met. There was a time I felt proud to be his son. The kids at school would say "Wow, your dad's a hero!" and I lapped it up. Then, when Mom got sick, my life changed so drastically, but for him everything stayed the same. He flew about, hunting killers and interviewing victims. All the while, I was battling to stay proud, to feel lucky. Mom was walking one day, wobbling another. Before long she was in a wheelchair. She was my favorite person. She deserved better. She told me that no matter what I grew up to be, she'd be proud. I hope she meant it.

Yawning, I battle to keep my eyes open. This traveling from state to state is starting to take its toll. Naturally, the reconnaissance, gathering of information on each new town, each new victim, was the type of challenge I gravitated toward. Figuring out how to commit each crime was exciting. It thrilled me every time my plans went off without a hitch.

As a child, I guess I was always planning, always thinking ahead. I found it oddly satisfying, snooping through his files, even when I didn't take them. I enjoyed examining the crime scene photos. They fascinated me. I reveled in listening into his phone calls, hearing him analyze the men he was hunting or interviewing. They became my own obsession. I thought those killers were fools, always planning how *I* would have done it differently.

I'll admit, with each kill my feelings toward taking a life have changed. Choking Joanna to her death was more tiring than I could have imagined, but even in the midst of tangled emotions, I felt untouchable, stronger and more in control than ever before. Once you get a taste of that power, it's addictive. I tapped into this unknown capacity. Beneath the average man and model husband lay a killer, and I relished that feeling. With each kill, that emotion, that initially felt perverse, became more welcome, until it has transformed into my new normal. With the urge to kill building, my need for sleep dwindles. I sit up again and roll out my neck. I reach for my laptop case and phone. I notice immediately that the motion detector at my house has been triggered.

It's time.

It's all coming together. Although I'm tempted to log in, I wait. This will allow the FBI enough time to set the wheels in motion on their end. I lay out my tactical gear and weapons before taking a long, hot shower.

CHAPTER 31

DEPUTY JONES

Della and a sour-looking Agent Clark arrived back in Wisconsin a few hours ago to a sheriff's station in the midst of a manhunt. With John at the helm, we called in all off-duty police officers, divided them into teams and sent them out to every hotel, motel, trailer park and airbnb in the Appleton area with a photo of our suspect. Hunter Fisher, son of a renowned FBI agent, and active serial killer, has the skills to survive in the wilderness. A major air and land search is set to get underway in the next few hours, including a press conference with all local and national news media. We know his name, we know what he looks like, and if he doesn't already, he'll soon know that the net is closing in on him.

"OK, listen up, everybody!" Della shouts over the hustle and bustle. Silence descends as she begins the speak. "Forensics teams at the home of Hunter Fisher have found a small wooden box in the crawl space. Inside, the skeletal remains of a vasa parrot have been found, along with over twenty photos of murdered women. Alex Fisher has identified them as images from cases he worked or from his research folders. These images have been kept by this man since he was a teenage boy.

They've also recovered a freezer bag. Initial findings suggest he kept the black feathers sealed and frozen for many years."

I shake my head listening to her fill in the blanks of our investigation.

"Do we know if the images are of our victims?" Walters asks.

She glances his way before addressing her answer to the room. "Yes. Five of the images are of women who survived a serial killer attack. Four of whom we know he has killed. The only person still alive from those photos is MacKenna Arnold."

"What does that mean, Perez? Will he run and hide?" I need to know.

"We know now that these murders have been fantasies of his for a very long time. But four months ago, he tapped into those deepest, darkest desires. His relationship with his wife may very well be the reason his murderous rampage didn't begin sooner in life."

"He killed her!" Clark interrupts.

"Exactly. He is unlikely to quieten those homicidal ideations. I believe he will continue on this road, try to see it through to the end. The murder of his wife was like killing the angel on his shoulder."

"Once the press conference airs, we are turning up the heat on a ticking time bomb!" Walters blurts out. "That could jeopardize Mac's safety." There's real concern beneath the stern edge to his tone. "I say we wait twenty-four hours before releasing information to the media. We need to get a step ahead of this guy."

"No, we go ahead with the public appeal." Clark cuts him off.

"We are talking about a few hours here," John pushes. The two men face each other across the oval table.

"No, we need to get his image out there. It's the quickest way of apprehending him."

"His own father said this guy could walk into the wilderness and have the skills to survive off the grid for months at a time. This will force him to go underground. We need time to get a handle on how to catch him," Walters argues.

"No, absolutely not."

"In a hurry to get your face on TV?" Walters' hands are on his hips, his jaw tensing with frustration.

"Need I remind you that the FBI now holds jurisdiction over this case?" Clark slams his hands down hard on the table.

"No, you need not!" Walters bellows back.

Della throws her hands up in the air. "Walters! Clark!" She glares back and forth between them.

I move to stand behind John, in complete agreement. This is bullshit.

"I don't like this anymore than you but we have orders, protocol to follow. You can take lead on the press conference if that's what this is about."

Her words shock me. Della knows as well as I do that John couldn't care less about taking credit or getting his face on TV. I don't miss how he jerks backward, his shoulders stiffening at the very idea of it.

DETECTIVE JOHN WALTERS

One hour ago, Agent Clark combed his hair into place and delivered his speech to the American public. The tipline has been ringing off the hook since, with people reporting to have seen him in Florida, New Mexico, Colorado, Chicago, and Ohio, to name a few. Then there are the calls coming in from the residents of Appleton, one woman believing he could be hiding out in her barn. We pulled officers from everywhere, including a patrol unit out on the Arnold farm to investigate the umpteen sightings. So far, we've come up empty and my stomach is churning with unease. Jones sets a coffee in front of me.

"What's on your mind, boss?"

"I can't shake the idea that he wanted us to find that car. He wanted us to think he was in Minnesota."

"I agree with you. It's been preying on my mind too, but we were already closing in on him. We would have gotten here without the car."

"True ..." My head bobs as I think. "But this guy knows FBI protocol and yet they're refusing to break it. He will have already anticipated their next move with the news media." I sigh.

I'm still considering the ramifications when Agent Ryan calls out. All heads look up or turn from whatever they're working on.

"Someone has logged in to his home security system!"

"Is it him?" I ask.

"Do we have a trace?" Perez is the first to move, her legs carrying her around to look over Ryan's shoulder. I quickly follow, watching as he punches letters and numbers furiously onto the screen.

"Yep, it's him."

The room stands still. The only sound is the clicking of Ryan's keystrokes.

"I have the ISPN. I'm running it now ..." He gives us a play by play of everything happening. My breath catches in my chest as I listen. "It's encrypted. If he stays on long enough, I'll be able to run a trace ..."

We wait on pins and needles. "Aw, fuck. He's logged off!" Ryan jumps up, knocking his chair over in his frustration.

The entire room groans in disappointment. Ryan paces with his hands behind his head.

"Wait a sec ... " Ryan stops in mid-step, zigging back to his laptop. "Maybe ... I created a virus earlier this evening and set it on his home system. It may have been enough to get access to his current ISPN. ... Once he logged on, it should have opened a back door. ... Yes! It worked; we've got him. He's currently connected to a public Wi-fi, here in Appleton ..."

I grip the edge of the table. The room pulses with energy as we wait.

"He's logged onto the Wi-fi at the Cedar Stay Motel, just outside of town ..."

"Madre di Dios! I stayed there last year!" Della gasps. We all spring into action. Guns are holstered, jackets thrown over shoulders, car keys ripped from the coffee-stained table. Ryan quickly closes his laptop. Whipping it off the table he rushes behind me as we all stream out of the conference room.

Perez and Clark surge ahead toward the exit. My blood sizzles with anticipation. This guy is dangerous. We hit the parking lot at a jog, the brisk evening air only fueling our pace.

"Jones, you're with me."

"Walters, do not go in until we get there. Remain vigilant. This is a skilled air force officer with nothing to lose. Taking out a few cops will be nothing to him," Perez is shouting across the hood of her SUV.

"Let's just get there!" Jones taps the roof impatiently. I jump in. We pull out last, following the SUV and two Outagamie patrol cars. In total, there are nine men on route to the Cedar Stay motel.

"We need back up to the Cedar Stay motel ... " Mandy's voice from dispatch is crackling over the radio as sirens and red-and-blue lights flash around us. My foot is on the gas, my eyes fixed ahead with Jones next to me.

"John ..." there's apprehension in Jones's voice.

"You OK?"

"You got me thinking about the car. He wanted us to believe he was in Minnesota, but he's here in Wisconsin."

"Yeah ..."

"We're all rushing to the opposite side of town, away from Mac and the farm ..."

My eyes look from the road to him. "He knew the FBI would trace him."

"He's too smart to get caught this way." Jones swallows slowly. We're the last car in a long line of law enforcement heading away from the Jones family farm. The kid's hunches have been right before, and I see the logic too.

I slam on the brakes. The car skids, smoke rising from the tire marks as I slew the car around.

"We could be wrong," I say.

"There are enough of them to catch him if we are. We need to get to the farm!" he says.

"I agree. Try to get through to your dad. Give him the heads up."

HUNTER

*I**diots.*

There must be something in the water around here, it's the only way to explain the stupidity. Hiding her out here on a farm with two junior deputies and two geriatrics. It's laughable. Ten minutes of recon told me all I needed to know. The uncle is camping along the treeline, playing sentry.

I'll get to him once I've finished with this group.

Entering the property from the main road was easy. A quick sprint across the open field and I was behind the barn.

There's no movement around the back of the house. The two cops are sitting in their squad car, windows rolled down and eyes on the house.

Sitting ducks.

Taking my knife into my right hand and moving to the driver's side, I strike fast and hard, plunging my knife into the driver's chest. The officer next to him fumbles for his weapon, his mouth falling open when I rip the knife free from his partners chest, spraying blood across the dash. He's too shocked to react quick enough for me. Diving through the open window, I drag the blade across the his neck.

Their eyes, full of fear and shock, send my blood sizzling with pleasure.

I push the driver forward, gurgling, struggling, and helpless, adding two more stab wounds to finish him off. I only brought one black feather, and it's for MacKenna.

It took me four seconds to take them out, then another five seconds to reach the basement window. Some hollering from inside the house is enough to cover the sound when I break the glass. Another five seconds, and I'm in the basement.

"Whistle for Sailor. I'll go up for Mac." A woman's voice calls out from above me. I'll need to be fast, strike now.

My eyes find the fuse box. I'm on schedule. Now I need to finish this before the old man makes it back for his supper.

"SAILOR! HE'S HERE!!" The urgent roar comes from the ex-cop.

Shit. He must have found the deputies.

I cut the power. Last check, all my equipment is ready to go. I dart up the stairs into the main house.

CHAPTER 32

Detective James Jones Senior, Retired

Summer nights in Bingham are always the same. Dark skies, dotted with stars as far as the eye can see. When the moon is full, like tonight, its glow illuminates the fields and bush. The crickets and katydids turn up their volume too, as if they're howling at it. If not for the danger that lurks under the same cover of darkness, I might be lulled into a pre-dinner nap right here on the open porch.

"Jim, supper's almost ready." The smell of fresh bread floats with Ruby's voice from inside. I'm a lucky man. Gripping my shotgun, I lean heavy onto the butt, using it as leverage to pull myself standing.

I'm getting old ...

"Jim?" She hollers again.

"Yes dear, I'm coming."

"Whistle for Sailor. I'll go up for Mac."

My eyes find her through the net curtains moving out of the kitchen and up the stairs. I whistle shrilly on two fingers, out toward the treeline in the direction of Sailor's camp. With Jimmy out on the trail of this maniac, it's just us four for dinner. When I see Sailor emerging from the edge of the forest, I groan my way down the steps to the squad car around the back of the house. The boys have been sitting here all day. A little night-time snack might keep them right.

As my boots hit the dusty gravel, a sensation, a frisson of fear seizes my gut. I recognize it immediately: it's a feeling so distinct, so primal in nature and one I haven't felt it since retirement.

It's eerily quiet ... comes to mind. The thought is confirmed by the sight of blood, splattered across the windshield of the squad car. Rheumatism forgotten, I run to the deputies. Pulling open the door, my heart leaps into my throat, lodging itself there. I gape in horror.

"Oh Jesus ... Hold on boys, hold on."

Grabbing the radio on one deputy's shoulder, my urgent call drowns out the desperate gurgling sounds of the two men struggling to breathe.

"MAYDAY, MAYDAY, MAYDAY! WE ARE UNDER ATTACK OUT ON BINGHAM FARM. SEND MEDICS, OFFICERS DOWN! SUSPECT STILL ON SCENE ..."

I assess them. One's throat is slit, the other is slumped forward with knife wounds to his back. There's no time. Whipping off my shirt, I press it to the young deputy's neck. His terrified eyes beg me to stay.

"I gotta go help the ladies. Hold this to your wound." My voice breaks.

Lord, watch over these boys ...

Hastening to the driver side, I wrench open the door and pull the second deputy toward the ground. With his legs still in the car and his head on the dirt, I leave him, hoping that gravity will stop his lungs from filling with blood.

"SAILOR! HE'S HERE!!" I'm running with the speed of a thirty-year-old man, adrenaline flooding my body and spurring me into action. Sailor sees me, hears the urgency in my voice and begins his own sprint toward the house. Just as I reach the porch, the electricity in the house cuts out.

"HE'S IN THE BASEMENT!" I scream to Sailor, kicking open the back door. My shotgun is tucked to my shoulder, loaded and ready to fire as I enter.

"Jim, what's going on?" Ruby calls from upstairs.

"Ruby, he's in the house. Get the rifle from our closet and go hide with Mac." I don't look up toward her, instead focussing on the basement door swinging open.

He's up ...

"Oh Jim, be careful!" Her whispered admonition fades toward the back bedroom. I'm at a disadvantage, he knows my location. The house is small, his goal is to get up the stairs. I listen intently, my head swiveling between the living room and the kitchen doors. He could be coming from either direction and I'm slap bang between both. There's nothing to do but guard the stairs and hope backup gets here soon.

"Mac!" Sailor calls out, rushing through the front door. My finger comes to my lips before pointing overhead to let him know where she is. He nods, stepping cautiously over the threshold and into the farmhouse. Slowly, he moves toward me.

"You go up, secure the ladies ..." I'm whispering, when a gentle creak on the floor alerts me. In a flash, a dark figure emerges from the living room, his black eyes zeroing in on the shotgun. My finger pulls the trigger. The gunshot blasts around us, the pellets blowing a hole in the wall.

Missed.

Smoke rises from the barrel. I cock the hammer again. I sight along the smooth bore of the gun, seeking him in the darkness. He snakes behind Sailor, who twists back, catching him with a blow to the face.

Damn it! no clear shot ...

Keeping the gun trained on their fight, I glance over my shoulder to the top of the stairs.

Don't let him past you ...

Sailor is holding his own, until a large hunting knife is drawn from a strap on the attacker's thigh. He lunges toward Sailor.

I can't risk a shot: Sailor might get hit ...

Without further thought, I enter the fray. With a knife at play, it'll take the two of us to protect them. I swing the barrel, bringing the butt around hard at the side of his head missing again when he drops to his knee. He swivels on the floor, turning in my direction and punching me in the gut. The blow knocks me back. Lifting the gun, I lash out again, but this time he twists away, landing another blow to my side.

Sirens sound in the distance. Sailor leaps on him. The knife, now covered in blood arcs up in the air.

"Sailor!"

The knife comes down, stabbing him in the back. My vision blurs, and I fall back against the wall.

God help us ...

Sailor drops next to me. Sirens and lights, almost at the house, illuminate the bastard as he takes off out the door. The girls are safe. Relief fills me.

"He stabbed you. How bad is it? ..." I say, trying to push up to help Sailor.

I can't feel anything ...

"DAD! Oh my God, Dad..."

Jimmy's here?

He's lifting me from the floor, turning me over. He turns to someone out of my sight.

"It's bad ..."

What's bad?

"I'm OK, where's Mac? Your mom? ... " A new wave of fear, like a bolt of lightning courses through me. I struggle to sit up.

"It's OK, Jim. The girls are safe, you kept them safe ..." Sailor's saying. Jimmy's holding me in his arms.

"Dad, we need to stop the bleeding."

"Bleeding? I took a punch to the stom—" My words are cut short by a round of violent coughs that burn in my gut.

"Shh, Dad, you're hurt. Don't talk ..." His eyes fill with tears. Ruby's clambering down the stairs, suddenly frantic. "Jim! Please God, no ...!" She drops to her knees, her hands gripping my shirt.

"Help him!" she hollers.

"I'm OK ..." The words are spluttering from my mouth on another wet cough. It's the metallic taste of blood dribling from my mouth that connects the dots.

I was stabbed.

In the distance, Walters is screaming for an ambulance. Mac is crying next to Sailor.

"Dad, please. Hold on." My beautiful family is praying for me. My eyelids feel heavy, the need for sleep becoming overwhelming.

"I love you both ..." I can hardly breathe.

"Oh, Jim! Please hold on, please, for just a minute more, honey ..." My wife, as beautiful as the day I met her, is whispering in my ear.

"Jimmy, keep them safe ... " I reach for his face. I'm so proud of you son ...

"Dad, I will. Please ..." He grips my hand, squeezing it in promise.

"Ruby, I ...love ..." I can't breathe. ..."I love ..."

I love you.

CHAPTER 33

DEPUTY JONES

Standing among the crowd of onlookers is a little boy. He's holding an American flag with one hand and covering his heart with the other. His eyes light up in fascination at the procession of motorcycles and patrols cars that escort the hearse. Leading us through the wrought iron gates of the cemetery, their sirens blare in Dad's honor.

"How are you holding up?" Mom, pale and shaking, squeezes my hand.

She hasn't stopped shaking since he passed.

"I'm—" The lie is too thick, too big to make it past my lips. My jaw wobbles, my eyes water just to set it free. There is no relief in tears, just more pain as my chest squeezes. The pain, too unbearable to contain curls me forward. I rock, my arms resting on my knees.

"Oh Jimmy, oh son ..."

The image of the little boy outside the window, idolizing the policemen, probably wishing he could be one of them, sends me spiralling into despair and shame.

I did this.

"Mom, I don't think I can say goodbye." My lungs burn, my ribcage rattling from the onslaught of raw emotion.

Why couldn't I just leave him out of it?

The cars stop. I can't get out. I can't face everyone.

How can I look them in the eye knowing what I've caused?

"I'm ... sorry—" My head is shaking. My tears stream freely down my face.

"Jimmy ..." Her voice is so gentle, so soothing.

How can she forgive me?

"I need you. I can't do this without you," she begs me.

I look out the window. People are walking to the open grave. Walters, Perez, Mac and Sailor are lingering by the funeral home's limosine door, waiting to support us.

"I should have found another way ..." I continue.

"Jimmy, don't you do that!" Her words are manic. My eyes whip to hers. "He saved those two deputies. They're alive because of his quick thinking. He intervened and saved Sailor too. He saved me and Mac, and all because he was a great cop. But above all that, he was an amazing father, a wonderful husband, and a hero to this entire town. There was never another way. Don't you take that from him."

My heart believes everything she is saying but my head can't quite catch up.

"OK." I'm trying to pull myself together, for her. A light rap on the window draws our attention to Walters's somber stare. He nods once before opening the door and sliding into the seat across from us.

"You both holding up?" he asks.

"We're just about ready." Mom has regained her composure. I can't look him in the eye.

"Jones, you hold onto your mom, and I'll be right behind you."

His voice is strong, controlled and exactly what I need. He opens the door again. Sliding out, he holds it open for us. I get out first, holding out my hand for Mom. She takes it, before wrapping her arm around my waist and holding on tight. Mac stands next to Della and Sailor, dressed in black and as pale as Mom, her eyes filled with the same shame I feel.

Please, don't ...

Unable to look at her without breaking, I drop my gaze to my feet and follow the path. Walters keeps his hand is on my shoulder until we reach the graveside.

MAC

Nine days ...

Since Mr. Jones was brutally murdered in his own home.

Nine days ...

Since I almost lost Sailor to that monster.

Nine days ...

Since I lost Jimmy.

He hasn't come by, hasn't called, or checked in. I've tried to reach out, begged Detective Walters to tell me where he is, but Jimmy's with his mom and I'm under FBI protection.

"He'll call soon. Give him time," Agent Perez tells me every day, but I know it's not true. I know he'll never look at me again, at least not in the same way. I can't close my eyes without seeing him covered in his dad's blood, without hearing Mrs. Jones's wails when they told her he was gone. Those memories haunt me day and night but remembering how Jimmy looked away from me at the funeral haunts me just as much. There's a gaping hole in my chest. No amount of yoga or therapy can fill it.

Only Jimmy, only he can ...

My fingers tremble. My entire being feels like it's being sucked into the hole. Pacing back and forth, wearing out the carpet of the hotel room they're hiding me in, isn't helping either.

I can't stay here. I can't breathe ...

A sudden knock on the door startles me, excites me, fills me with hope that today will be the day he comes. Rushing to it, and forgetting to check the peephole, I drag the chain across the track and turn the locks. When the door swings open, my hands fly to my mouth.

He came.

"Oh Jimmy ..." My arms are around his neck, my face buried into his shoulder. "I wanted to call you but they said you needed time. I was so worried, are you OK?"

He doesn't respond, and it's then that I realize he hasn't hugged me back, hasn't leaned into me in the same way. His entire body is ramrod straight; his strong jaw tilted away from me. My heart shatters. My arms fall from his neck. Stepping back, I look at him, really look at him.

He's lost weight ...

I twist my hands together at my stomach, waiting for him to speak.

"How've you been?" He glances briefly at me before his eyes return to the floor. My entire body trembles. My words are shaky when I speak again.

"Jimmy, please talk to me. Please let me in ..."

"That's ironic, coming from you!" he spits, "I've been asking you to let me in for twenty years! And *now* you want us to share?"

I deserve this.

"I was hurting, just like you are ..." I try.

He's so angry. My lips wobble, then press together. I'm too afraid to say another word.

"Perez thought it would be a good idea for me to come by, update you on the case. He's still on the run. Every media outlet has his photo, but for now, you'll remain here until we catch him."

So, there's no real update.

"Jimmy ...?" My voice is so weak. The fear coursing through my body is unlike any terror I've ever known. I thought dying scared me, but losing this man, losing his faith in me, is a fate far worse than death. He won't even look at me.

"Jimmy? Please, look at me ..."

"What, Mac? What do you want to say?" He turns red eyes in my direction. They're swollen from grief, but he doesn't look away. Not when my eyes water too, not when the tears we've both been holding back fall, and not when I say:

"I love you, you know. I just want you to know that, in case—" My throat constricts.

"In case what?" He takes one step closer.

"In case he comes back ..." My shoulder lifts as I try to find words. "In case you never want to see me again."

"He'll be back. But he won't get close enough to hurt anyone I love, ever again, Mac ..."

He towers over me. The tremendous weight of his pain becomes mine. It unfurls in the depths of my soul and manifests itself in gut-wrenching sobs.

"When Mom died ..." Tears are streaming down my face ... "I found you, Jimmy. Please, find me now. Let—" My sobs turn into short, shallow gasps. "Let me save you in the same way you saved me."

He looks away. "I can't do this ..." He turns to the door. "I can't stay here." Reaching for the handle, he struggles over his decision to leave.

Please stay ...

"You know I loved you too ..."

Loved.

The past tense is a dagger to my heart.

"It took me some time to understand your pain, why it made you so cold ..." He turns, eyes blazing my way again.

"What I'm feeling now: this ache ..." He thumps his chest. "This fucking endless rollercoaster of guilt, shame, loss, and love for you, for my dad, for my mom, is making me sick. I want to set fire to every happy memory I have, because I don't deserve them. I don't deserve to have anything good."

If grief had a check list, he'd be ticking all the boxes of how I experienced mine. How I justified my treatment of him. The truth is, I've never felt worthy of him. It scares me, knowing what's coming next. My heart braces for the final cruel blow, that he'll say to isolate himself and not have to deal.

"Don't," I hear myself say. "Don't do what I did, Jimmy. You've always been stronger, a better person than me. Please, don't let this monster harden you."

When he was fourteen years old, he asked me to dance and got a bloody nose. He found the courage, even after I'd cut him off. He deserves that from me now. Stepping into his space, into all possible rejection, I wrap my arms around his waist, breathe in his warm scent and whisper, "Knock, knock?"

He tenses, his heartbeat pounding against my cheek.

"I can't, Mac ..."

"Please ..." I squeeze tighter.

"Who's there?" he croaks.

"MacKenna ..."

"MacKenna who?" His shoulders slump as the tension starts to drain, his weight relaxing into me. I hold tighter.

"Mac-can-I love you?" It sounds awkward and not at all in line with our jokes, but it's my last-ditch attempt at reaching him. His body shakes. I think it's anger at first, but then I hear his soft laughter.

"That was so lame. You're the worst at jokes." I raise my eyes to his. Sadness still resides there, but for the first time since he arrived today, I see a glimpse of Jimmy Jones.

"I am not!"

"You should have said 'Jimmy a chance to love you.'" His eyes roll.

"That would be demanding. But ..." I swallow against my parched throat. "I meant it."

"*Can* you love me, knowing that I intend to kill him, Mac?"

His words send another wave of emotion to the back of my eyes.

"I know a good place we can bury the body." My lips twitch until he smiles, lacing his fingers with mine.

"I bet you do. But I mean it, Mac: there's no way I'm letting him close to you again."

His grip tightens, the connection sparking new life within me. My pulse calms, years of fear peels away, leaving me languid, even drowsy in his protection.

"And when he's gone? Will you still be here?"

Catching my chin, his fingers tilt my head back. Warm lips, full of promise, gently press against mine as his fingers graze up and down my bare arms.

"Jimmy ..."

"Mac ..."

When the salt of his tears tickles my tongue, my arms come around his neck, my tongue gently coaxing his mouth apart. He wraps his arms around my back, lifting me from the floor. There's no madness in the urgency of our kiss, just a tender need to feel the other's closeness.

My feet dangle as he carries me to the bed, both of us falling together. His body presses against mine, his weight on my chest the only pressure I want there ever again.

"Jimmy …?"

At the sound of my sniffles he lifts worried eyes to meet mine.

"Are you all right?"

"I love you." The need to tell him again and again overwhelms me. "You're the only girl I've ever loved."

My heart swells. "I want to be the last, too."

His weightless gaze lifts. "You got it." He smiles, before allowing me to hold him, cry with him.

CHAPTER 34

DETECTIVE JOHN WALTERS

Dust has settled on the crime scene in the nine days since Jim was murdered. My chest aches for Jones, and for the man who gave his life for the people under his care. Appleton won't ever be the same again. Standing over the dried blood of the fallen hero brings hot tears to my eyes. Clearing my throat, I blink them away, shifting my focus to the hole in the wall created by his missed shot. My fists curl with the urge to punch a hole right next to it. That missed shot was just one more, in a long line of missed opportunities to end this fucker's spree.

He knew our every move, knew all along where Mac was, and played us for a bunch of fools. Jim's murder is a devastating reminder that while we carry a gun on our hips and good intentions in our hearts, all it takes is one act of evil to catch us off guard. And someone dies. Though it brings little comfort, my hand rests over my holstered gun as a new wave of sadness joins the unescapable guilt that lodged itself in my chest nine days ago. Sucking in a lungful of air, I release some of the weight with a whispered promise.

"I'll get him, Jim."

The words linger in the empty farmhouse, following me from the hallway into the living room. It's a promise I intend to keep with me until I fulfil it. My feet move across the creaking floorboards, bringing me to the mantelpiece cluttered with family photos. Jones, as a little boy, sits next to a young MacKenna Arnold around a campfire. They're both holding a S'more and smiling toward each other. Jones at high school graduation, his graduation from the NWTC Law Enforcement Academy, and standing next to his patrol car on his first day on the job. There's so much love and pride for their only son. Overcome, I look at my feet. I can't even begin to comprehend what he must be feeling. Perez is with him today. In all honesty, I couldn't face another day of telling him we have no news. There's no word on the man who murdered his father.

Jones did everything right, but he's a mess. Mac is too. She blames herself. They both need each other but he's stayed away. Perez is trying to encourage him to visit with her. We all need something to hold onto to these days.

I'll hold onto the goal of catching Fisher...

With that in mind, I shift my mind back to investigator mode. This is not the home of a colleague, this is a murder scene. And every scene holds some answers. Stepping back, I consider the entire scene. Neither Ruby or Jones have been back yet. Everything is exactly as they left it. I run through what we know.

He gained entry through a basement window.

Turned off the power, climbed the stairs and moved through the kitchen, into the living room.

Attacked Sailor at the other end of the living room.

He was quick, full of confidence when he came here.

How could he be so sure there were only two deputies outside, and none inside?

It's unlikely he had entered the farmhouse before that night, which means he was coming in blind. He couldn't have known the layout of the house, but he must have had some insights as to where things were.

But how? There was no way for him to surveil this house.

Alex Fisher has been on the phone with Della and Clark often. They're gathering more and more information about this man daily. He was a twisted kid, killing the family bird, stealing photos of dead women and hiding in his father's office, listening to his phone calls. He was voyeuristic from an early age. Surely, he must have used those skills here. Which once again begs the question of *how?*

Nothing seems out of place. The old farmhouse, with its dated furnishings, sits untouched since the tragedy. My musings take me through into the kitchen. Dinner plates sit on placemats around an empty table. Pots and pans are still on the stove, a loaf of bread, long past stale now, is carved into slices on the kitchen island. Mac's red purse brings a splash of color to the sorry scene and an old familiar feeling to my gut. Reaching into the pocket of my slacks to grab my cell phone, I call Agent Perez.

"It's Walters. There's nothing here. I doubt he's still in Appleton. Tell Jones he can come on home," I tell her, before hanging up and heading straight to my car.

DEPUTY JONES

Walters told me it was time to face the inevitable.

"You're not alone, Jones. I'm here, every step of the way," he promised, slapping my back. Della stood next to him.

"And I'm one call away. You won't be alone," she agrees. With one last encouraging nod from them both, I climb into my truck and head out to the farm.

It's after sundown when I arrive. Parking, I sit, staring at the house. The electricity hasn't been turned back on. All the life was snuffed out of this place in just a few minutes of violence.

I can't go in ...

A world of shame grabs hold, squeezing the air from my lungs. Swearing and gasping against the feeling, I slam open the truck door and stumble into the night.

"Just breathe," I hear Walters say. It feels as though everyone is listening, watching my grief weaken me at a time when I need to be strong. For Mom, for Mac. Inhaling deeply, I square my shoulders and my eyes return to the house. I still can't believe he's gone, that he's never going to come out and meet me on the porch again. Dad deserved a peaceful death; to die old, in his bed with Mom at his side. Every time my eyes close, images of him, covered in blood, play out in my mind.

It's time.

Fear is the most natural thing to feel in moments like this, but as I step onto the porch, walking across the wooden structure, I feel him. I hadn't thought too much about the afterlife before this, but since his death, it's given me some strength to believe he's with me. That he forgives me. It reminds me that despite my own self-loathing and guilt, his good nature and big heart still exists. Deep down, next to the desire to punish myself, is the knowledge that he wouldn't want me to.

Turning the key and stepping over the threshold is the easy part. Seeing the spot where he died, too much. I look away quickly, my feet taking me through the dark house into the living room. The stale reek of the unemptied kitchen garbage lingers in the air.

"I can't be here alone," I say aloud. My voice fills the empty house. The need for support, for *someone* to help me through this, is overwhelming. I punch the familiar number into the phone.

"Hey, I'm out at the farmhouse," I croak to the receiver.

"How are you feeling?" Her voice instantly takes the edge off, reminds me of the reason I am here.

"Alone." It's the truth. "I think it would be safe for you to come by, maybe sit with me?"

"Are you sure?"

"Yeah. I'm going to take out the trash and tidy up, try get the electricity back on. I'll be here a few hours. It would be nice to have company."

"I'll be there in thirty." She hangs up.

Moving to the kitchen cabinets, I take down three candles and light them, before emptying the bins and the refrigerator. Just like I said.

Thirty minutes later, Mac's Jeep Cherokee pulls up.

HUNTER

In all honesty, the fact that this group is still alive doesn't sit well with me. To come back here, knowing how easy it was for me to gain access? Knowing how far off the beaten track they are, to come here again and assume that I'd leave a job unfinished, is quite frankly, insulting.

They deserve to die, for that alone.

When I entered Mac's home, on that very first day, I was cagey enough to put a bug in the lining of her purse. I've been listening to her every step of the way. In the mall, making her plans to go camping, sitting around the table and playing cards with the Joneses. I listened to her boyfriend and his dad discuss all those old cases, desperately trying to find the link. When she left it behind at the farmhouse, I thought my luck had run out. But thanks to Detective Walters, the boyfriend has finally come home, and he's foolish enough to have invited her over.

I was forced off grid. I've been sleeping rough in the wild, hiding from the countless search parties. I broke into vacant homes to charge my equipment, fleeing back into the wilderness on foot, listening, waiting for news about her whereabouts.

I approach the same way as before, parking along the main road and waiting behind the treeline. When her jeep pulls up, every sinew within me fires to life. My heart pounds. I'm ready to end this and get out of this hick town. She jumps out, long dark hair pulled back in a pony pulled through a blue baseball cap. She sprints to the door in her yoga gear, jumping into his arms, before he swings her inside.

I hear "How was the ride over?" His voice is faint, her response muffled. They're too far from the purse.

"I'm going to go down and try get the electricity on. Why don't you light some candles upstairs?"

This is too easy.

I hear more noises through the mic as they move around. When I'm certain he's in the basement, I dart for the house. The back door is unlocked, the handle turning with well-oiled ease.

I pause at the door to the basement. Should I take out the bigger threat first? Even if I catch him off guard, it's too much of a risk to attack from this position. Mac is the main target. If she hears the fight, I risk her escaping again.

This is my last shot.

With that in mind, I take the stairs two at a time, then silently make my way along the hallway. There's a window at one end. Looking over my shoulder and listening for movement downstairs, I open it to give myself a quick escape route, if needed. Candlelight glows from under a bedroom door.

How romantic.

Drawing my knife from the strap on my thigh, I move to the bedroom door. It's already ajar. A gentle push creaks it slowly open. She has her back to me, looking out the window.

"Hello, Mac."

The heady rush of power burns its way to my every extremity when her back stiffens. I can't restrain my chuckle. This is absolute rapture.

I'm going to savor every second.

"Oh good, you came."

She turns, raising her head. Green eyes, full of grit and bright with satisfaction lift from under the brim of the baseball cap.

FBI Agent Della Perez has her gun in hand and has a clear shot.

Fuck!

CHAPTER 35

DETECTIVE JOHN WALTERS

No doubt about it, it's a cruel game of cat and mouse.

From my cramped position across the floor of Jones's truck, I can't help but feel I've stooped to an uncomfortable level. He's about to walk into the house where his father died, facing it for the first time on his own. My desire to catch a killer wars with the instinct to be his friend.

A woman's purse wouldn't usually pique my interest, except that Mac carried it everywhere she went. We already know Fisher hacked her home security system and has a penchant for listening into conversations, so the notion that he was listening to the Joneses doesn't seem too much of a stretch. Although, ever since setting this plan in motion, watching Jones step forward without hesitation, I've been plagued with doubt.

Maybe I'm way off base.

Yet, pulling the plug on the whole operation felt like a bigger mistake. Call it a hunch, but I can't shake the thought of Fisher's confidence walking through those doors, fearless, as he attacked a home occupied by four people. Mac had only been there a few days, and he found her. Now, she's been in protective custody for nine days, *without her purse*, and he hasn't made a move.

Is he running scared? Or is he in the dark now that she's away from her belongings?

There were two ways to know for sure. Check her purse for a bug or leave it untouched and hope that he's listening.

"How's he holding up?" Della's voice sounds through my earpiece, pulling me from my doubts. She, and over thirty Outagamie deputies and FBI agents, are two minutes away on a neighboring farm. Once we know he's on site, they'll descend from all sides and surround the farmhouse.

He's not getting away again.

"He's exiting the truck now," I say, knowing every officer is listening in. Off the radio, I whisper to Jones, who's looking distressed.

"Just breathe."

Moments later, he's in the farmhouse. The plan is simple: he'll begin by speaking out loud, letting our killer know he's there, before making the crucial call to "Mac." Della will be on the other end of the line. The hope is that he won't be able to resist the opportunity to take another shot at her. I'm shifting position to stretch out my cramped back when I hear tires crunch along the gravel. A car door slams shut, quick footsteps climb the porch stairs. The screen door swings shut when Della and Jones walk inside. Suddenly, my position on the truck floor feels even more constricted. My heart pounds and the hairs on my arms stand, while I'm forced to stay still and simply listen as Della and Jones exchanged muffled conversation. The idea is to let Fisher know that she's there but to avoid raising his suspicions.

They split up to lure him in, as per our plan. Seconds later, a shadow moves past the truck. My entire body stills, listening as the gravel crunches under stealthy footsteps that move toward the house.

"He's here," I whisper into my radio. "Hold position until he enters the house." I slowly turn my body until I'm hunkered at the door, my fingers gripping the handle, readying myself to jump out at Della's word.

"He's inside," Della whispers, less than five seconds later.

I've got the truck door open. I leave it swinging as I sprint to the back of the house.

"Hello, Mac."

A chill runs down my spine, hearing his icy tone over the radio. He's closer to Della than I am. It dawns on me that he could well be carrying a gun, or he could get the upper hand before I get to her.

"You fucking bitch," he snarls.

Jones and I crash into each other as he bursts from the basement. We push through the narrow kitchen door. Jones is three steps ahead of me as he takes the stairs two at a time.

"SEND BACK UP, NOW!" I bellow, loud enough for Fisher, the team standing by, and the whole of Wisconsin to hear.

DEPUTY JONES

"FREEZE!" Perez's scream rings through the house. My legs feel heavy as I pound up the stairs, reaching the top in time to see him flee from *my* room, the room where he thought he'd find Mac. My dad's face, my mom's grief, Mac's fear and the terror he's caused us all. These images drive me into the darkest place, unknown territory, but a place I knew myself to be capable of on some level. I'd do anything to protect the people I love. Fury fuels me as he dives toward the open window at the end of the hallway. Throwing police protocol to the wind, I lunge at him. I make solid contact with his back and tackle him to the ground. He's fast. He twists sideways, his elbow connecting with my jaw. That blow knocks the last shred of my self-control. I pound on him with both fists. He fights back, bucking beneath me, managing to turn onto his back.

"Freeze, motherfucker." Walters's voice is deathly calm, and barely audible. My rage is drowning out his words, and Perez's, as they call for me to stop. I know they're circling me and this murdering son of a bitch as we grapple on the floor, but I don't care. He tries to sneak a knife from the strap on his thigh. Grabbing hold of his wrist with one hand, I pound at his jaw with the other. We roll, tugging back and forth for control of the knife.

"FREEZE!" Walters is louder this time.

I manage to whack the knife from his hand. All rational thought, all reason and thought of risk evaporate in the blazing rage coursing through my body. The cracking of bone echoes. I punch harder, spurred on and unable to stop.

"Jones." Walters's tone is firm.

My fist comes up again.

"JONES. ENOUGH!" he hollers now.

Not until I draw blood ...

Beneath me lies the man who murdered my dad, the need for vengeance consumes me. Walters grabs my arm mid-swing. The blow, meant for this bastard, catches his lip. Walters falls back and I take one last furious swing: right hand whacking against his cheek, left hand against his jaw.

Blood spurts from his lip before Walters finally drags me off. Perez is calling for the medics. Flashlights blind us as FBI agents and deputies surround us.

FBI AGENT DELLA PEREZ

He's in custody. Jones gave him quite a beating, but once the paramedics gave the all clear, he was cuffed and placed into the back of Clark's SUV. He'll be transported immediately to the Green Bay Correctional Institution, the closest high security facility. He'll most likely stay there until his trial.

"You did great." Walters comes up from behind to stand next to me. We watch Agent Clark climb into the SUV, two other agents already inside to escort the prisoner. Two Outagamie patrol cars drive ahead, another two behind, their tires kicking up dust, illuminated by the blue and red flashing lights that disappear down the drive. Leaving us alone.

"How's Jones?" I finally ask.

"He's on his way to the station. Mac and his mom are waiting for him."

"How's the lip?" My eyes glance sideways, checking his swollen lip. Jones gave him quite a whack.

"Kid's got a good right hook." He lifts his fingers to the cut, wincing, before finally looking me in the eye.

"Not sure he'll let you live that down."

"I'll let him away with it ..." A crooked smile creeps up his face. "This time."

My heart swells, with jealousy creeping into the new unoccupied space. The emotion bores and exhausts me at once. I'm so tired of living on the edge of everyone else's life, watching from the outside as bonds form while I'm moving on to my next case.

Just like before, I'm about to become a memory to Detective Walters.

"So, what's next?" he asks, nudging me with his elbow.

Back to business.

"He'll be questioned by the FBI, then local law enforcement will get a crack at him. After that, there are four states looking to take a shot at prosecuting this guy. I'm sure there'll be extradition requests, and a lot of red tape to wade through before any trial gets under way. With some luck he'll plead guilty. That would save the families from having to go through the trials."

"I meant for you."

Oh ...

"I'm not sure ..." I turn, glancing toward the farmhouse. "I'll head back to Virginia. My position is unclear, moving forward."

"It's bullshit, Della."

"Maybe I belong in the field ..."

"Maybe, but you're beyond capable of overseeing that division. It was a dick move to demote you," he growls. It makes me smile.

"Not the first dick I've dealt with, won't be the last."

"I'm sorry for how I behaved in Virginia," he begins. I lift my hand to stop him.

"Don't, John ..."

"No, I—" His body tenses, his jaw rigid. "I was angry."

"No shit! I was there. You know, John, this is my job and I'm *sick* of men telling me how to do it, treating me like a fragile doll because I'm a woman! He attacked me. So what?"

"So what?!" His eyes blaze incredulously.

"You took two bullets last year. Did I get angry? Accuse you of being unprofessional? Question your judgment?"

"No, you fucked off back to Milwaukee!"

"Oh, now I'm the bad guy for doing my job, too! Should I have been more concerned? Leaned into the feminine role, checked to see if the big, strong man was OK?"

"I thought you might." He shrugs.

"Why?"

He looks away, into the night.

"WHY?" I demand "You made it clear; you didn't *want* me to care!"

"I *don't* want you to care." He rounds on me, just as angry. "*I* don't want to care! I was angry in Virginia, *not* because you're a fragile doll, *not* because you can't do this fucking job just as well, if not better, as any man I've worked with, but because my first thought wasn't to contain the situation, it was to *kill* the fucker who hurt you!"

His confession shocks me into complete silence.

"You're a distraction, Della. One that scares the shit out of me. And if I allow myself to be carried away …"

"You'll chase down the most dangerous men on this earth, but you're afraid of *me*."

"*They* can't hurt me!" he growls.

"They could kill you!" My voice rattles with emotion.

"Being dead and feeling nothing is far easier than giving into this!" His finger waggles between us.

"Wow." My eyes well up. "That's a first, John. Being told that the man I care for, would rather be dead than risk a relationship with me." I turn to storm away but am yanked back and against his chest as he glares down with eyes full of fury.

"Don't twist it. I'll ruin it, I always do. I work long hours, I don't want children, I'm not the kind of man that you should want."

"Yeah, you're right, John. I want someone who feels all the fear and takes the leap anyway. You're not the only one who works long hours. And I don't remember you asking if I even wanted kids. I don't remember you thinking of anything other than yourself. You're a coward."

"It would never work. You live in Virginia, you travel ..."

"Anything else?"

"What about Clark?"

"What about him?"

"Did you ...? Are you and he ..." He has the decency to blush at the question.

"Yeah, John, we did. We spent one night together!"

"After we ...?" His fingers release their grip around my arm as his body moves away from mine.

I can't believe this. "After we *fucked*?" I spit.

"It's none of my business. I shouldn't have asked." His eyes fill with contrition.

"It was months ago. And you're right: it's none of your business. I'm going home."

"Della ..." He calls after me as I stride to Mac's jeep.

"No, Walters. You were right. You will ruin it. You already have."

I close the door, blocking out whatever else he has to say. My heart throbs, aches and trembles all at once. My foot hits the gas, my eyes fixed ahead as I drive away, leaving him to stare after me. Country miles melt into highways as the space between us widens.

I park Mac's car back at the sheriff's station. I say my goodbyes to Jones and Mac before meeting up with Clark and Ryan in Green Bay. Clark doesn't object to giving me some annual leave. I need time.

I'm going home.

CHAPTER 36

MAC

The wait at the sheriff's station sent me spiralling into a world of fear and dread. Mrs. Jones, Sailor and I sat holding hands, between bouts of weeping and pacing the floors. Finally word came over the radio, the plan had worked. Hunter Fisher was under arrest.

Ruby and I hugged each other, crying hard for ten minutes. Holding on tight, as we sobbed for Mr. Jones. Sailor stood over us, his hand resting on Ruby shoulders the entire time. I've been through it enough to know that the arrest is only the beginning of the healing. We all have a long road ahead of us. Thirty minutes later, Jones comes through the doors. His eyes are red and puffy, his knuckles bloody. Relief propels me into his arms. Mrs. Jones wraps her arms around us both. Together, we all cry again.

"Your dad would be so proud," she croaks.

"I wanted to kill him," he gulps.

"I know, but it's over now, son, it's over ..." She wipes his tears. I feel honored to be part of such a private moment.

"What's next?" I ask.

"Now we go home."

"Where's that?" I laugh. Jimmy's large arms hug us both to him again.

"We'll stay in my apartment here in town, for now. After that, wherever you all are, is home."

His sweet words, meant to include Sailor, ease away the last of the fear. The tail end of adrenaline leaves my body, my limbs relaxing against him.

"OK, let's go home." I sigh. With his mom in one arm and me in the other, and Sailor at my side, we leave the sheriff's station just as Detective Walters is walking in.

"How're you holding up?" He stops us, eyeing Jones with a concerned expression.

"I'm fine. I'm going to take the ladies and Sailor home. I'll shower and come back ..." My fingers bunch a handful of his shirt. I was hoping to have some time with him.

"No, take the night. Get some sleep and I'll see you tomorrow," Walters insists. I could hug him.

"Sorry about—" Jones begins, but stops when Walters holds up his hand. I take him in. He looks tired, weary even. His lip is swollen but it's his shoulders that look weighted down, despite Fisher being behind bars.

"Just go home, and take care of yourself," Walters says. Jimmy nods and resumes walking.

"Jones?" Walters calls after us. "You did good, kid! You're going to make a hell of a detective."

There is no mistaking the raw emotion and truth in his words. Jimmy tenses, his eyes filling again as he stares at his mentor.

"Thanks, John."

"Goodnight," he says again, before turning from us, heading into the station.

His usual confident stride is gone, and for the first time I realize that Detective John Walters should be going home too. There was something about him that I liked the moment I met him, something in him that I recognized in myself. I wasn't sure what it was until now.

"He's a good man," Ruby says, as we watch him leave.

"He's a great man," Jones counters.

He's a lonely man.

CHAPTER 37

DETECTIVE JOHN WALTERS

She left me choking on dust as she sped away.

I walk back toward the house, my head hanging low. I spot something blowing across the drive.

It's laughable that his black feather would appear at this moment. Reaching for it, I pluck it from the ground and carry it with me to the foot of the porch steps.

I twist the feather in my hands and replay the conversation with Della over in my mind. I can't help but wonder if I'm making a mistake.

Is it worth the risk? Or is this feather a reminder that the work must come first?

Maybe she's right. Maybe I am a coward. On a deep sigh, I haul myself back up and head to the station. Whatever the answer, I have reports to write and a killer to check in on.

The Next Day

HUNTER

Rage plagues me. It's coursing through my veins and wreaking havoc with my breathing and my concentration. The dull aches from Deputy Jones's beating are nothing, compared to the tightness in my chest every time I recall seeing Agent Perez's face beneath the rim of her cap. Thoughts of my mistakes have been running rampant through my mind all morning, eroding my self-control. My hands miss the weight of my knife. I keep squeezing the empty space where the hilt should be. Another reminder that the only blood shed last night was my own.

They've caged me at the end of a long corridor on the second floor of the Green Bay Correctional Institution, where the stale stench of bleach and body odor thickens the air. The distant sounds of guards changing shift is interrupted by the echo of approaching footsteps. The steady steps pique my interest at this early hour. All night, guards passed my cell, pausing outside each cell on their rounds. Lifting my head from the hard mattress, I sit up as the visitor nears.

My bruised muscles scream as my feet drop to the floor. I straighten, suppressing a groan, to see Detective Walters. He lazily scans my surroundings before his eyes snap back to mine.

"It seems the big mystery of why you chose your victims has been solved."

"Oh? Enlighten me."

He steps closer to my cell. "I'm not sure the profilers will agree with me—"

"They'll say I chose them because my father either worked their case, or investigated them for his book."

"Thing is, he worked cases and interviewed survivors in almost every state."

"I'm aware."

My bored sigh seems to amuse him. The smug bastard grins before he speaks again.

"Yet you chose victims from only states that have abolished the death penalty."

"Your point?"

"My point is ..." He steps closer again, until his shadow stretches to my feet. "You're a coward. Behind those tough-guy eyes is a frightened, little boy, crying for his daddy to come home."

"Some might say I'm being smart."

"Not smart enough."

"I'm still breathing, Walters."

He chortles, a deep rumble in his chest that shakes his shoulders and slices through my restraint. I'm on my feet level with his narrowed gaze through the bars.

"I amuse you?"

"You know the media's calling you the Parrot Killer? You're nothing more than a caged bird, and will be for the rest of your life. In a few weeks, you'll be yesterday's news. And while the rest of the world moves on, you'll be here, still squawking for daddy's attention."

He steps back before I can reach my hand through the bars. Grabbing hold, I pull myself flush against the cold steel and watch him saunter off.

"You made a mistake coming here, John! You hear me?"

He doesn't look back.

DETECTIVE JOHN WALTERS

I move back through the North cell block to the admin building. There I pass through the metal detector and collect my badge and gun before signing out and leaving Hunter Fisher and the GBCI. He'll likely spend the rest of his life in the maximum-security prison. I only glance back one time before leaving it in my rearview mirror.

My next stop is the Jones family farm. I've got a bucket and cleaning supplies on the backseat. Jones and Ruby won't be returning any time soon, but at least when they do, Jim's blood will have been washed from the floor, and the hole in the wall will be patched.

I pull up outside the house and step into the early morning. Dew on the grass and leaves mingles with the scent of wildflowers in the air. The farm looks idyllic, and hides the horrors of Jim's death, especially on such a beautiful morning. With every step toward the porch, my stomach winds into a tighter knot. Hunter Fisher is behind bars, but this case left too many casualties in its wake. Images of Jim's death flood my mind. Regret stabs through me as I turn the key and enter his home.

Inside the door, my eyes land on the bloodstain, the hole in the wall. The scent of Old Spice lingers in the air as I walk past the open door to his office. Sunlight streams through the window and lands on his roll-top desk in the corner. Leaving the bucket at the door, I turn toward the leather chair, still holding the imprint of his body, and the open files on his desk. This was the last thing he read here.

My curiosity wins out, and I pick up the top sheet of paper. It's a suspect interview report. The suspect is one Roxanne Monroe, the last-known person to see Logan Webster, before he disappeared on December 15th, 2007. I recognize his name, know that this boy now a man, is still missing. Worse dead. I can't turn back time to prevent his death, but maybe picking up the leads on Jim's only unsolved case will give both Jones and I something to refocus on. Nothing like work to distract you from troubles.

Distractions.

Della's eyes, full of disappointment and hurt the last time she looked at me, fill my mind. With another deep breath, I squeeze away the memory and shift my attention to my next battle.

THE END

THE THRILL BEGINS HERE...

Thank you for embarking on this thrilling journey with my characters! Let's keep the suspense alive.
For exclusive sneak peeks, behind-the-scenes content, and the latest updates on the upcoming heart-pounding book 3, join my newsletter today!

www.christinewinstonauthor.com

Acknowledgements

There are, as always, so many people to thank. So, let's dive straight in!

The release of book 2 experienced serious delays, so my first acknowledgement is to my readers who have reached out with support, encouragement and who have patiently waited for this book. It makes all the difference on the hard days to know that there are readers waiting on my next book, and I can't thank you all enough. I hope you love this story and the characters as much as I loved writing them.

Thank you to my family and friends who have endured my rattling on about characters, book releases, book titles, book cover designs and even rewrites! Without your love and support I'd be lost. With a special acknowledgment to my mam and dad.

Alison, thank you for ALL the book cover designs. You must have created at least 10 great designs to help me home in on my genre and a cover that fit, not just the market, but the story and me as an author too. I loved every one of your designs but I'm so happy that I was finally able to pick 1!

Nicole, at Emerald Edits. I always say it but without your feedback, support and encouragement, this book could not be the story it is today. Thank you.

Jill, at Bright Owl Edits. My favorite line and copy editor! Like

Nicole, you not only produce high quality editing but also give feedback on the story and my characters to help elevate the book further. I truly appreciate you going above and beyond your duties to help and support me. Thank you.

Orla, at Doyle Edits at home! (LOL) Thank you for volunteering your time, energy, and effort to proofread for me. You've been with me since the Undone days, I'd be lost without you. Thank you.

Dee, my read-through editor! A title invented especially for you and one that is well deserved. You gave up so many evenings to read through this book, discussing the characters, plot, dialogue and so much more. It has made all the difference to this book! I'm so grateful to you. Thank you.

Finally, my beautiful daughter Isabelle. I work a lot and writing eats into our time together. Thank you for pushing me to keep going even when it means you see me less. My heart fills with so much pride for the young woman you are becoming. Thank you, baby, (you'll always be my baby).

Printed in Great Britain
by Amazon